"Why are you here, Trey?"

Lisa asked the question before she could stop herself.

"Uh, we're looking for your grandfather, remember?" He was laughing at her again.

"No." She leaned forward. The room was no longer cold, and she was warmed up from the inside out. "In Telluride. Why did you come to Colorado? You're not from here."

"What gave it away? The boots?" He grinned at her, stacking his feet on the old coffee table. His boots were across the room and she glanced over at them, noting the scuffed leather. Well-worn, the dark brown boots had seen better days.

"That—and the accent. Texas, right?"

"Yeah." He stared down into his drink. Was he wondering how much to tell her? If he should lie? Was this all a lie...?

Dear Reader,

When word came that the Harlequin Superromance line was closing, it was a sad day for me. My series A Chair at the Hawkins Table was nearly finished and I was looking forward to hopefully adding to it, as well as bringing new characters and story lines to my readers. The uncertainty was a challenge, but the editors at Harlequin were wonderful and worked to make sure no one missed out.

I was thrilled when the last of the original six books, *Addie Gets Her Man*, was released as one of the final books under the Harlequin Superromance banner. It was a bittersweet but special last hurrah. Things got even better when the Harlequin Heartwarming line offered me a new home *and* extended the invitation to continue the series.

Many of you will recognize Trey Haymaker from the series, most specifically from *Cowboy Daddy*. He has been strong in my head from the beginning, and readers have wondered what happened to him. Well, now you'll get the chance to learn his story. I'm so grateful to Harlequin Heartwarming for welcoming both Trey and me. And luckily for Trey, we also found Lisa. She's a perfect fit—and contrast—for him.

I love to hear from readers, and I look forward to introducing the Hawkins clan to a whole new group with Harlequin Heartwarming! Thank you for inviting me and joining me on this new journey.

Angel Smits

AngelSmits.com

angel@angelsmits.com

HEARTWARMING

A Cowboy at Heart

—

Angel Smits

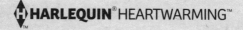

Recycling programs
for this product may
not exist in your area.

ISBN-13: 978-1-335-51072-3

A Cowboy at Heart

Printed in U.S.A.

www.Harlequin.com

Angel Smits shares a big yellow house, complete with gingerbread and a porch swing, in Colorado with her husband, daughter and Maggie, their border collie mix. Winning the Romance Writers of America's Golden Heart® Award was the highlight of her writing career, until her first Harlequin book hit the shelves. Her social-work background inspires her characters, while improv writing allows her to torture them. It's a rough job, but someone's got to do it.

Books by Angel Smits

Harlequin Superromance

A Chair at the Hawkins Table

A Family for Tyler
The Marine Finds His Family
Cowboy Daddy
The Ballerina's Stand
Last Change at the Someday Cafe
Addie Gets Her Man

Visit the Author Profile page
at Harlequin.com for more titles.

To all my Super Sisters, for inviting me in, sharing your wisdom and mostly for the wonderful friendship you've given me.

And as always, for my forever hero, Ron.

CHAPTER ONE

OLD PEOPLE DIDN'T tend to barhop, at least not in Trey Haymaker's experience. They tended to find a barstool and plant their backside on it for the duration of their stay. This afternoon, one of the three regulars took up space along the polished wood, which meant the other two couldn't be far behind.

"What can I getcha, Win?" Trey asked the skinny septuagenarian parked on the corner stool. Winston Ross was one of the few people Trey had known before moving here. The old man owned the cabin up in the mountains outside town that Trey, and his grandfather, had frequented over the years.

Those memories had made Trey reluctant to contact the man when he'd first arrived in Telluride. He hadn't been sure he wanted to face the past, the pain that always came with the reminder of his grandfather's betrayal. But fate had had other plans when she'd given Trey a job in the very bar that Win frequented.

Funny how small towns worked like that.

Looking at Win now—his weathered face, his stooped shoulders, his dimmed blue eyes—Trey saw time's evidence.

Win had grown up here in Telluride, in the center of the Colorado mountains. He'd been a boy before the ski boom, before the old mining town had grown into nearly a city. Trey remembered hearing stories about how Win's dad had run the gas station, and how in high school, Win'd started working there. Win's knack for fixing a car had been the secret to not just working for his dad at the station, but to eventually becoming a partner, and ultimately the owner. Townsfolk and tourists alike had kept him in business for years.

Today, though, the old gas station was long gone, and a convenience store stood on that prime piece of real estate. Win was now retired, spending his days with his cronies, instead of under the hood of a car.

For the thousandth time, Trey wished Win could be his granddad, instead of that old—

Trey shook his head, focusing on Win's words instead of the old pain.

"Same as usual."

"You got it." Trey pulled the highball glass out, and, as he fixed the drink, he kept one eye on his friend. "You okay?" Was Win paler tonight, or was it just the lighting?

"I'm fine. Or at least I will be once you finish pouring." He rubbed his gnarled hands together in anticipation, the rough rasp of his outdoor-worn skin loud even in the noisy bar.

Trey slid the glass over the polished bar, the ice softly clinking when the glass came to a stop at Win's elbow. "The others coming in tonight?" Usually, Hap and Sam were here before Trey finished pouring.

"S'posed to be, but I ain't seen 'em yet." Win stared down at the drink. Was he also wondering where his buddies were? They were getting up in years…

The door opened then, and a cold wind came in with a flurry of snowflakes. Sam held the door open for Hap, who pushed his walker slowly through the doorway. A pile of snow caught on the front of the tennis balls he'd shoved on the metal feet, and a puddle quickly formed as it melted. Trey made a mental note to wipe it up.

"Where ya boys been?" Win called, lifting his drink in a silent salute before taking an exaggerated, taunting sip.

"Ah, shuddup," Hap grumbled as he reached the barstool beside Win. He nodded at the drink. "Gimme one of them, Trey." He glared at Trey. "Maybe two."

"Yes, sir." Trey fought the smile. He didn't take Hap's glare personally. Hap glared at everyone.

Sam, on the other hand, grinned wide and took the farthest barstool, lumbering his big frame up onto it. The sheriff's badge on his coat glinted as he shrugged the garment off. "I'll stick with beer."

That wasn't new, either. Trey couldn't remember the man ever drinking anything else. Once he'd finished serving their drinks, Trey leaned against the back bar, watching the trio.

What had they been like back in the day? He wished he could have seen them. Known them. They had to have been quite a wild bunch. And even though he was quite a bit younger, Sam told tales of how he'd tagged along with the older boys. Trey smiled at the image.

He glanced over the half-dozen others in the bar, and then to the window where snow fell on the other side of the glass. Thick, big flakes of cold and damp. It was going to be a quiet night. He could afford to kick back and watch.

"Whatcha think about that?" Hap interrupted Trey's thoughts as he leaned forward to catch Trey's eye. "I think he's full of baloney."

Though Trey hadn't heard the whole conversation, he didn't have to ask who or what Hap was referring to. Win and Hap had this same argument every time they came in here. The razzing went on as usual.

"I don't listen to all your crap," Trey said, a smile to contradict his denial firmly in place.

"Ah, come on." Win slammed the empty glass to the bar. "Sure, you do. Yer a bartender. Best listeners on the planet." He shoved the glass toward Trey. "Bet you got plenty of stories to share."

Trey shook his head and refilled the glass. "I might listen, but I don't gossip."

"Good man," Sam said. He nodded and took a healthy swig from the long-neck bottle.

"Humph." Hap finished his drink, too, and mimicked Win's movements to ask for another.

While Hap waited, he turned awkwardly, digging in his pocket, and for an instant, Trey thought the old guy was going to fall off the stool. "You ain't foolin' us, boy."

Hap finally turned back around and pointed a bent finger at Trey, who breathed a sigh of relief as Hap regained his balance.

Hap had grabbed an envelope from the

pocket of his jacket. It was worn and crumpled, like someone had tried to destroy it at one time.

Ancient cellophane tape had yellowed in several places. "What's that?" Win leaned toward his friend and indicated the envelope with a hitch of his chin. "Looks older than dirt. Hell, looks like it's been *in* dirt." He cackled as if his comment was actually funny. "You out diggin' in the cemetery or something, Hap? High school reunion?" Macabre humor was never beyond these guys.

Was that a growl that left Hap's throat?

Whatever had been written on the outside of the envelope, if anything legible *had* been, was nearly worn away. Lifting the tattered flap, Hap pulled out another ancient piece of paper. Carefully, as if it were something precious, he spread it out on the bar top.

To Trey, it resembled some kid's scribbles more than writing. Hap reached into the envelope again and pulled out a second sheet of paper. A half page.

"A telegram?" Win asked. Hap nodded. "When did you get that?"

"I didn't." He glanced at Win. "Your dad did."

"What?" Win frowned.

"I was a-cleaning up the back porch. Millie

is nagging me to think about that retirement community they're a-building up the road. Now, I ain't sayin' I'm willing to go there, but I gotta make her believe I'm at least considering it."

"Would you get on with it?" Sam prodded.

"Hurumph." Hap pushed the old telegram another inch toward Win. "I just found this. It was in a box I'd packed up years ago when I retired from the shop. Haven't looked in it since. Thought it was all mine. Didn't know there was any of your stuff in it."

Win hesitated before reaching for the telegram. Trey put one of his bartender superpowers to work—reading upside down. There wasn't much on the page, so it wasn't hard. *Sent a map of our find. Will be in the post soon. Yours and Mom's if I don't come home. Love, Duncan.*

"Duncan? Your brother Duncan?" Sam asked.

Silence was the only answer for a long minute. Win stared. Sam waited. Hap glared. And Trey pretended not to notice any of it. Finally, Winston took a deep breath. "Yeah." He looked up at Trey. "My older brother. He didn't come home from Vietnam." He said it with the rhyme of a curse word.

The word caught Trey's ear, and he froze, his smile vanishing.

"Vietnam." Hap repeated it and Trey saw the other two nod. Were these guys vets? They were the right age. Same as his grand-dad. Trey cringed. Was that how Pal Senior had met Win? He'd never heard that story.

Trey's mind tripped back to all the other stories his grandfather had shared with every man who'd ever worked on the ranch. Back to a time when he'd believed every word the old man said.

A bitter taste rose up in Trey's throat, and he shoved away from the bar. His heart picked up a beat, and he curled his hands into fists. Curses echoed in his mind. This was so not why he was here. He'd come to Telluride so he could be totally on his own, to leave his past behind.

Trey grabbed a mop and headed to clean up the puddle Hap had made coming in, but that did little to distract him as their voices still carried across the nearly empty room.

"What's he mean by *find*?" Sam asked.

"I don't know." Win reached out and grabbed the page of scribbles, the crinkle of the paper cutting through Trey's well-intentioned escape.

Win turned the page around half a dozen

times before saying, "Nothing on this 'map' looks familiar to me."

"Are you kidding?" Hap said. "This here— it's the peak over near the falls. Just past where they're a-building that retirement community Millie's so in love with."

"How can you be so sure of that?"

"I've seen enough brochures of the place— I can find it in my sleep. And look." He turned the makeshift map into the light. "Here's the highway and this is that old ski run. See?"

The two men leaned forward and tried to see what Hap was showing them. Trey gave up trying to keep his distance and went to join them. Curiosity just might kill him.

"You know anything about this?" Sam asked Win.

The air hung thick and full of something Trey didn't want to take time to identify.

Finally, Win shook his head. "I was a kid when he left." Win's faded eyes grew distant. "I remember goin' to the funeral more than I remember him." He chuckled softly, not happily. "Jumped half a foot when the twenty-one-gun salute echoed across the valley. All the grown-ups were crying." He shook his head and reached for the glass Trey set in front of him. His hand wasn't as steady this time when he took a deep swallow.

Trey saw more than that in Win's eyes, which met his briefly before skittering away. With a whispered curse, Win climbed down off the barstool. "I'm done, boys." He shrugged his jacket on and walked slowly to the door. "Put the drink on my tab, Trey. See ya." And he disappeared into the night.

"Well." Hap sighed. "That was a waste of time."

"What were you trying to do, exactly?" Sam asked.

"Get information about this 'find.' It's gotta be a treasure."

"You're an old fool. What do you need a treasure for?"

"Are you nuts?" Hap smacked a gnarled hand on the metal walker at his side. "To keep me outta one of them places."

Sam pursed his lips and lifted his beer to drink. He didn't say any more. When the bottle was empty, he stood. "Come on, Hap. Let's go. The weather is getting rough out there."

"But I ain't done drinking."

"Yeah, you are. Let's go." Sam tossed a couple of bills on the bar. "Keep the change," he said to Trey.

Hap grumbled but grabbed hold of his walker anyway. The papers were still on the bar. Trey picked up the glasses and pushed the papers closer to the edge so Hap could reach them.

"Just toss those in the trash," Sam told him. "No one's looking for any stupid treasure." He gave Hap a meaningful glare.

"You always were a stick in the mud, Sam." But Hap didn't grab the papers. He turned the walker toward the door and headed home.

Trey stared at the old pages. No way was this the end of it. After putting the glasses in the sink and wiping down the polished wood surface, he carefully folded the old pages and put them back into the envelope. He wasn't buying the idea that there was any treasure, but there was no way he'd be the one to toss Hap's dreams into the trash.

No way. He hit No Sale on the cash register and shoved the envelope in where the checks normally went. There was plenty of room as no one used checks these days. Tomorrow, he'd give it back to the three men.

LISA DUPREY HURRIED across the parking lot, praying the wind wouldn't catch her skirt. As it was, she was freezing. The calendar might say spring was coming, but the breeze blowing off the Rockies was still full of winter snow.

Finally, she reached the big glass door emblazoned with the frosted image of a steaming pot of soup and a ladle. She loved the company's logo. Simple, yet it looked warm and inviting. A Taste of Home—Catering and Heartfelt Events.

Who was she kidding? It wasn't just the logo; she loved everything about her job and her life right now.

Stepping into the lobby, Lisa hurried in, but halfway to the kitchens, froze. Where was Trudy? The receptionist always sat at her desk. When Lisa came in every day, every time she went out to an event, every night when she went home, Trudy was there. She often teased the older woman that she had a bed stuffed under the desk and didn't really go home at night.

But Trudy wasn't there now.

Silence surrounded Lisa, and she stood still for a moment, listening, waiting. And then she heard voices. Distant voices. One male, deep, commanding. Marco. The other soft, feminine. That had to be Trudy. They were in the kitchen.

Hurrying down the short hall, Lisa pulled open another glass door and stepped into the gleaming white kitchen area—Marco's pride and joy. Sunshine poured in the south-facing wall of windows, glowing off the polished floor and counters.

"But you can't mean it, Marco. That's so… so wrong."

"It's the truth, Trudy. I'm sorry." His voice was no longer commanding. It sounded—*he* sounded—defeated.

"But what am I going to do?"

"Pack up and start looking for another job," he said softly. Was that a hitch in his voice?

"Marco? Trudy?" Lisa called their names to get their attention. Both of them spun around, staring at her, as if surprised she was there.

"I'm sorry I'm late," Lisa said, pulling off her coat and draping it over the tall chair at the raised counter. "What's going on?"

"M…Marco says we're closing." Trudy's voice shook as she clasped and unclasped her hands together.

"What?" Lisa froze, her breath stuck in her chest. "What do you mean, closing? Like, for the day?" Was there some holiday she'd forgotten?

"No. Forever." Marco's voice faded on the last word.

"But…what about all the new clients? The events we're scheduled to handle?" They'd all been so thrilled when Robert had brought the contracts in. Marco had even taken them all to lunch to celebrate. She moved closer to stop beside Trudy and look at the papers spread out on the table. She hadn't started working on most of these jobs yet, but she was supposed to meet with Robert in the next few days to get the details.

"All gone. All lies. A ruse to distract us while he stole everything." Marco threw his hands in the air, and, turning away, he stalked across the big expanse of the prep area. "I've got some calls to make. To tell the few real clients we have that we can't cater their events." And with that, he disappeared into his office. The door slammed with a loud wham, and, in the quiet it left behind, she heard the lock click.

"Trudy? What happened? We were just voted Best of Denver." Lisa looked around, as if the appliances or counters held some answers. "Where's Robert?" Marco's partner was usually here well before any of them got in.

"That's the problem." Trudy threw her hands up in the air, similar to Marco's dramatic move, only more defeated. "We don't know." She reached behind her, to the stack of papers that sat on the counter. She tossed them dramatically into the air. "These are fake. Lies. All lies." As the papers fell around them, Trudy's eyes filled with tears. "He took everything. The money Marco gave him to buy the supplies, he just took it. Cleaned out every penny from the accounts. No money. No supplies. No customers." Trudy stumbled to the door, toward her abandoned desk. "No job." Her sob broke the silence.

Lisa swallowed. No job? No. It wasn't possible. She loved this job. She *needed* this job. Silence was Lisa's only answer. What was she supposed to do now?

An hour later, the meager contents of her desk packed into a couple of vegetable boxes, Lisa sat in her car staring at the beautiful brand-new building. Marco had poured everything he had into designing this place. He loved it. And when he'd hired her last fall to be the event coordinator, she'd been so happy, she'd cried in his office. His success had given her a place to build the career she'd only dreamed of before.

Now all of it was gone? A gust of cold wind shook her little car, and she shivered. Still, she didn't start it and drive away. She smacked the steering wheel.

How could someone fake doing a job? What was wrong with actually *doing* your job? There were plenty of customers wanting

Marco's amazing food, her decorations and entertainment. They created magic together.

Magic that was apparently no more than dollars to Robert.

She'd been an idiot! She'd worked with him every day for months. How had she not seen that part of him? Thinking back now, she realized she didn't really know anything about him.

He hadn't told her anything about himself, hadn't shared any personal information.

Lisa's hands shook, from cold as much as from her anger, as she reached for her purse. She would have to—she froze, almost literally...do what?

Rummaging around in her purse, she pulled out her phone. She needed someone to talk to. Someone to spill her hurt all over, who'd listen and not chastise her for trusting so blindly.

Jack's face came to mind. But her ex-none-too-supportive-idiot boyfriend had told her not to leave her other job. Thank goodness, he was her ex and she wouldn't have to tell him anything.

A weird sense of déjà vu made her cringe. She'd thought she'd known Jack, too. But just like Robert, Jack had been a liar.

No, she couldn't go back to that. Back to where Jack had left her. Back to… No!

As if on cue, her phone rang. Not Jack, thankfully. Her mother. Lisa gulped.

"Hello." She might as well break it to her now and get it over with. She'd have to talk to her mother about this at some point anyway.

"Hello, dear." Mom's familiar voice was a welcome long-distance hug. "How are you? I haven't heard from you for a while."

"Oh, uh—" How did you tell your mother that the job you'd been raving about for months was no more? That it was all over.

"Oh, Mom!" Her carefully planned conversation turned into a whimper. "I lost my job." And a wail.

"Oh, hon. What happened?"

The words stuck in her throat for a moment, then came rushing out. "The boss is closing the business." She tried to regain control of her emotions, with little success. "One of my coworkers was a dirty rotten crook and took all the money. Marco can't keep the business open."

"I'm so sorry, dear. That's awful. I know you really liked that job."

"I did." Sadness swept through her. "I don't know what I'll do now."

"Everything will be fine. You'll get another

job quick. I'm sure of it. You can always go back to Dusty's."

No way. No way was she returning to her old job. Not just because Jack was there, though that was part of it. It would mean admitting defeat. She might be down, but she wasn't out.

"I'll find something," she declared.

"That's my girl. I'm sure you'll land something better."

"I hope so. Thanks, Mom." Her mother always had a way of making things seem much better than they really were.

"Lisa, the reason I called…" Her mother took a deep breath. "Have you talked to your grandfather lately?"

"Uh, no." That was a bit out of left field. "Should I have?"

"No. But I haven't heard from him and I'm a bit worried. I usually call him every Tuesday, but this week he didn't answer, and he hasn't phoned me back."

"Do you think there's something wrong?"

"I hope not. I'm sure Hap or the sheriff would get in touch with me if something had happened. No, I'm afraid he's up to something and you know how that goes."

She did. Everyone did. Grandpa was the king of schemes. He'd always been a dreamer.

He'd been one of her biggest champions, encouraging her to follow her own dreams. Her mother and grandmother had talked of all the ideas he'd had over the years, few of which Grandma had ever let come to fruition.

"Maybe—"

"Maybe what?" Somehow, Lisa didn't think this was a good maybe.

"Now that you're unemployed for a bit, maybe you could take a trip up to Telluride and check on him."

"Mom, I don't have the time—"

"For your family?" There was an edge to Mom's voice that made Lisa remember "the look" her mother had given her whenever she'd done something naughty. "I'd go, but you know your father and I are leaving for the cruise this week. Your sister can't go because the kids have school, and your brother is working."

Lisa sighed. *Remind me to get a family and a job soon.* "I'll check on Grandpa," she agreed, but not without a heavy sigh. The nagging bit of worry was only part of the reason she agreed.

"Oh, thank you, dear. You know I'd do it myself if I really thought it was a serious problem." And she would. Mom was a great mother and a good daughter. Family was important to her.

As long as the dreams weren't too big.

CHAPTER TWO

LISA SLIPPED HER PHONE back into her purse just as Trudy came out the front door. As Lisa had, she carried a battered box of belongings—the contents of her desk crammed into a single square foot of space. Her purse, the suitcase version, hung off her shoulder. Where was her coat? Did she even have one?

The older woman looked as lost as Lisa felt. Lisa couldn't let her leave without a decent goodbye.

Despite the cold wind, Lisa climbed out of her finally warm car and hurried over to where Trudy struggled to heft the box into her trunk. A faded brown coat nestled on the floor of the trunk.

"Let me help." The wind tried to rip her words away, but Trudy's nod told Lisa she'd heard. Together, they managed to get the box settled in the trunk.

The older woman forced a smile through her slowly freezing tears. "Thanks, hon. I'm just so—"

"I know." She got Trudy's arms into her coat and helped her zip it up. "Where are you going now?"

Trudy shrugged and looked out over the nearly empty parking lot. Marco's car was the only other one left. "I guess…home."

"So, you do have one." Lisa joked, trying to make the woman smile. It almost worked. "How about I buy you a coffee?" She pulled her own coat closer around her. "I'm—I'm not ready to be alone yet."

Trudy appeared relieved. "Me, either. But I'll buy my own. We're both going to be without a paycheck soon."

"Come on." Lisa headed to her car. "I'll drive."

Trudy shook her head. "I'll take my car." She looked back over her shoulder. "I don't want to come back here to get it."

"I understand." Lisa headed to her car and they each drove to the coffee shop down the street. Lisa pulled into her usual spot, her eyes taking in the familiar facade. How many times had she come here on break or for lunch? This might be her last visit. Lisa blinked her eyes. It wouldn't do any good to sob in her coffee.

Trudy pulled up beside her, and they braved the weather again to step into the warm, coffee-scented café. It was busy—the whirr of the coffee machines, the soft conversations and the piped-in music filled the air around them. So familiar.

Trudy squared her shoulders and shoved the gigantic purse up more firmly on her shoulder. "I don't know about you," she looked sideways at Lisa, "but I'm going to just pretend this is my lunch break."

"Denial sounds like a lovely plan." Lisa nodded and followed Trudy to one of the back booths. It might be a long lunch break today.

"Hey, ladies." Mindy, the young waitress who worked here most days, carried the coffee carafe to the table with a smile. "The usual?" she asked Trudy.

"I—I'm not sure yet."

Mindy's smile faded. "Are you okay?"

Trudy's eyes filled with tears, and Lisa put her hand over Trudy's. She looked up at Mindy. "Yes, the usual for Trudy. And I'll take…" She glanced at the menu in front of her. "I'll take a number three." It was a big meal but why not? She had to eat today. They both did.

"Sure." Mindy nodded. "I'll get those started." She left and headed to the kitchen.

"I'm sorry," Trudy whispered. "I'm being

silly. It's not as if I can't afford to retire or take some time off."

That didn't surprise Lisa. Trudy worked constantly. When did she have time to spend any of the money Marco had paid her? And he'd paid her well.

"But?" she prompted.

"I don't know what I'm going to do with myself." She shrugged. "Work is all I have. My kids have scattered around the country. My husband is gone. I'm—" Trudy picked up her napkin and wiped her eyes. "I'm all alone."

That explained why Trudy was always at work. "No, you're not. You've got me."

"Thank you, dear, you're sweet, but you have your own life. You have things to do. I'm sure you'll get another job soon."

Mindy appeared just then, setting tall ice waters in front of them. Once she left again, Trudy tried to smile at Lisa.

"You'll be busy job hunting yourself," Lisa pointed out.

"I doubt I'll have much luck. Few companies want to hire someone over fifty, much less over sixty."

"There's a lot to be said for experience."

"I agree. But they don't always think like we do."

Trudy's sadness gave Lisa something to focus on, to work on. So, for the next hour as they ate, she tried to cheer the other woman up.

Finally, when Mindy had brought their checks and cleared away most of the dishes, they couldn't stall any longer. Trudy sighed and glanced out the window. "I guess I should be getting home to Fred and Ethel."

Lisa nearly gave herself whiplash staring at the woman. "Who?" Trudy didn't have any family at home—hadn't she just said as much?

Trudy hesitated only an instant before the words spilled from her lips. "My prize-winning cockatoos." For the first time all day, a genuine smile formed on Trudy's face. She reached for her phone. "Here." She turned the screen toward Lisa.

Two big white birds, with bright blue rims around their eyes and a plume of feathers on each of their heads, posed for the camera. "I—" Lisa was stunned. "You never even mentioned them before."

"Oh, dear, of course not." Trudy's smile faded, and she leaned closer to Lisa, lowering her voice. "The competition is fierce, and my pair are now quite valuable. I couldn't risk anything happening to them."

"Oh." Lisa frowned, too. "Why are you telling me now?"

Trudy shrugged. "I'm so proud of them. And it is hard to stay quiet about something this exciting. I trust you. You've really helped me today. Thank you."

Trudy slid her finger over the screen. "Here we are when I won Grand Champion with them last year."

"That's stunning." And they were. But so was the fact that Trudy had never said a word about them.

Lisa smiled. "You asked me what you should do now?" She pointed at the phone. "Focus on that." She reached out and squeezed the woman's hand. "Do what you enjoy. You've earned it."

Trudy nodded, and this time her smile didn't fade. "Thank you, dear. I'm going to miss you."

"Oh, you're not rid of me yet. But I need to get going, as well. My mom asked me to help her with something."

"What's that, dear?"

"My grandfather lives up in Telluride. This is a good excuse to go see what he's up to. She hasn't heard from him for a while and she's a bit concerned." That was putting it mildly.

"Oh, my dear, I hope he's okay."

Lisa smiled. "I'm sure he is. My mother worries about him, but he loves those mountains. Me, too."

Trudy gathered up her purse. "That sounds like a great idea." She stood, and Lisa followed. "I'm so glad we did this."

After a heartfelt hug, they settled their bills and headed to their cars. Lisa watched until Trudy had left the parking lot before she started her car.

Looking in her rearview mirror to back out of the parking spot, Lisa met her own gaze. "At least I know you," she said aloud. Maybe she should be more like Trudy. Less open.

She frowned. She wasn't a liar, and wasn't a lie of omission just as bad? Confused, she put the car into gear and got moving. Maybe a trip up to the mountains would do her good. It would help her clear her mind, and, once Grandpa came down from the hills, he'd help her focus on where to go next. He'd always been a good sounding board for her.

Four hours later, when Lisa finally reached Telluride, she walked between the piles of snow on either side of her grandfather's sidewalk. Someone with their trusty snowblower had come through here, clearing a path from house to house. Nice of them, since she knew her grandfather didn't have a snowblower.

The mystery scooper had even cleared the walk going up to Grandpa's front step. Only the last dusting of snow covered the stone.

But where the neighbors' walks were packed down from footsteps, the walk to Granddad's was still somewhat pristine. Her footsteps were the first ones there. Halfway up the sidewalk, she reached into her purse and pulled out the single key she kept in the inside pocket. A cowboy-boot-shaped key ring saved it from disappearing into the depths.

She pulled the screen door open and put the key into the lock. The little pressure she used was just enough to nudge the door to creak open slowly. She stared. What the—

Darkness was all that lay beyond.

Stale, closed-up air wafted out, bringing warmth out against the cold afternoon. But it wasn't the usual warm, welcoming scent of her grandparents' house. This scent held time in it.

"Grandpa?" she called, almost hoping she wouldn't hear his voice. If he was in there, with the house shut up like this, so dark and sad, that would not be a good thing.

Slowly, she angled the door just a bit more and called for him again. Still no answer. Then she heard something. Footsteps? Heavy.

Quick. Distant. "Grandpa?" She took a couple of steps through the door.

Glass crashed somewhere in the other room. Had he fallen? She rushed inside toward the sound. *Please let him be okay.* Him falling—even though he was a healthy, agile man for his age—could be disastrous.

She reached the doorway to the living room and stared at the empty room. No one was there. But cold, snowy air was blowing in from the window, making the old-fashioned sheer curtains dance. She hurried over to find the window broken. A movement at the corner of the yard startled her. Someone, certainly not her grandfather, leaped over the back fence. Footprints showed dark across the snow-covered yard.

"Hey," she yelled, wasting her breath as it fogged in the cold air.

She shivered as much from the cold as the realization that someone had broken into—and apparently out of—Grandpa's house. Was he okay? Was he here? She ran through the few rooms on the lower level, finding nothing. She hurried up the stairs, checking rooms until she finally reached her grandparents' bedroom.

It was as deserted as the rest of the house. And cold. The bed looked like it hadn't been slept in for ages. She frowned, gazing at the old-fashioned dresser and vanity that her grandmother had loved and polished each week with lemon oil. Grandma had been gone over a year now, but that faded sweet/tart scent still tinged the air.

Even though a light coat of dust covered everything and danced in the light that filtered in.

Grandpa wasn't here. No one was.

But someone, who wasn't her grandfather, had been.

Hastily, she pulled her phone from her pocket and dialed 9-1-1. Slowly, checking around each corner as she moved, she went back downstairs and waited just inside the kitchen door.

Near the knife rack.

The dispatcher answered, and Lisa gave the address, telling the woman her suspicions that someone had broken in.

"Are they still there?"

"No, but I'm not sure there isn't someone else hiding somewhere."

While she waited on the phone, her mind raced. Where was her grandfather? When her mother had mentioned Grandpa had disappeared again, most likely into the hills, she hadn't seen the house, hadn't felt the emptiness that permeated it.

Why hadn't he let anyone know where he was going? Maybe he had, just not them. She'd have to check with his friends.

What if something had happened to him?

THE THIRSTY EAGLE SALOON sat smack on Main Street. It faced the ski slopes that dominated the view from all over town. Trey stared out the big plate-glass window at those slopes, wishing he was on his new pair of K2s instead of sitting here counting change.

Last night's snow had put down a good foot of powder, and even from here, the white plumes flying up behind the skiers were clearly visible.

"Hey, boss," Gabe called from the kitchen. "We're low on tequila. And there's only two cases of burgers left in here." Gabe's voice sounded muffled so Trey figured he was inside the walk-in freezer.

Trey sighed. Trey couldn't do much about restocking. He wasn't the owner.

Hap Southers was. And while the old man loved the place, apparently being a mayor—or former mayor—and a bartender wasn't a good mix, even in a wild mountain town like Telluride.

Hap relished showing off and one-upping his cronies, but he was cheap. Before anyone could order supplies, they had to call Hap and ask. Hap refused to give any of the staff a budget or any kind of idea what they should spend.

Trey hated having to ask for anything. He was used to being in control. He always had been on the ranch, and when he'd left Texas and his family's ranch behind, he'd stopped asking anyone's permission to do anything.

Until he'd started working here, that was. "I'll ask Hap about the order after I get back from the bank." He grabbed the bank bag with the deposit he'd already counted and headed out the door. It was a nice day, and the walk to the bank would be good for him.

Even though the sun was still out, the mountain's shadow had fallen over the town. Sitting in a box canyon, some part of Telluride was always in the shade.

The breeze cut through the afternoon, and he shivered. Lord, this place was so different from Texas.

His phone rang just then, and he pulled it out of his pocket to look at the screen. The ranch. Just the thought of the home he'd left behind seemed to summon his past. He pocketed the phone again, not even bothering to silence the ringer.

He'd only answered a call from the ranch once, the first week he'd been here. He'd foolishly thought there was some emergency. Someone was dying, maybe. But it had just been one of the hands asking for Trey's input—and for help getting his father, Pal Junior, to change his mind about something. Trey had hung up.

He'd left that all behind.

He needed a life without his grandfather's legacy or anyone's influence. If he was going to build a new life, he had to completely leave the old behind.

And the old had to let him go. They, apparently, found that harder to do than he did, since they kept calling. He'd eventually check his voice mail, but not today, and not any time soon.

"Afternoon, Trey," Linda, the head teller, called from her station as he entered the bank. She didn't bother to stop counting the stack of twenties in front of her. The woman could, and probably did, count money in her sleep.

"Hey, Linda." Trey moved to her counter to make the deposit. "How come you aren't up on the slopes? Looks like a good day for some runs." Trey and Linda had met on a black diamond ski run his first week here, and had shared several conversations about their love of skiing when he came into the bank.

She was pretty, and he'd even thought for a minute and a half about asking her out. She'd be a perfect fit for him—at least the him he wanted to be. But something didn't feel right.

In the past, he'd have asked her out without even thinking twice. He liked women but— He stood there watching her...and had no desire to make any move. Dating was a commitment he wasn't ready to take on yet.

"Yeah." The rubber band she put around the stack of cash snapped into place, breaking into his thoughts. Thankfully, Linda was oblivious to what he was thinking as she reached for his deposit. "But just like you, I need to eat and keep a roof over my head."

"I hear you." He nodded and waited until she'd finished putting all the assorted papers and pieces away before handing him back the bag.

Stepping outside, he gave one last longing glance at the slopes and the skiers flying down the hill. He wished he were there, losing himself in the cold, the sun and adrenaline. But he headed back to the bar.

"Hap's on the phone," Gabe called as soon as Trey stepped inside.

He hadn't even removed his coat, but he took the phone. "Afternoon, Hap."

"Afternoon, Trey. Gabe said you were ordering supplies?" Trey looked over at his cook, who'd obviously heard and simply shrugged.

"Just got back from making the deposit." He knew what was really important to the old man. "I planned to give you a call, but yeah, we need supplies." Gabe deserted him, going into the kitchen.

"Let me see—"

"Big weekend's coming. New powder made the news. We'll be swamped." He knew how to get Hap's attention. "Could be a profitable week."

"Hmmm. You think so? I'm not sure."

Sometimes Hap was too much like Pal Senior—too damned cheap. Trey nearly cursed aloud. No one was as bad as the old reprobate. "Look, I can run this place on a shoestring, but that's going to make your deposits smaller. Today's was good. I think you'll be pleased."

"I'll log on." Through the phone, Trey heard the sound of Hap tapping computer keys. Hap kept tabs on him by checking the bank account online each day. "Well, what

do you know. That's lookin' good." A few
more keystrokes.

"So, can I get some more supplies in?" Trey
hoped Hap didn't hear the way he gritted his
teeth.

"Yeah. Make an order. But don't make it
too big. Just enough to get us through the
weekend. Don't want anything left over to
just sit there and go bad or anything."

Trey refrained from telling the old man that
alcohol didn't go bad sitting for a few days
and most everything else would be frozen.
Now that he had the go-ahead, he ended the
call quickly so he could make the orders before the suppliers closed for the day.

"We getting the stuff?" Gabe ventured
back out of the kitchen.

"Thanks for the support there. Yeah." Trey
logged on to the computer. "Ordering now."

Gabe leaned against the doorframe. "You
think he's greedy or cheap?"

"Who?"

"Hap."

"Your guess is as good as mine." If Trey
could answer that, maybe he wouldn't be here
now. Hap reminded him too much of people
and places he wanted to forget. He silently
prayed, as his fingers flew over the keys.

Don't ever let me be like that.

CHAPTER THREE

THE SOUND OF TIRES on the street outside had Lisa staring anxiously out the screen door. She'd stayed in Grandpa's kitchen, waiting, listening, prepared to run like hell if anyone else came out of the shadows or any of the rooms.

The dispatcher had recognized her grandfather's address and put her straight through to the sheriff himself, Sam Coleman.

Sam and her grandfather had been best friends for years. He'd offered to stay on the line with her until he got there, which thankfully only took five minutes. He'd tried to calm her by discussing the weather and odd bits of gossip.

When Sam's tall, burly figure rose from the squad car, strong and reassuring, she let out the breath she'd been holding and hung up.

"Whatcha doing in here?" he growled when he saw her sitting at the kitchen table like it was dinnertime.

"Waiting for you."

"You don't think someone else is here?"

"Nope. They'd have come out by now," she rationalized, ignoring the glare he sent her.

"Well, stay put." He pointed at the chair, then reconsidered. "Better yet, go sit in my squad car." He re-aimed his index finger at the door. "Lock the car until I come back out."

"I'm fine right here." The person who'd run had been in Grandpa's house for a reason, and she wanted to know who they were and what they'd been after.

Sam just turned on his booted heel and started looking through the house. She could keep track of him by the sound of his footsteps and the echo of doors and cupboards opening and closing. He was very methodical in his search.

"You're right. I don't see anyone," he finally said as he returned to the kitchen. "But the bedroom window upstairs is open. You open it?"

She shook her head. "Which room?"

"The master. That one's pert near the full two stories up." He frowned. "Still one treacherous jump." He stared at the stairs as if trying to figure something out. "I closed it, but I'd like one of the guys to come out and dust for fingerprints."

That explained why it had been so cold in the room. "They didn't go out that window."

He stared at her then, his thick brows gathered in a frown.

"The living room window. I heard glass break and when I looked out, I saw someone in the yard." How had he missed the broken window?

Glowering, Sam turned on his heel again and spent several minutes in the living room.

He walked slowly back into the kitchen, his gaze trained on the floor. Finally, he stopped and looked up. "Did they run back in here?"

"I—" Why did he think that? Then she followed his gaze.

She gasped. "Is that—?" There was a faint trail of something dark across the tile that she hadn't noticed. "Oh, God. Sam—" Her voice broke, and her mind filled with every horrible possibility. "Is that blood?"

"I ain't sure." He shook his head. "I'll have a deputy come check it out." He walked over and grasped her elbow. "Let's head outside."

Gently, Lisa pulled away, trying to stand her ground, even though she was trembling hard. "Don't lie to me, Sam. Please." She tried to tamp down the worry that threatened to choke her. "If that's Grandpa's blood, do—" She swallowed, her mouth suddenly dry.

"Now, don't go jumping to conclusions." His words didn't match the worry in his eyes. He cleared his throat and tried again, still unsuccessfully, to guide her to the door.

"Do you notice anything missing?" he asked, clearly trying to distract her.

And, even though she knew what he was doing, it worked. Maybe there was a clue in the house. Lisa looked around but had no idea what to even search for. "I—I don't think so." She shrugged. Suddenly, the weight of the last few hours settled hard on her shoulders.

The morning had started out so bright. Marco's pronouncement about the business closing seemed ages ago. Lunch with Trudy… The drive up here… Now this. It was almost too much.

Should she have called Sam earlier, when Grandpa hadn't answered her mother's calls? Should she have come to visit sooner? More often?

She'd been so busy the past few months with the job, she hadn't been up here much, nor had she spoken to her grandfather in a while.

Guilt raced through her. Would it have made a difference if she had?

Would he still be here? Would something have happened to her, too? Her stomach churned.

"Sam, when did you see him last?"

"See who? Win? Oh, now, don't go fretting, Lisa. He had drinks with Hap and me yesterday over at The Thirsty Eagle." Their favorite bar.

Lisa shot to her feet and paced. "But Sam, look at this place." She waved her arms around. "He seems to have been gone longer than one day." She ran her finger over the counter where a layer of dust dulled the dark tone of the marble.

"Lisa." The older man stepped closer. "Your grandma's been gone almost two years," he unnecessarily reminded her. "Your grandpa would never be accused of being a housekeeper."

"But—" She looked around, more closely this time. She stalked over to the refrigerator and yanked it open. The light came on, washing over the room, reassuringly normal. A gallon of milk, a carton of orange juice and several other normal items sat inside.

She didn't want to, but she opened the milk and sniffed. Not spoiled. Thank goodness.

Maybe he hadn't been gone long. Maybe she was jumping to conclusions. Still… "Then where is he? It's getting late." Another glance at the clock told her it wasn't that late by her city standards. But here? For her grandfather? It was very late.

"Don't go borrowin' trouble." Sam put his big, rough hand on her shoulder. "I'm sure there's a simple explanation. We'll find him," he reassured her, and she wasn't sure if he believed what he was saying or not.

Sam pulled out his phone and was soon talking to someone about securing the house. "Bring a sheet of plywood." He paused and listened. "There's a couple of sheets out in the shed. Got a broken window here, and Win ain't around to fix it. Yeah."

Once he'd hung up, he turned back to her again. "Okay, let's get you settled at the hotel."

"What?"

"It's too late for you to drive to Denver tonight. And you're not staying here by yourself."

"Sam, I'm a grown adult. I'm not a kid anymore."

"I know that." He put his hands on his hips. "Someone broke in here for a reason. If they didn't get what they want, they could come back. Nope, you're not staying here." He shook his head, and she saw his familiar stubbornness flash in his eyes.

Sam wasn't going to let her stay in the house. Despite the fact that she didn't *want* to stay here by herself, she wasn't admitting that to him. She let her stubborn glare speak for her.

"No." The big man strode toward the screen door and held it open for her. "Not only no, but hell, no." He shook his head.

"I can't go to a hotel." She hadn't had time to tell him she couldn't afford it. She *had* lost her job today. She glanced at her watch. Yeah, still today. She followed him outside and watched as he closed and locked the door.

"Win would kill me if anything happened to you." He finally stopped next to her car and crossed his arms over his chest. Stubborn never looked so human. Or immovable. "Evelyn down at The Guest House always has a room for dignitaries. We'll set you up there."

"I can't—"

"Gonna make me tell Win on you?" His left eyebrow lifted, and she recognized that he'd stay here all night long and argue. And she wouldn't win.

"Oh, fine." She huffed to her car. "But only for tonight."

"We'll see." He waited while she climbed in and closed the door behind her. Walking back to his car, he waited until she started her own vehicle and headed toward the small downtown hotel. He followed close behind.

The Guest House was one of the oldest buildings in Telluride. The two-story building, with an old-fashioned false front and big glass windows all across the street side, was a landmark. Built during the original mining boom back in the 1890s with new mining money, it'd been meant to impress.

And it still did.

She'd always wanted to stay here. Why did she feel like she was taking advantage of a bad situation?

As if she had any choice? Sam sat in his car outside and waited until she walked through the big glass door. Glancing at him and waving, she hoped he investigated crimes in this town with as much tenacity as he used keeping track of her.

She looked around the vast lobby in awe. It had seemed silly to stay here when her grandparents had always had a perfectly good guest room. That guest room was still there—just not an option right now. She shivered at Sam's earlier warning that the intruder could return and she continued farther inside.

She had to force her feet to keep moving. It was so beautiful. Two huge antique crystal chandeliers hung from the high ceilings. Light fell in prisms over the old-fashioned wingback chairs and Chippendale couches, and in pools on the lush gray carpet.

Brass handrails edged the steps she descended into the sunken lobby area. But what caught her eye was the staircase. It curved upward, over the heads of diners in the small bar, and continued to create the ceiling over the check-in desk. Gleaming brass rails followed the same curve and nestled in the crease of the carpet on each stair.

It was beautiful. Too pretty to actually use, and too expensive for her to afford, she was sure.

Straight ahead, a tall counter made of dark wood dominated most of the far wall. Two staff members in formal tuxedo-type attire waited for her to step up.

"Oh, hello." An older woman came out from behind the desk. Her neatly-cropped silver hair bounced, and her eyes smiled behind the dark cat-eye glasses she wore. "You must be Lisa. I'm so sorry to hear about the break-in."

Sam wasn't much for keeping secrets.

"Sam told me about Win. I'm sure he's just off in the hills." She put an arm around Lisa's shoulders, comforting and warm. Lisa almost let herself believe the woman's reassurances.

And she might have if she hadn't seen

that trail of dark blood on her grandfather's kitchen floor.

"Th-thank you," she whispered and let the woman lead her to the check-in desk.

Half an hour later, Lisa was settled in a room on the second floor. While the furniture was new and almost modern, the building made it all look antique. Where there had been renovations, the old brick wall was left exposed.

The windows were old, or seemed to be, and thick drapes were pulled back so she could look out. She did that as she sat down on the edge of the bed. What was she supposed to do now?

After a few minutes, she grabbed her phone and checked, just in case she'd missed a call from Grandpa.

Nothing.

No one. Not Trudy. Not Marco. Not Sam. Not her mom, nor her grandfather. She suddenly felt very lost. And alone.

Standing, Lisa made herself break out of her pity party. This was ridiculous. One bad day—okay, a really bad day—did not define her life.

She walked over to the windows, intent on pulling the shades. She might as well try to get some sleep. But as she reached up, she saw a movement in the alley below.

Leaning close enough to feel the cold coming from the glass, she watched a man go to the Dumpster. Curiosity made her lean closer, her forehead bumping the window pane.

Was that Sam? What was he looking for?

He was using a piece of wood to rummage around in the Dumpster. From here, Lisa couldn't even make out his face, but saw him shake his head. Finally, he stood back and put his hands on his hips, much like he had at Grandpa's house just a short while ago.

The star on his chest glinted as he moved in and out of the moonlight.

Did Sam's odd search have anything to do with the break-in at Grandpa's house? She leaned closer.

After several long minutes, she watched as he threw his hands up in defeat, an all-too-familiar gesture. He reached into his pocket and pulled out a phone. What was he saying?

Slowly, carefully, because she really wasn't eavesdropping—really—she turned the lock to open the window. Thank God this wasn't like the hotels in Denver where the windows were sealed.

A cold breeze slipped in between the wood frame as she lifted the window. She heard the echo of Sam's deep, time-worn voice. "Nah, it ain't here." Silence. "I know we told him to throw it away. Doesn't mean he did," Sam snapped at the person on the other end of the phone before there was more silence.

What had someone supposedly thrown away? Something relating to Grandpa? Or something else? Surely the break-in wasn't Sam's only case.

"I am not climbing into the damned Dumpster for a piece of paper." Sam turned to leave. "You shoulda made a copy." The sound of his bootheels was loud, like they had been when he'd been walking around the house, only this time, it was against the stone of the alley instead of ancient wood floors. "Or taken a picture with your phone. You do know how to use it, right?"

The other person must have said something loud as Sam pulled the phone away from his ear. "I heard you. So did half the city. Just calm down, Hap. Don't worry. We'll find it. I'll check with him tomorrow. Maybe by then Win'll show up and you can ask *him*!" Finally, Sam let the lid of the container slam down and slowly walked away. The echo of his footsteps faded as he headed down the alley and disappeared into the night.

It did have something to do with her grandfather! Not only had Sam mentioned him by name, but Hap was the third leg of their troublesome trio. Those three always knew each other's business. Always.

Lisa resisted the urge to run after him but ultimately gave up. What the heck? She pulled open the door, making sure she had her key card before stepping out into the deserted hall and pulling the door closed.

She took the stairs, nearly falling on her face when she hit the bottom too quickly. She slammed the crash bar on the door, the sound exceedingly loud in the night. Immediately, the cold bit into her skin, and she realized she'd left her coat in her room. Stupid.

Okay, this had better be a quick trip. She hustled across the alley and peered over the edge of the Dumpster. The thing was nearly half full. And the aroma… She stepped back and covered her nose. Eww…

Dishes clattered nearby, and she turned to look through a battered screen door in the old brick wall. A kitchen was on the other side, the white fluorescent light barely reaching through the shadows. Ah, food scraps—to the extreme—made that odor.

More prepared this time, she turned back to the Dumpster. Sam had mentioned a paper. She grimaced. Paper wasn't going to survive that mess. No wonder he hadn't wanted to look any closer.

"GREAT. JUST GREAT," Trey grumbled as he slammed the receiver down. Nothing like an old-fashioned landline to vent his frustration with. The one waitress scheduled for tonight had just called in sick. She'd probably gone to the same party his cook Gabe had gone to last night. At least he'd toughed out the hangover and shown up.

Trey headed to the kitchen to strategize with the cook. "Hey, Gabe," he called as he stepped through the swinging metal door. He walked around the corner, into the big industrial kitchen. The long metal tables were bare, and there wasn't any heat coming from the gigantic stove. The vent fan was silent. "Hey, Gabe," he called again. Still no answer. Where had the idiot gone?

Trey could make the burgers, but dang it, he couldn't run the bar, the kitchen and wait tables by himself all night. He cursed and flipped on the grill.

Heading to the big walk-in freezer, he yanked the door open and tossed a box of burgers up onto one of the tables. He pulled everything else to make the burgers as well as a packet of the frozen fries that landed on the same table with a thunk. Maybe if he served enough drinks, they wouldn't care how long it took to get their food. Happy Hour, it was.

A sound came from the back doorway. "Gabe, I hope you're out there." He stalked to the door and shoved the worn screen open. "I need your—"

A young woman was leaning into the Dumpster. Long, shapely legs led up to a nicely curved waist. The rest of her was in the shadow between the lid and the metal wall.

"Hey!" Trey yelled, not sure why he was so surprised. Homeless people came here to Telluride, too. They drifted through the Dumpsters, hoping to find something to eat or sell. "Get out of there. If you get hurt, it's not our fault." He hustled over toward her.

She yelped as the plastic lid came down and smacked her in the head. She shoved it aside and stood up. A pair of angry green eyes glared at him. "You scared me," she accused him.

"Better than shooting you."

She frowned and tilted her head just a bit sideways. "You'd shoot me for getting into your Dumpster?"

He almost laughed. "No. But I'm nicer than most people."

She turned back to what she'd been doing. Leaning over again, she stood on her tiptoes. He reached out and grabbed the belt loop at her waist and pulled her back. "I said—"

"You said you weren't going to shoot me."

"I'm rethinking that." He glared down at her. "What are you doing?"

"I'm—uhm—looking for my—uh, brace-let."

"For what?"

She didn't meet his eyes, which told him she was lying. He crossed his arms over his chest and waited for her to answer.

She stood there, her hands on her hips, glaring at him. She actually tapped her foot. "You know—a piece of jewelry that fits around your wrist?"

"Not funny." He leaned toward her, hoping his glare intensified enough to make her take him seriously. "Ever hear of asking if someone found it? Maybe it's inside and not in some smelly Dumpster."

The lie flashed in her eyes. "Oh, did you find it?" she asked, gripping his arms. She was laying it on a little thick.

"Well, no, but—" Of course he hadn't.

"Why did you get my hopes up?"

"I just suggested it." What was wrong with this woman? "But you didn't even ask."

She rolled her eyes and turned back to the Dumpster. "Don't let me bother you." She waved toward the still-open door. "I'm sure you have customers."

He did, but leaving her out here to get hurt wasn't a good idea.

Maybe his cynicism was clouding his judgment. Maybe she was telling the truth. Why was a bracelet so important to her? Was it valuable? Sentimental value? "Surely you can get another bracelet."

She spun on her heel, glaring at him. "Spoken like a person who has money to burn."

"I don't have money to burn. But it's just a bracelet."

"Just a bracelet?" Her voice went up a good octave. "It's the only one I have, and the only one I'm likely to have. I need it."

"Why?"

She hesitated. "Because—" She swallowed and didn't meet his gaze again. "I planned to, uh, pawn it. Yeah, that's it."

He looked a little closer and even in the shadows of the alley he saw the stress in her eyes. "You an addict?"

She glared at him.

"You drink?" He thought about the waitress who'd just called in "sick." Which reminded him that he needed to get back in and start making orders.

"No," she denied. "Though a glass of wine now and then with dinner is awfully nice." There was a wistful note in her voice.

"If it's money you want, maybe I can help you out. You know how to waitress? Cook?"

He'd startled her, he could tell. "What do you mean?"

"I run this bar. My cook is missing, and my waitress just called in sick. I can't do it all by myself. You want a job? I'll give you a shot."

"Are you crazy?"

"Sometimes, I seriously think so." He sighed. "I need the help. You in?" He waited while she thought about it. He wanted to push her, wanted to just grab her and drag her into the kitchen. But he just waited.

"I can cook. How hard is it to be a waitress?"

He reached out and curled his hand around her wrist. "You're hired. Let's go."

CHAPTER FOUR

WHO WAS THIS GUY? Lisa looked at him first, and then around the bar with interest. She hadn't been here in a while. It was old, with pictures of skiers up on the walls, along with beer signs and advertisements for local events. Wood covered the walls, the floor, and a long, polished hunk of it made up the bar top. Only a couple of tables were occupied, and none of the people seemed interested in anything but their own conversations.

"So, if I'm working for you, who are you?" she asked, coming to a stop at the outer side of the bar.

"Guess it would be fair to introduce myself." He smiled and extended a hand to her. "Trey Haymaker, bartender and manager here." She took his hand. She noticed the calluses on his palms and the firm grip of his hand.

He was tall, though part of that was the raised floor behind the bar. Like everyone else here, where ski slopes dominated the town, his face had a windburned hue to it, and his dark blond hair was tousled from that same wind. When he smiled, it was warm enough, but his eyes didn't hold that same warmth. Welcome, but distant.

"I should let you know," she continued. "I've never waitressed before. Not really. I've worked events, but nothing like this." She needed to be honest with him, and herself.

"I didn't think you had." One of the customers at a table across the room waved at him and he moved to talk to them. Nodding, he returned and started fixing drinks. "All I need is someone to do just what I did. Go to the table, ask what they want and give me the information. I'll fill the order and you can carry it back out. Simple."

She could do that. "Do you want me to take payment?"

He nodded. "If you can."

"I can." She'd done plenty of that in both her college days working retail and definitely working with invoices for Marco.

"Good." He nodded. "Here's an apron. Sink's in back to wash up. Then you can deliver that to the table on the left." He slid a round tray with three drinks made and ready to taste toward her.

"Okay, here goes nothing." She laughed,

and smiled at him. He didn't smile back, but he didn't frown, either. That was a good sign, right?

For the next two hours, they developed a rhythm. Orders, making drinks or food, serving. She couldn't say she loved it, but the tips were nice, and it was a job. A temporary job, she reminded herself, that would give her money while she waited for her grandfather to return, or she found something else.

"I'll show you how to close down tomorrow night, if you're planning to come back," Trey said once the last customer had gone and the door was locked.

"Why wouldn't I come back?"

He laughed, and it was the first time she'd heard him do that. "Not everyone does." He walked behind the bar and hit a button on the cash register. He started counting the money. "You got a place to stay?" He asked it nonchalantly, not even looking up from his task.

"Uh, yeah." That seemed like a strange question. "Why would you think I didn't?"

This time he did look up. "Well, I did meet you rummaging around in the trash."

True. She frowned. "No. I've got a place to stay." Two to be specific. She almost told him that, then remembered her earlier decision to be more like Trudy. To be less open and trusting.

He wasn't local, since she didn't know him, and there was a hint of a Southern accent in his voice. "You're not originally from here, are you?" she asked before she thought twice about it.

He glanced up again. "Nope, but I'm here now."

That wasn't much of an answer, and it didn't take long to realize she wasn't going to get much more. He was clearly a private man. Every other time she'd tried to chat with him tonight, he'd answered just as succinctly. No elaboration, no explanation and no effort to get to know her.

The red flags that filled her mind were worth paying attention to. She'd had enough experience already with people who weren't open and honest with her. She'd do well to remember that.

The next morning when her phone alarm went off, Lisa smacked it to silence the noise. She'd forgotten to turn it off last night. For half an instant, she panicked that she'd be late for work if she didn't get moving.

Then reality hit her. She didn't have a job to get to. Wait... Had she dreamt last night? The Dumpster? The way Trey Haymaker, her new boss, had grabbed her arm, and before she could think straight, hired her to waitress? Until two in the morning?

She'd been too stunned to say no, and because of that, she did indeed have a new job.

Groaning, she rolled over. Might as well sleep in since she now apparently worked the night shift. She closed her eyes, putting the pillow over her head to block out the morning light. But returning to sleep was out of the question. She'd been getting up early too long to break the habit in a day.

Slowly, she sat up and shoved her hair out of her eyes. But when she put her feet on the floor, she yanked them back. Pins and needles stabbed her abused toes. When was the last time she'd done that much standing and walking? "Never," she mumbled and hobbled into the bathroom.

Thankfully, the shower came on hot nearly immediately, and she stepped under the spray with a sigh. Warm. Comforting. Leaning back against the tiles, she let the water wash over her.

What had happened to her life? Two days ago, she'd had a job she loved—a career job, not a waitress job—her grandfather was safely situated in his little house and life was good.

Now none of that was true. Closing her

eyes, she tried to force herself to relax. This might be her last chance to do that.

Had she really told Trey she'd be working again today for a whole shift? The man did intrigue her. Tall. Athletic. Cowboy boots and jeans were never a bad thing. His image was fresh and clear in her mind—his voice, deep and warm, echoed in her thoughts.

Stop that! She grabbed the soap and lathered up. Now was the time to focus—and not on some guy, no matter how good-looking.

Still, if she was working at the bar, when was she going to job hunt? Heck, when was she going to find her grandfather? Or some decent shoes? She needed some support for her poor arches if she was going to be a waitress.

She was *not* going to be a waitress forever, she reminded herself. It was just…temporary. She was an event planner with a life in Denver, not here.

Turning off the water, Lisa grabbed one of the big, fluffy towels. Another reality. She couldn't afford to stay here, not on a waitress's salary, though she had gotten some really nice tips last night.

She'd have to stay at her grandfather's place until she found him. But what if the intruder came back? What if she was asleep when they did? She couldn't stay awake all the time. She shivered and stepped out of the shower.

Oh, what was the purpose in fretting? She quickly dressed and headed down to breakfast—it was free, after all. Images of an old lady she'd seen at a buffet once, sliding food into her purse, came to mind.

Was that why grandmas always had huge purses? To slip food into, just in case? No, no, she reprimanded herself in her best mental impression of her grandmother.

Free breakfast here, and Trey had told her she could get lunch if she came in early. She'd be fine. Her stomach growled in a loud taunt.

She'd been destitute for all of twenty-four hours, and she was already turning into a pathetic shadow of herself. Shaking her head, she went downstairs in search of food and her sanity.

Evelyn was up bright and early. The older woman bustled behind the serving table, directing a couple of young girls to refill the serving trays. Lisa's heart hitched. That was her job. That was what she was supposed to be doing. Damn Robert and his greed.

"Good morning, dear," Evelyn greeted her. "Did you sleep well?"

"Uh, yes, I did." Once she got to bed. Three

in the morning had been way past her normal bedtime. She headed for the coffee first.

"So glad to hear it." Evelyn moved on down the line, stirring the food and directing the girls. "Better help yourself quick. We'll be done soon." She smiled at Lisa before disappearing into the kitchen with a nearly empty tray of potatoes.

The food did smell delicious, and Lisa heaped a plate full. Her panic returned to taunt her, but she pushed it away. She would find a solution to her current situation.

Evelyn came in with a set of to-go containers. She set them on the end of the long buffet table.

"Who are those for?" Lisa asked, not seeing anyone else in the room.

"We package up all the leftovers and take them to the church. They offer them to some of the parishioners who need help."

"Oh, that's nice." Lisa's voice faded. Was she destined to be one of those people? What if she couldn't find a job? A real job, she amended. What if she was stuck here?

Now, cut that out!

She couldn't be stuck here, she reminded herself. She had an apartment—and rent due in two weeks.

She took a deep breath with the next bite of eggs. She was being ridiculous.

"Morning, Ev. Lisa."

Sam? What was he doing here? "Did you hear from Grandpa?" Her own situation and appetite forgotten, Lisa looked up at the big man.

Sadly, Sam shook his head and slid into the seat across from her. "No, hon. I came over to check if you had. Did he call you?" His eyes seemed sad, almost haunted, like he'd lost his best friend. Which in reality, he had. Her stomach dropped, and she set her fork down.

Then she remembered that last night she'd turned her ringer off and had shoved her phone into her pocket as soon as she'd waited on the first table. She'd been too tired to check it last night.

Would she have even heard it ring in the noisy bar? She struggled to pull the phone out of her purse then thumbed on the screen. Her heart sank. No calls.

"No." She stared at the screen, hoping maybe it would ring now just because she wished it. It stayed silent. "Nothing."

"Did you find anything else out last night?" She'd seen him by the Dumpster and knew he hadn't found what he'd been looking for there.

"Nothing new about Win," he answered.

Did the big man actually look sadder? What wasn't Sam telling her?

"Unfortunately, his isn't the only case I've got right now." He looked at her then, the sadness of a friend gone from his eyes and the distance of a working lawman in its place.

TREY WATCHED HIS brand-new waitress move around the crowded room. She wasn't homeless; she'd given him a very brief explanation on her situation. If she was staying at The Guest House—the nicest place in town—she was far from homeless.

Tonight, Lisa was wearing black cowboy boots with a pale peach dress that skimmed the tops of her pretty knees. He watched the skirt sway and swirl. Watched her smile shine down on the customers at each booth and table.

Who had taught her how to dress for a mountain winter? With the snow swirling outside, she should be freezing, but she'd been running back and forth, filling orders for over two hours. A sheen of sweat glistened on her brow, and earlier she'd pulled her blond hair back into a loose braid that was now little more than an idea.

It was still pretty, though he reminded himself he shouldn't notice. He was her boss, for

God's sake. Well, technically, he was a supervisor and Hap was the boss. Except all Hap ever did here was drink with his buddies.

She was graceful despite the boots that should have made her just the opposite. At least, she couldn't sneak up on him.

"Hey, give me two whiskeys, neat, and a couple of daiquiris for the lightweights with them." She leaned against the counter and watched as he pulled the drinks together.

"You should take a break." Trey shoved ice into the blender wishing she—and her amazing scent—would move away. Then he wouldn't have to keep tearing his gaze away from her. He could actually focus on his job.

"I'm good." She grinned at him as she refilled the napkins and straws on her serving tray. "I don't think I'd know how to take a break."

"I'm not against you giving it a shot."

When her laughter overshadowed the noise of the bar, Trey realized he was in serious trouble. Warm and rich, the sound reached too deep inside him. He couldn't help joining in.

Hastily, he shoved the drinks across the smooth bar. She set them on the plastic tray and wove her way back through the crowd. She'd definitely done something like this before. Maybe not waitressing exactly—she'd screwed up enough orders to tell him that—but something similar. She knew how to work a crowd.

He'd have to ask her... No, scratch that. He wasn't asking her anything. She was temporary help. She'd eventually move on. For the millionth time, he wondered why she was here in Telluride.

She delivered the drinks with a smile and a heavy dose of sass. She was definitely in her element. People loved her, and she seemed to love them, too.

Later, after the crowd had finally thinned, the door opened again. The wind caught the wood-and-glass frame and slammed it against the wall. The man who came in just then grabbed it and fought the wind to get it closed. Finally, it latched, and the guy turned around, surveying the room as he straightened his expensive wool coat.

Lance Westgate. Trey frowned. The land developer who was building the retirement community that Hap was always talking about. He often came to the bar for an expensive drink and to flaunt his success.

He stood there in the doorway, surveying the room as if looking for someone—or pondering the peasants. There were empty tables now that the rush was over. "Take a seat anywhere," Trey called across the room. "We'll be right with you—"

Trey glanced around the room, his mouth open to speak to Lisa…but she was nowhere to be found.

LISA WAS FAIRLY CERTAIN that back in high school, Lance Westgate had been voted most likely to be found dead in a back alley. Polished, cleaned up and almost handsome now, he made her stop and stare. And duck down behind the bar until she could figure out what to do.

Facing him was not an option. Hadn't he moved away? What was he doing back here looking all successful just when she…wasn't?

It wasn't like she was embarrassed or anything about losing her job—well maybe a little.

She didn't know many people her age here anymore, having only visited her grandparents a few times a year, and meeting mainly their friends. But she knew Lance.

There'd been one summer when she'd met a lot of people her family hadn't introduced her to. Sam had found her once and brought her home to her grandparents. Grandpa had made sure to warn her about Lance.

He runs with a rough crowd, girl, he'd said. *Don't get mixed up with people like him.*

The warnings had only made Lance more intriguing. Until she'd gotten to know him. His friendly smile had faded quickly into a sneer, and one night in particular popped vividly to mind.

She'd been so young, naive and trusting. She'd stood her ground when he and his friends had pressured her to take a drink, though. She hadn't given in to their pressure to smoke either, even though she'd been scared when they'd tried to intimidate her.

Heading back to Denver a few weeks later, she'd moved on, but never really forgotten. Had he changed? Grown up into a decent, responsible person? Matured?

Now he was on the other side of the bar drinking top-shelf whiskey. And she couldn't face him. Not yet.

"Evenin', Trey." They knew each other? How well? Wasn't that interesting? Lisa glanced up at the man beside her.

He leaned against the bar, his arms outstretched, shifting smoothly as he made the drink without seeming to even think about it.

From down here, he looked incredibly tall. He wasn't short by any stretch of the imagination, probably five-ten. His jeans were worn, and fit like they were tailored for him…

Okay, Lisa, get your eyes off him. Think about something else.

She needed to move away. But if she crawled away, Lance would see her. What would he think she was doing down here if she popped up like a jack-in-the-box? She was losing her mind…what was left of it.

"Hey, haven't run into the old guys here for a while," Lance said.

Old guys? That got her attention.

"Didn't know you paid them much mind." Why was Trey's voice thick with his Southern accent all of a sudden? She'd heard it faintly last night, and had asked him where he was from. He'd reluctantly answered but hadn't elaborated.

"Not usually." Lance shifted on the other side of the bar. Was he leaning forward? She tried to melt into the back of the bar, scooting as far as she could beneath the shelf. "Just seems odd without them."

"It's a bit late for the older crowd." Trey moved away from her, picking up dirty glasses from the other end of the bar. Was he trying to distract Lance?

"Yeah. Guess I have to learn about the habits of the elderly. You heard about the development project I'm working on?"

Development project? She listened harder.

"A little. Hap mentioned it."

She made a mental note to ask Trey about that project.

"Hap?" Could she actually hear a frown? "Oh, yeah. One of the old guys." Lance laughed. She heard the glass move against the wood surface. "He's the one with the walker?"

"Yeah. Used to be mayor? Owns this place?" Trey clattered the glasses in the sink. "He and his wife are looking at the retirement villas."

"Good. Good. They are going to be mighty nice. I tell you, the architects and designers outdid themselves." Another slide of glass on the wood.

"One more? It's last call, so this is the end of the night."

"Sure. I'm staying over at The Guest House since I'm only here checking on the project."

The Guest House? Lisa clapped her hand over her mouth to silence her gasp. She'd have to keep an eye out for him.

Trey made another drink, though he stood farther down the bar to do it. He didn't slide it down to Lance, which made the other man either have to lean to get it or scoot a stool over. Lisa breathed a slow, silent, sigh of relief.

"Maybe I could come by when those guys are here?"

"Why?" Trey frowned.

"Oh, they're my target customers. Maybe I could talk about the development. Get their backing."

"Maybe." Trey focused on wiping down the bar again. "They don't have a regular schedule. You know. Retirees." Why was Trey saying that? She could set a clock by those three and their eating and drinking habits—except lately, since her grandfather had been totally out of his routine.

"Yeah. Here's my number." The sound of the card stock snapping on the wood seemed loud. "Maybe give me a call if you see them come in. I'll come over and chat up my project."

Trey picked up the card, nodding as he read it. She watched, mesmerized, as he slid the card into his back pocket.

"I'll keep it in mind." His voice startled her.

"You do that." The silence grew, and Lisa heard the clink of ice. The sound of the high-ball glass's thick base returning to the bar top was loud in the nearly empty bar. "Thanks for the drinks. How much do I owe you?"

Trey stepped over to where she sat, and she nearly squealed as he stopped right in front of her. What had she been thinking, ducking down right by the register? She curled in on herself, leaning her head on her raised knees.

"See you around, Lance." Trey's accent went even deeper. "I'll let the boys know you were asking about 'em."

"Thanks. I appreciate it." Lance's voice was farther away now. "I'm sure our paths will cross." The sound of footsteps against the wood floor receded, and Lisa heard the door open and then close.

Neither of them moved.

Slowly, Lisa opened her eyes and looked up. Trey's denim jeans were still right there. She glanced up, noting his big belt buckle—maybe he was from Texas?—then moving her gaze even farther up to the muscular curve of his chest, to his chiseled jaw…and blue eyes staring down at her.

"Is he gone?" she whispered.

"Yeah." Trey stepped back as if just realizing how close they were. "You can get up." He extended a hand to help her stand.

She stared at it, hesitating. Then, swallowing hard, she put her hand in his. It was rough and warm and solid and big. Her mouth dry, she couldn't speak for a minute. "Th…thank you."

"Oh, no. It's not that simple." Trey leaned back against the ledge behind him, crossing his arms over that impressive chest. She'd taken stock of everything else, so why not appreciate the bulge of his biceps along the way?

Shaking her head, Lisa turned and reached back to untie her apron. Of course, the strings had become a knot.

"I want to hear what that was all about." Trey stepped closer, and, after gently pushing her fingers away, worked at the knot himself. She closed her eyes again, trying to tamp down her awareness of him. What was wrong with her? He was her boss!

Finally, the knot loose, he flicked the apron off and pulled the right side. The fabric whispered over her before falling away.

She had to face him. Taking a deep breath, she got control of herself. "There's nothing to tell. I was just surprised to see him, is all."

Trey was back to leaning against the bar, her apron bunched up in one hand.

Feeling a bit foolish for her impulsive actions, she reached under the bar and grabbed her purse and coat. "I gotta go. See you— uh—tomorrow?"

Before he could say anything, she ran out through the kitchen, the screen door smacking loud in the night, the snow emphasizing the echo.

She glanced back over her shoulder and was surprised to see Trey standing in the doorway. The light from the kitchen outlined his body, casting him in shadow so she couldn't read his expression. She wanted to turn around, see what he might say and do if she faced him, if she let her feelings show.

Instead, she focused on making her way across the alley and up to her room. Earlier today she'd planned to head over to her grandfather's place and stay there. Sam didn't think anyone was coming back, but it was too late to check out of the hotel now. "Just one more night. Then I'll leave."

Flashing her key card at the door, she hurried inside and up to her room. By the time she made it over to the window and parted the curtains, Trey was gone. Had he really been there? Had she imagined him?

Why did she feel disappointed that he hadn't followed?

CHAPTER FIVE

AN HOUR AFTER CLOSE—and too long since Lisa'd run away from him—Trey topped off a shot glass with the house's best whiskey. And just like every other night, he placed it in the middle of the bar. And let it sit there.

A silent reminder. A not-so-silent taunt.

Leaning on the polished bar's smooth surface, he stared at the untouched drink. Tonight, it almost looked pretty with the glow shining up through the copper liquor. The lights around the bar were dim, but outside, snow covered the ground and the light of the high full moon reflected off the drifts. Winter's pale, white glow illuminated the room.

Tonight, though, his thoughts were what had drifted.

What had gone through Lisa's head as he'd stood there, just inches away from her, at the register? She'd been hiding from Lance for some reason, and Trey had been more than curious to find out why. Had something happened between them? She hadn't seemed afraid exactly, but her discomfort was enough to set off his protective side.

Fool. He'd come to Telluride to get away from tangled personal relationships, not get involved in another one.

He almost downed the whiskey just to drive the ache away. But staring into the liquor, he reminded himself what it meant, what it stood for. What it was. And what it wasn't.

Needing to escape his disturbing thoughts of Lisa, he stared at the drink and forced his mind onto something else—anything else. For the first time in months, Trey pictured the place he'd been struggling to escape. *Home.*

Everyone on the ranch was fast asleep by now, the nightly ritual that plagued him long forgotten in their dreams. He glanced at the clock. They'd be getting up to start tomorrow in an hour or two.

As soon as he'd been old enough to hold his own glass, Trey had joined the men of the ranch for their nightly toast—though his had held milk and later root beer. The drink hadn't been what mattered. What had mattered was belonging, being seen as one of the men. Together they'd toasted the end of another successful day.

Trey grimaced at the memory.

He'd been twenty-one the first time his

grandfather, Palace Haymaker, had poured Trey a shot of whiskey. Granddad had poured two fingers, just like this. Pal had thumped him on the back, full of pride.

The words were always the same. *To a good and productive day, today and tomorrow.* Even now, Trey whispered the words aloud.

Trey had been saying them long before Granddad had handed him that first shot glass.

His dad—Pal Junior—had been there, too, along with half a dozen of the men. They'd cleaned up before Grandmother would allow them to even think about sitting down at the table, even though it was in the big ranch kitchen. With their hair slicked back, their bare foreheads where their Stetsons sat all day long were as white as newborn baby's skin. Otherwise, their faces were tanned and leathered by the elements.

Each man held a shot glass, the glass engraved with a big letter *H*. It had been mid-August, the heat shimmering on the horizon even late at night. Through the front window, the moon, full and gold, much like tonight, sat on the edge of the hills and wavered beyond the summer air.

It's your time now, boy. Granddad walked

across the room, a shot glass in each hand. One for himself. The other—Trey's hopes that the other glass was for him rose and nearly toppled over in his pride as the old man extended his hand. *You've proven yourself well.*

Pal Haymaker had been an impossible man to please, and Trey, Pal Haymaker III, as his only grandson, had struggled more than others. The bar had been higher, harder to reach. Somewhere above perfection.

You sure?

The old man glared at him. *You second-guessing me, boy? I don't offer until I know.* Trey half expected a cuff upside the head. The old man surprised him by simply extending the glass again. Trey took it without another word.

The men all lifted their drinks high, the old man speaking those ritual words. Then in a fluid motion, they all tipped the shots back and drank.

Trey did just as the others did. He knew that cuff upside the head that he'd expected earlier would come without warning if he so much as flinched.

But the burn… He'd heard about it. He'd expected it. With a mental curse, he swallowed the reflexive cough. His eyes burned. His throat ached, and his gut caught fire real fast.

The others all set their glasses on the tray near the door, the one Grandmother had put there for just that purpose, and headed back to the bunkhouse.

Soon, the only people left in the room were Trey, his father and grandfather. Pal Senior walked over to the bar and poured himself a second shot. He didn't offer either of them another. Pal Junior excused himself and headed up the wide, winding staircase to bed.

For an instant, Trey wasn't sure what to do. He set his shot glass on the tray and took a step through the wide doors.

Boy?

His grandfather's voice sent a shiver up his spine. He turned back around. *Sir?*

You done good tonight. Pal laughed. *Thought you were gonna embarrass me by choking.* His laughter was more of a cackle. The old man spun around and pinned Trey with a nasty glare. *Where you been learning to drink?*

Trey met the old man's glare with one of his own. He'd just gone through the last rite of passage to be accepted as one of the men here. He wasn't giving up all that he'd gained—and so he'd lied.

For the first time, he looked the old man in the eye, held his gaze and lied straight to his face. *No drinkin', sir.* He didn't dare even think about all the parties down at the river, of the men in the bunkhouse who'd tried to prepare him for this minute. His friends had known what the old man expected, and he wouldn't betray that support for anything.

He wouldn't cost one single man his job, or one friend his grandfather's respect.

Looking back now, Trey remembered how he'd idolized his grandfather. The big, boisterous Texan had owned one of the largest ranches in the Lone Star State. He'd been a decorated Vietnam vet, and a shrewd and tough businessman. But he'd been equally generous with the people he loved.

And he'd loved Trey, or so Trey had believed, spoiling him with toys and privileges. Fat lot of good that did him now.

Closing his eyes, Trey reminded himself why distance was his shield.

Late last year, Trey had left that all behind. Betrayal put a nasty taste in his mouth.

"Get the hell out of my head," Trey growled. Now he sat—he stared—and finally, he strode to the sink and dumped the expensive whiskey down the drain. "Still not ready to have that drink with you, old man," he whispered to the empty room.

This time, not even memories answered

him. With a curse, he smacked the No Sale button on the cash register just a bit too hard. He'd finish up the deposit and get out of here.

The drawer sprang open and he counted the change. Like every other night, he lifted the change tray, checking for the non-existent checks. Win's papers were still there, just as he'd left them.

Why hadn't the old guy come back to get them? He'd vaguely noticed the trio hadn't come in, but he hadn't really thought about it. Not until now. He'd been too busy.

The papers intrigued him, and he pulled them out. A yellow tinge to the paper showed time's evidence. Carefully, he unfolded the crude drawing. Was it what Hap had said, a map? A treasure map?

The hills around this town were full of gold and silver. The history books were full of the tales about people who'd gotten rich in the area, as well as those who'd lost everything. What treasure could possibly be here that the gold fever had managed to miss?

Was there a treasure? Or was the map just another hoax? He turned the paper over. Nothing more on the back. Trey stared at the pages for a long moment. What if it really was a treasure map? What if…

Trey cursed. It was just an old homemade

map. A myth. A scam. Nothing more. Probably a joke someone had pulled on a mark back in the gold-rush days.

There were no hidden treasures up in the Colorado mountains. But if there were... Would it be the answer he needed, the key to his independence? A new start?

Putting the map back, he finished the deposit and stuffed the bag into the safe to take to the bank tomorrow. He'd had enough for tonight, and all he wanted to do was get some sleep. Time to close up.

His bootheels echoed loudly as he walked across the old wooden floor. At the end of the bar, Trey grabbed his Stetson—another holdover from growing up in Texas—and locked the door behind him.

Outside, the snowdrifts on each side of the walk were nearly hip high. The newly-fallen snow crunched and squeaked under his steps—loud in the frosty middle of the night. He headed around the building to the old fire-escape stairs.

His small studio apartment was technically in the same building as the bar—there just wasn't a direct passage from one to the other. Part of the deal—he couldn't have planned it better.

A few snowflakes fluttered over him. He

couldn't tell if it was new snowfall, or if the wind had caught the stray flakes and tossed them around. He turned up his collar to keep the cold from slipping down his neck. Fresh powder did have its price.

He'd just reached the top of the old stairs when voices broke the stillness. He stopped, listening. Who else was out this late? Nothing good could be going on at three in the morning.

"Hey," a voice called out of the darkness. Trey leaned over the old rail, thinking the words were aimed at him.

A big burly man came out of the shadows below, his back to Trey as he looked down the alley. In the distance, Trey saw a smaller, thinner man awkwardly hurrying away. For an instant, Trey considered going down again. That wiry, lanky frame seemed almost familiar...

"Hey!" the bigger man yelled again, thankfully tearing Trey out of his thoughts.

There was menace in the man's tone. Menace and something else. Demand? Anger? The big guy lumbered toward the other man, and Trey almost took a step. He'd always prided himself on taking care of the people around him. But the people around him had always been familiar to him. Family. Friends.

Neighbors. Haskins Corners, Texas, was a long way from Telluride, Colorado.

He continued watching the men. Watched to make sure nothing happened. When the big man reached the smaller man's side, Trey leaned farther over the rail. But the men shook hands, and he breathed in relief. The smaller man reached into his back pocket and pulled out an envelope.

Pale moonlight reflected off the paper, but from here, Trey couldn't make out anything—of their expressions or their words. They were talking, and the big man nodded as he looked at what the other man handed him. What were they doing? Their voices didn't carry across the night air, even though there was little to stop them.

Trey turned to go inside, and the sound of his movement echoed through the silent night. Both men glanced up toward him then, but the shadows still obscured their faces. Familiar? Older than he'd expected. Had he seen them in the bar? He couldn't say. The place was often jam-packed.

They stared at him as if they hadn't realized he was there.

Skimming the brim of his hat with a familiar, two-fingered Texas salute, Trey turned and continued inside. He was tired. He didn't want to be involved with anyone.

The fact that Lisa's image flitted into his mind only ticked him off. *Not her, either.*

He unlocked his apartment door and shoved it open. Silence greeted him, engulfing him as he stepped inside. His footsteps were muffled by the worn carpet. At the window, he glanced out. Same view, different angle.

The men were still there, talking, the bigger man gesturing to emphasize the words Trey still couldn't hear. Words he swore he didn't *want* to hear.

However, curiosity continued to knock on the door of his brain.

Shaking his head, Trey flipped on light switches as he moved farther inside. Warmth reached out and reminded him of how cold it had been outside. The men had distracted him from it for a bit.

He hung his coat on the hook by the door, his hat beside it. He glanced out the window again, but the men were gone. Where were they? Gone back home? Somewhere else? Headed for trouble?

The night was empty, the moonlight falling unimpeded on the snow. Trey shivered. Danged old fools. Just like his grandfather had been, they were up to something. Trey shivered, and reminded himself he'd come here to start over, to escape the mess other people made of their lives.

Not find more of it.

THE SUN WAS BRIGHT TODAY. Lisa had decided late last night, as she'd tossed and turned, that she wasn't going to sleep her day away. She had plans and work she needed to accomplish if she wanted to do something besides serve drinks and burgers for the rest of her life.

Not that it was horrible—especially with Trey Haymaker's face flashing through her mind. But it just wasn't for her. It wasn't her dream.

Today, she was going to check out of the hotel, nice as it was. But not until *after* she finished breakfast.

Then she'd move her few things over to Grandpa's house and see what needed to be done there. One of Sam's deputies had boarded up the broken window, and thankfully no one had returned to the house since the initial break-in.

The only fingerprints they'd been able to identify were Grandpa's. There'd been a few others, but no information yet on whose they might be. While Sam wasn't thrilled about her staying at the house, he hadn't been able to convince her to change her mind. If Grandpa were here, he'd stay. She'd told Sam to send a deputy around to check on her if he needed to, but she was going to stay there.

Once she was settled at the house, she planned to run over to the library and check her email and some job sites. She needed to focus on *her* life, *her* goals and find a way to get back on track so that once she found Grandpa, she had a life to return to.

Pulling her small wheeled suitcase behind her, she headed to the elevator. The doors slid open smoothly, and she froze.

Lance stood there staring back. She shivered, hoping he put it off to the cold weather, not her discomfort with him.

"Lisa?" he asked, putting his arm across the doors to hold them open for her. "Lisa Duprey, right?"

She stared for a long minute. "Uh, yeah." She tried not to wonder if he'd be so friendly if he'd seen her avoiding him last night.

"Lance Westgate." He moved closer, his arms wide like he meant to give her a hug. "Remember?"

"Lance." She dodged his attempt at an embrace. This was not the Lance Westgate she remembered. That guy had been a boy, with long hair, a slightly stooped stance and a bit of a chip on his shoulder. A boy who'd lived too far on the fringes, trying to find his place with the least desirable elements.

This man was tall, with perfectly trimmed and styled dark brown hair, a faint shadow on his jaw and straight broad shoulders. He wore a long trench coat, open to show the lapels of an expensive suit.

No, this was not the Lance Westgate she remembered. But looking into his eyes now, there was still something familiar there. She suppressed a shudder at the memory of him and his friends on that long-ago night.

His words from then still had the power to haunt her. *Come on. Try it. Trust me.*

Trust him? She'd barely known him. But she'd been tempted. She'd wanted so badly to fit in. She'd been visiting her grandparents for the summer, and while she'd wanted to make friends, she hadn't thought about boyfriends. Okay, she'd thought about them, but in a distracted future sense. She'd been all of fourteen.

She'd finally refused and run home—spending the rest of the summer on her own—not with a group of friends as she'd hoped.

He might have changed physically, but her reaction to him hadn't changed. She still didn't like or trust him. "Oh, uh, yeah. Lance.

How are you?" She stepped into the elevator, leery of the way he seemed to loom over her.

"Oh, I'm doing well. Doing very well, actually."

"So, what brings you here?" She meant the hotel since she'd heard he'd moved away from Telluride.

"Oh, I always stay here at The Guest House when I'm in town. There's not a better place." He lifted an arm to gesture and encompass the entire building. "I'm sure you agree."

"Uh, yeah." He stayed here frequently? How much money did he make that he could afford frequent visits here? Envy, she reminded herself, was an unbecoming emotion.

"I'm sure you've seen the new housing development I'm working on at the edge of town."

"Uh…no, not really. I got here late the other night. It was dark. I didn't see much of anything."

"Well, you'll have to check it out." He laughed. "Not that you'll need it anytime soon. It's a retirement community."

"Oh." That was a bit of a surprise. "How'd you get into that field?"

"Worked my way up, of course." His grin was just a bit smarmy.

Thankfully, the doors slid open as silently

as they had closed upstairs. He let her go first, and she gladly stepped into the lobby.

"Care to join me for breakfast?" He waved toward the dining room.

Big spender—considering it was free. If they'd dated, where would he have taken her for a meal when they were kids? Not here, she was sure.

"Uh—" She wanted breakfast, but she didn't want it with him. "I have to get going. But, uh… Thank you."

Was that a flash of anger in his eyes? Had he seen her hiding from him behind the bar last night? Her cheeks warmed.

She'd acted childishly, she admitted it. But facing him hadn't been an option. The rest of her warmed as she recalled Trey's reassuring presence. Shaking her head to clear her thoughts, she stepped away. "Thanks for the invite. See you around." She hoped not.

Outside, the air was cold, with frost painting her car windows and every flat surface up and down the street. Her breath fogged in the air.

Lisa scraped just enough of the ice from the car windows to see as she drove the few blocks to Grandpa's house.

Not much looked different, except for the sheet of plywood nailed over the broken living room window. She'd have to make sure no moisture had gotten in.

Tentatively, she tested the front door, only slightly relaxing when the door was solidly locked. Opening it, she stepped inside, enjoying the warmth that wrapped around her.

More prepared for the state of the house this time, she headed to the small bedroom where she'd slept whenever she came here to stay. Down the short hall behind the kitchen, it had been her special place. And with her grandparents' room upstairs, she'd found it easy to sneak out.

What had she been thinking in those days? Lisa sighed. She hadn't—that was the problem.

As she set her suitcase on the bed, a sense of homecoming enveloped her. The old springs squeaked, and she smiled at the familiarity.

She focused on her few things. She needed to unpack at least some of her things. That kept her busy for all of ten minutes. After which, she decided it was time to investigate the damage in the living room.

Someone, probably Sam, had closed the old-fashioned pocket doors, so stepping into the room was like entering a freezer. She gingerly inspected the deputy's work, hurrying before she froze.

The wood was solid on the outside, but the wind whistled in through the open glass. She'd have to get the window fixed, or something put on the inside.

Maybe she'd go over to the hardware store. The owner, Lee, knew everyone in town. He could direct her to someone for the repair. She'd just grabbed her purse and was headed back outside when the shrill ringing of the phone broke the quiet of the house.

Lisa jumped at least a foot and let out a shriek that would have resulted in her grandmother's disapproval. After a deep breath, she reached for the phone hanging on the wall.

Should she answer it? What if it was Grandpa? Duh. Why would he call himself? She rolled her eyes. It was probably a salesman, or some stupid robocall. But just in case…

"H…hello?"

"Lisa?" her mother asked.

"Uh. Hi, Mom." She closed her eyes and leaned her forehead on the wall beside the phone. She should have called her mother as soon as she got here. Okay, so she'd been a little distracted.

"How's everything going?"

"Uh, well, uhm…" She wasn't quite sure where to begin.

"Lisa, that's not an answer." There was a bit of impatience in her mother's voice.

"Yeah. I should have let you know." She felt a bit guilty, but she didn't like the idea of her mother worrying. Among other things.

"Let me know what?"

"Well, I'm here."

"I realize that, dear."

"Grandpa isn't."

Her mother sighed. "Where is he?"

"That's the problem. No one's really sure."

"What?" There was a heavy silence. "Who have you asked? I'm sure he told someone where he was heading off to. He always does."

"Well, Sam was here the first night, and he has no idea. Someone broke into the house, and Sam came to check."

"What? Are you okay?"

Lisa was glad her mother was worried about her. "I'm fine."

"I guess I'll have to drive up there tomorrow and handle this myself. So much for my trip." Why was there a heavy sigh at the end of that sentence?

"Mom, Sam is handling it." How did her mother do that? Just one statement could make Lisa feel so incompetent. "I'll stick around until we figure out what's going on.

I'll keep you posted. You asked me to see what was going on, and I am." If her mother wasn't going to trust her, why hadn't she come up here in the first place? Lisa almost said so out loud, but bit her tongue instead.

It wouldn't do any good to antagonize her mother. At least Mom couldn't send her "the look" over a phone.

"I'm sure you are, dear, but they know me better than they do you. I'm sure they'll respond to my demands."

Belinda Duprey had been in charge of her business and the family entirely too long. Yeah, she'd grown up here, as had Lisa's father, but that didn't mean she'd stayed connected. And her mother's bossy, demanding personality didn't always encourage confidence. Or confidences.

Lisa loved her mother, but Belinda had wanted her children to stand on their own two feet. And that meant all by themselves.

And, on the whole, Lisa did that.

But sometimes, like now, as she looked around the beloved but empty house, Lisa felt just a little bit lonely. Before she disappointed her mother and admitted how she felt, she decided to wrap up the call.

"I gotta go now, Mom. I've got to get to

the hardware store to see about getting this window fixed."

"Window? What window?"

"The broken one." She shouldn't have said that.

"Who's fixing it? You can't. You aren't a carpenter."

"Yes, Mom, I know."

"Go see the guy over at the hardware store. Lee. Tell him I sent you. He'll be able to help."

"I'll handle it." Lisa tried not to grit her teeth. "Talk to you soon." She ended the call before her mother could give her any more unsolicited advice.

CHAPTER SIX

COLD SLICED THROUGH TREY. He turned up the collar of his jean jacket, once again cursing the fact that he'd left the warmth of southern Texas behind and had voluntarily come here to the deep Rocky Mountains. Winter only emphasized the stupidity of that decision.

Luckily, the streets were narrow and the old brick buildings created something of a barrier between him and the icy mountains. If it weren't for the wind following him down the street, he might have enjoyed getting out today.

He needed a distraction but hitting the slopes was unfortunately not an option. He had too much to do; besides, that would give him time in his own head. No, he wanted something to concentrate on. The leaky sink behind the bar was the perfect solution.

Trey pushed open the door to the hardware store that sat just a block away from the bar. "Lee," he called, guessing the owner was in the back playing solitaire on his computer. "I need plumbing supplies."

"You know where ever'thin's at." The disembodied voice came from the back room, as Trey had suspected, but Lee didn't.

"Yeah, but I need your expertise."

"Like hell," Lee grumbled. Still no movement.

Trey laughed and headed to the farthest of the half-dozen aisles. He was perusing the bins of elbow joints and drain traps when he heard footsteps. "You win the game, Lee?" he asked without looking up.

"Bah! No. You distracted me."

This time, Trey did glance up. "At solitaire? Really, man?" Trey straightened, standing a good three inches taller than the middle-aged store owner. But what Trey had in height, Lee had in bulk, and not around his middle. The man was in serious body-building shape.

Lee shrugged and faced the bins instead of Trey. "You finally fixing that back sink? Took you long enough."

"Hey, I asked for your help last fall."

"And here we are midwinter. Good thing it didn't freeze."

"Just help me get the right parts, man."

"Grumpy," Lee mumbled and rummaged through the assorted bins, the metal and plastic pipes making a loud clatter that filled the shop. "This'll work." He handed Trey a curved piece of pipe that looked like the one still on the sink—the one that was leaking. "And this." He handed over another piece. And several others, before he turned and smiled at Trey. "That'll fix you up real good."

"All this?"

Lee just stared him in the eye, and lifted an eyebrow as if to say, *You doubt my wisdom?*

Trey sighed. He'd wanted to get his mind off a certain new waitress and get the sink fixed. A win-win. Shaking his head, Trey followed Lee down the next aisle—the one filled with tubes of caulk. If nothing else, he'd learned the skills of a handyman since moving here.

"You ready to check out?" Lee asked.

"Yeah." Trey followed Lee to the counter and dropped the supplies. The old Formica gained a scratch or two, but no one would notice. "You sure I need all this?" He looked doubtfully at the man.

Lee pawed through the pile. "Maybe. Maybe not. You can bring back whatcha don't use." He grabbed the first pipe to ring it up. "You still asking for my help? I got time to-morrow afternoon."

"I'll call if I can't figure it out. You've taught me plenty."

Lee grinned. "Now I guess we see how much you listened."

Just then, the door opened, breaking into their conversation.

Lisa and a cold blast of wind rushed inside. She looked straight at them, and Trey couldn't tear his eyes away. So much for distraction.

WHAT WAS TREY doing here? Lisa paused just an instant before forcing herself to keep walking. "Hey, Lee." She walked up to the counter. "Trey."

"Hi, Lisa. Didn't hear you were back in town," Lee said.

She'd known the man most of her life, as Grandpa came here all the time. He was always fixing something, so she'd tagged along when she'd visited.

"I've been here a few days." She glanced over at Trey, hoping he hadn't shared any information about her new job with Lee. The older man didn't need to know she was working at the bar just yet. He'd learn about it soon enough, though, since word traveled fast in a small town.

"What can I do for you?" Lee asked.

She heard her mother's voice in her head.

"Grandpa's got a broken window, and Mom figured you'd be the best one to ask for help."

"How'd the window get broken?" Lee asked while he rang up Trey's items.

"A couple of days ago, someone broke into Grandpa's place."

"Well, that's not good!"

"No. And they broke the front window. Sam had one of the deputies board it up, but it can't stay that way—it's freezing in the house."

"Why isn't Win getting it fixed?" Lee asked, shoving the items into a bag as Trey scanned his credit card.

"Wait…" Trey stopped and looked back at her. "Win is your grandfather?"

"Uh…yeah." She didn't elaborate, but faced Lee instead. "Who can I trust to help me get the window replaced?"

Lee rummaged around in the mysterious underbelly of the counter, pulling out several ratty business cards and putting them up on the counter. As he pulled each one out, he shook his head. "Ah, here we go." He finally glanced up at her and smiled. "This is yer guy. He's one of the best repair guys in the valley. But I'm not sure what kind of stock he's got on hand. Those are some old windows."

It hadn't really occurred to her that because they were up in the mountains, not Denver, that'd be a problem. "He'd probably have to order them, wouldn't he?"

"Probably," Lee confirmed.

"Dang. I'd really like to make sure it's taken care of so Grandpa doesn't have to deal with it when he gets home."

"He's gone?"

"Uh, yeah." She dared a peek at Trey, who was still waiting for Lee to hand him the bag.

She didn't like admitting she didn't know where her grandfather was, but he and Lee were friends. Maybe he'd said something to Lee. "We think he took another of his trips into the backcountry. Did he mention it to you?"

Once again, Lee paused, almost as if he were looking on the inside of his own head for an answer. "You know—" He rubbed his chin. "He said something. Dang, I wasn't really payin' attention."

"Were you playing solitaire?" Trey added, a bit unhelpfully. She frowned at him then returned her focus to Lee. "Anything you can remember would help."

"I'll think on it. If anything comes back to me, I'll let you know. I was wondering about him since he hasn't been in this week. He's normally around enough that we chat, but it's been so blasted cold, I just assumed he was staying home."

"I wish." She picked up the business card. "Do you need this? Or should I take a picture?"

"That'd probably be your best idea." He nodded toward her phone. She quickly took a shot of the card and he put it under the counter again.

She'd head back to the house and see if she could get hold of the carpenter. Maybe he could come out today, though she wasn't hopeful.

Lisa looked over at Trey, then to Lee. "You don't happen to have time to come over and check it, do you?"

"I can't leave the store. My assistant is out for a funeral. He'll be in tomorrow."

She'd probably already have the carpenter out to check it by then. Oh, well. She could handle one night.

"Trey can check it." Lee suggested.

"What?" she and Trey said at the same instant.

"Well, you know Trey, right, since you work for him?"

"Yeah." Why she'd thought there was a

point in trying to keep it from him, she had no idea.

Lee took control. "Great. Trey, I'd appreciate it if you could give it a once-over. Those deputies are good at what they do, but carpentry ain't part of their skill set, if you get my meaning."

"Uh—sure. I don't mind." Trey moved away from the counter, grabbing the bag Lee finally handed him. The contents made a metallic rattling sound.

"Here." Lee moved from behind the counter. "Take this." He pulled out a thick roll of plastic from a big wire rack. "Just in case. There's some two-by-fours in the back room. You can tack it all up and at least keep the wind and damp out for now."

"How much do I owe you?" she asked.

"No charge. Consider it a favor for Win. Hope he gets back soon, safe and sound." The big man's face showed his concern for his friend. She couldn't refuse his offer of help.

"Thanks." This time when she looked at Trey, their gazes locked. "Uh, you, too."

"Sure." Trey broke the connection first and headed to the door. He held it open for her.

HALF AN HOUR LATER, Trey was up on the ladder in Grandma's perfectly arranged living room. Grandpa hadn't moved a thing since Grandma had died, and it still felt familiar and homey.

Except for the hole in the window and the icy cold air.

Lisa stood below, holding the other end of the two-by-four.

They were both wearing their coats since the temperature in the room hadn't risen much above zero degrees. She shivered and tried to keep her grip tight on the board.

"Only a couple more nails and we should be good," Trey said, and she heard the shiver in his voice.

"Thanks for helping."

"Like I said before, no problem." They didn't speak any more as he nailed the board in place, then climbed down. "I'll put the ladder away."

He couldn't seem to get away from her fast enough. Or maybe it was just the cold. Thankfully, the old house had pocket doors that closed the front room off from the rest of the house. As she pulled them shut, the room seemed warmer. At least the wind wasn't howling through it anymore.

Trey came back in just then, tromping snow loudly off his feet. "All put away."

"Thanks." Silence, awkward and heavy, settled between them.

"Well, guess I'll be going." He turned toward the door.

"Wait!" Why didn't she want him to leave? Was it because she didn't want to be alone in the house? Or was it because she liked him being here? Being with her. "Let me at least make you lunch for your trouble."

"You don't have to do that."

"Don't tell me you aren't sick and tired of eating grilled burgers nearly every day."

He laughed, but not with much humor. "Hey, they aren't half bad."

She rolled her eyes and pulled out her grandmother's big skillet. "I don't have a lot of groceries yet—just what Grandpa had— but I can whip us up a decent brunch." She smiled at him. "Come on. Don't make me eat alone."

He smiled back and rubbed the nape of his neck as if deciding. Finally, he met her gaze. "Sure. If it's no trouble."

"No trouble at all." And it wasn't. She was hungry now that she had company to share the meal with.

It didn't take long to fry up some eggs, the bacon Grandpa always had in the refrigerator and hash browns. Her favorite breakfast for lunch. Trey volunteered to make the coffee and toast.

"We work pretty well together," he joked. "I should probably hire you. Oh, wait—"

"Very funny." She set their plates on the table and settled across from him. "Now eat up before it gets cold."

Trey dug into the food and barely came up for air. "You're a good cook. Remind me of that the next time Gabe calls off."

"I'm not running that kitchen." She pointed her toast at him, and he laughed.

Finally full, Trey leaned back in the chrome chair and settled his coffee cup in his hand. "That was delicious. I don't think I've had a meal that good since I left home."

"And where's that?" Texas was a big state.

Silence was the only answer she got. She glanced up from her meal and found Trey looking at her, but the distant glaze in his eyes said he wasn't seeing her.

"Trey?"

"Uh, yeah." He shook off the stupor, but didn't answer her question. He let the quiet of the house slip in, and she didn't push him. He clearly didn't want to answer her. Instead he changed the subject.

"Your grandfather was in the bar the other

night. With Hap and the sheriff." Trey stood, picking up his dirty plates.

That got her attention. "What were they doing?"

"Mostly just harassing each other and drinking. Have you asked them if they know where he is?"

She nodded and stood with her own plate. "Sam's the one who came when I called about the break-in." She tilted her head toward the front room. "I'm sure he talked to Hap. They're always together."

"Yeah, they are." Trey smiled. "You know Hap owns the bar, right?"

"I knew he used to. Thought maybe you'd bought it."

He laughed. "No. I'm not ready to commit to something like that." He rinsed the dishes and stacked them in the dishwasher.

"Thanks." She was pleasantly surprised at his help. "For helping with the dishes, and the window."

"My mom would smack me upside the head for being a rude guest if I didn't help clean up." He reached out to take her plate.

"Guess you should remember that, too, the next time Gabe calls off." She smiled, turning his joke back on him. He laughed and the honesty of the sound made her stop moving. Warmth washed over her. She liked it.

"You should do that more often," she said.

"What?"

"Laugh." She put the other utensils on their plates and faced him. "It's nice."

He nodded, though he didn't return her smile. He took a step back and crossed his arms over his chest. "You're a puzzle."

"Why's that?"

"You're from here?"

"Sort of. My mom and dad grew up in town, so I've spent a lot of time in Telluride with my grandparents. I grew up in Denver, though, really."

"The other night. Why did you hide from Westgate? You obviously know him." Trey asked the question with his usual quiet directness, but something about his voice, and how he asked, was different. She couldn't put a finger on it, but there it was, right in front of her.

"I—" Why had she hidden from Lance... really? She'd nearly convinced herself it was because Lance had always been a jerk, and she hadn't wanted to deal with him. But if she were truly honest with herself, her pride had gotten in the way.

If they had talked, Lance would have asked

her about her life. And while he stood there in his fancy jacket, wearing the imported wing tips, and sporting a high-end salon haircut, she'd have had to admit that yes, she was working full-time in the bar now, and yes, she'd lost her dream job in Denver.

Humiliation was not her favorite outfit.

She moved over to the coffee maker and refilled her cup, lifting the pot in the air toward him. He shook his head and waited while she sat back down on the old chrome kitchen chair and leaned her elbows on the table, her chin in her palms. "Guess I'm a chicken."

Trey frowned and carefully leaned against the counter, crossing his ankles.

"This from the woman I found searching through a smelly Dumpster, who's apparently friendly with both the sheriff and the former mayor? Who avoids drunks in the bar like a pro and stands up for everyone but herself? You are far from a chicken."

That was the longest speech she'd ever heard him make. She stared at him. "That's not courage, that's just…determination."

"Well, whatever it is, keep it up." He pushed away from the counter, grabbed his coat from the chair. He'd left the Stetson by the door and now he settled it on his head. "I'd better get going. We've got a bar to open in an hour, and I haven't even started working on that sink."

"Sorry I interrupted your work."

He laughed and she smiled in response. Still a nice sound. "It's kept for a few months now. Another day or two won't matter. See you later?"

"Yeah, I'll be there."

He headed to the door, then stopped, his hand resting on the knob. "Thanks for lunch. Maybe we can do it again sometime."

Without another word, Trey yanked open the door and stepped out into the cold.

Through the window in the door, she watched him walk away, and suddenly realized he'd never answered her question about where he was from.

Those boots were a dead giveaway that he hadn't come from any city. The leather was too worn, his gait too comfortable in them.

At the end of the walk, he turned up his collar and lifted his face up to the sky. He might not be from here, but he was certainly at home here in the snowy mountains.

Still, it was odd that he seemed to avoid any questions about his past or where he was from. It reminded her of her history with Robert. And just one of the many reasons why she should let Trey Haymaker walk away.

CHAPTER SEVEN

SKIING HAD ALWAYS helped Trey clear his head. At least it had in the past, and was part of why he'd moved to Telluride. It required concentration on just one thing—his body. How it moved. How the equipment worked with that movement. What the mountain felt like beneath his skis. How he made sure he didn't end up on his back in the snow. Full focus and concentration on nothing else.

The only downtime to think was on the lift, and if he was lucky, those minutes were filled with inane small talk with a stranger. It was distracting and safe. And lasted only a short while.

Then he was back on the slopes, fighting gravity and winning his war against his troubles 90 percent of the time.

He'd fixed the sink—without having to call Lee for help, thank you very much. Today his relief bartender was opening the bar. Rick worked ski patrol most of the winter, but picked up a shift here and there for Trey. He'd gladly taken the hours when Trey called him.

Working last night with Lisa had been difficult. Only because his parting words after she'd made him brunch kept echoing around in his head.

Leaping off the ski lift, he moved to the side of the run. He'd been skiing since almost the same time as he'd started to walk. Learning to slide down the side of a mountain, with nothing to stop him, had been his first taste of freedom and speed. Back in Texas, he'd found that adrenaline rush on the back of a fast horse, and then later behind the wheel of a car. Flat, straight stretches of highway had been his addiction.

Now, just before noon, Trey stood at the top of the slope. The crowds were light. The powder was thick after last night's storm. He let the pair who'd gotten off the lift behind him move ahead. He wanted to enjoy the view from here and not worry about where others were. He was only going to get a couple more runs in before he had to head to work. He wanted to enjoy them.

Wanted to wipe his mind clean.

Trey closed his eyes for an instant, drawing in a deep, burning-cold breath, then let it out in a white cloud. He should see darkness behind his eyelids, but instead he saw *her*. Lisa had somehow leaped, full of life, into his mind, shattering the calm. He put his poles hard into the snow and shoved off.

What was wrong with him? Trey let the cold air wash over him, hoping it would knock some sense into him.

Swoosh. The sharp edges of his skis cut through the powder, sending a white plume out behind him. Out of the corner of his eye, he saw the sun catch the crystals before they fell back to earth.

The icy wind kissed his face and slipped through his hair. He should have worn a hat. But this felt too good and blew out the cobwebs in his mind.

But even with the demands of the mountain beneath his feet, he couldn't escape his thoughts of Lisa.

Helping her with the window and letting her fix them a meal had been a mistake. He'd thoroughly enjoyed himself—that wasn't the point. The problem was that he'd enjoyed himself…and wanted more.

Moguls rose up on the slope, and he nearly stumbled. How many times had he taken this slope? Too many to make that kind of miscalculation. Catching himself, he focused and took them with the skill he'd worked years to achieve.

Flowing with the terrain, bending, straightening and leaning when needed, he raced down the mountain. He tasted the frosty snow and relished the scattering of flakes on his skin.

An instant later, as Trey neared the next turn on the manicured slope, a figure barreled past him. A man Trey hadn't seen up top, dressed all in black, cut too close. Trey might enjoy adventure and adrenaline, but he wasn't an idiot. Dodging the man's next pass, Trey slowed, letting the man go ahead. Watching him descend, Trey didn't think the other man looked out of control, but that pass had been too close.

What was going on? He stopped at the edge of the hill, near the tree line. Standing there, his poles planted in the snow, Trey waited, watching. The black-clad figure wound his way through the mogul field with clear expertise.

He'd have admired the guy's skill, if he hadn't nearly sent Trey flying into the trees. The danger of that made Trey shudder.

Once he was certain the man was long gone, Trey shoved off again and headed down.

He slowed his normal speed. His concentration was off, and he didn't dare risk a fall.

The trail wound down the side of the mountain, and just as he reached the final, major turn, Trey saw the dark-clad figure near the tree line. The stranger executed a fast turn and pulled to a stop.

Was the guy resting, or waiting for someone? For him? Trey wasn't interested in playing cat and mouse, but he hesitated to pass the guy. Darn. He had neither the time nor the desire to deal with stupidity.

Shaking off his uncharacteristic paranoia, Trey headed for the last turn. He'd make this his final run for the day and head to the bar from here.

He'd just come up even with the guy when Trey saw him push off. What the—?

This time, he didn't come toward Trey, but kept pace with him. Trey didn't race. That was stupid and dangerous, especially on slopes where other skiers could come out of nowhere. But there wasn't anyone around, and the guy wasn't backing off.

Fine. Let's get this over with. Trey pushed harder and bent lower toward the terrain. He knew this hill and easily pulled ahead. He tamped down the adrenaline rush that tasted sweet. He pulled his focus in tight, letting the glide of the skis, and the feel of the cold air rushing past his face, be all that registered.

Focus.

Something hard, solid—a person—hit him in the side. His balance and focus gone, Trey tumbled. Even though fresh powder lay on top of the run, the snowpack beneath was hard as a frozen rock. His shoulder hit first, then his hip, then finally his skis snapped loose. He came to a sudden and painful halt just feet from the ponderosa pines.

Sucking in the frigid air hurt. He didn't think anything was broken, but he couldn't be sure. There were going to be plenty of bruises to investigate later. "Darn," he said aloud and heard it echo back at him from the deserted slope.

He sat there for several minutes, though, making sure there weren't any injuries he'd missed. Finally, once he'd caught his breath, he reached for his skis. Stepping back into them, he finished the run without incident. And without any company. Where had the guy gone?

At the bottom of the slope, people were moving everywhere, their voices loud, their faces unfamiliar. Half of them wore dark clothing.

He'd never be able to pick the guy out.

His taste for the slopes tainted, Trey took off his skis and propped them on his shoulder. It ached from his fall, and he made a mental note to take some pain meds once he got to the bar.

Hyperalert, he made his way the short distance to the bar. His cowboy boots were in the back room, and he hustled to get the ski boots off. Finally, in street clothes again and with his cowboy boots on, he sat and took a breath.

He'd been skiing long enough to know the rules of the slopes—to give other skiers space and respect. He'd never had anyone challenge or target him that way before.

Who was he? He recalled the men in the alley the other night and was sure it wasn't either of them. They'd been older. This was a much younger, thinner, more agile man. Someone who moved easily on the slopes.

Those two would have struggled on the demanding ski slopes. But was it because of them? Someone they knew?

Shaking his head, Trey stood and headed into the office. The bottle of painkillers he kept in the desk drawer rattled as he pulled it out. Usually he took them after too many hours of bookkeeping, or from standing behind the bar on an especially busy night.

Not because the slopes had been too rough.

On the plus side, at least he'd forgotten about Lisa for a while.

A WEEK HAD PASSED since Lisa had driven into Telluride. She had yet to hear from her grandfather, and she'd only made it to the library twice to check her email and do any job hunting.

At this rate, she'd be here permanently.

Dread and disappointment threatened to take over, and she wasn't sure what to do. She wasn't even sure if there was anything she *could* do.

So, just like every other day, she trudged through the snow and headed in to work. The routine was starting to feel comfortable and safe.

Her shift started light, and while the ski crowd would be in later, she was glad for the reprieve. Still, she hustled. Trey wasn't in yet, so Rick was behind the bar. Gabe was in the kitchen, and she ran back and forth, though thankfully she wasn't running as much as walking today.

An older couple came in for a warm lunch. She chatted with them and was happy to share information about the local history and some of the tourist sites they might like.

They had driven up from Denver and were

scheduled to see the new retirement village later in the afternoon. "I'm sure you haven't checked it out," the man said with a smile, "But I'm sure you've heard about it."

"Oh, I have." Lisa forced herself to smile. It wasn't their fault the developer had been a jerk to her when they were kids. "Enjoy your visit," she said as she took their payment to the register.

Few people wrote checks these days. Since she'd started working here, this was the first one she'd taken. Trey hadn't explained anything about how he wanted them handled. She'd written down their phone number and driver's license info. She hoped it was enough.

The cash register was old, and when the drawer popped open, she wasn't even sure where to put the check. The coin tray lifted up easily and she figured she'd put it under that. She needed to remember to tell Trey that she'd put it there, or his deposit would be off at the end of the shift.

She was surprised to find a couple of other pieces of paper under the tray. Maybe she should look and see if there was info she'd missed on the check. Reaching in, she pulled the papers out. They weren't checks.

The papers were old. The word *telegram*

was printed across one of them. She'd never seen a real one before. The words looked like they'd been written on an old typewriter. The names were familiar, and she frowned, trying to place them. From the last name, it had to be someone in her family. Was that her great-grandparents?

The other page was a hand-drawn map. It was rough and hard to understand. She recognized a couple of the landmarks, so she knew it was a drawing of an area around here.

The screen door squealed open then, and Trey came in. Startled, she shoved her hands and the papers into her apron pocket. All her thoughts ceased as he came through the kitchen and toward the bar.

He'd been skiing. He said he tried to take a run or two before he came in each day. His face was sun- and wind-kissed, and his hair had been ruffled by that same breeze. Her fingers itched to mimic the wind.

His ski jacket made his shoulders seem wider... She tore her gaze away.

"Hello, Trey," she said.

"Hey, boss," Rick called out as he finished the drinks she needed to deliver. Trey mumbled something that could be hello or good-bye—she couldn't tell—as he headed to the office, his steps heavy and loud.

"That's your problem," she whispered to herself, thankful the bar was loud enough to cover her words. "Boss. Think boss," she said, trying valiantly to get the image of his broad shoulders out of her brain—and failing.

SHUTTING OUT THE EVENTS on the slopes, Trey got through the rest of his shift. Like every other night, he pulled open the cash drawer and lifted the change tray to count down.

Hap had called earlier and asked if he still had the map and telegram, or if he'd thrown them away as he'd asked. Not that Trey had any intention of giving them to him, but the guy did own the place. He could come in here anytime, though Trey would probably hear him, and that blasted walker. Still, Trey decided to put them someplace else, someplace safer.

They belonged to Win, and that was who he intended to give them to.

Except they were gone. He cursed. Setting the coin tray on the counter, he bent down to look deeper in the drawer. Maybe the papers had gotten caught and pulled back behind the drawer. No sign of them there. He checked around the register. Under the counter. Even reached for the trash can, sifting through the receipts and papers he'd tossed in there during his shift. Nowhere.

"Looking for something?" Lisa's voice startled him.

He spun around to find her standing there, a couple of pieces of yellowed paper in her hand. "Yeah." He put the change tray back. "But you know that." He crossed his arms over his chest and leaned against the bar.

She lifted the telegram and the map a bit higher. "These aren't checks."

"Nope. A customer left those. I put them there for safekeeping until he comes back to get them."

"By customer, you mean my grandfather?"

He looked harder at her and nodded once. "Yes, though Hap was the one who brought them in." He took the telegram and map from her fingers and returned them to the register. "They told me to throw them in the trash. I figure Win might change his mind."

"Trash?" That got her attention. "When?"

"A while ago. The night I met you, actually."

"That's what Sam was searching for!" Lisa reached past him and pulled the papers out again, examining them more closely. "This is it."

"What are you talking about?"

"That's how I ended up in the Dumpster." She pointed to the back alley. "I was in my hotel room and saw Sam digging through the trash. This—" she shook the pages until they made a crackling sound "—this had to be what he was looking for."

"Could be." Trey wasn't sure how much he should tell her—but what if she knew more about the treasure Win had hinted at? "Does anything about it seem familiar?" He'd leave it open, see what she'd volunteer.

"No. But I recognize the names."

"You should. They're your family." She nodded as she reread the old words.

Trey took his time looking at the map over her shoulder. He fought to focus on the page, struggling as the faint perfume she wore reached out and teased him, whispered for him to notice her.

Lisa turned around then, and for an instant, they were within breath-sharing distance. She gazed up at him, her eyes wide, that darn perfume weaving around him.

He didn't look away. Neither did she. Time froze.

Suddenly, Lisa stepped away, breaking the spell and the connection. Trey cleared his throat and took his own steps back away from her. Maybe he'd imagined it.

Mental eye rolls were starting to become too much a part of his day.

Lisa opened the register again, the ring loud even in the noisy room. She carefully replaced the map. "Why did you put it here?" She turned around and pinned him with a direct stare. "Why not the safe in the office?"

Trey shrugged. "I figured he'd come back and get it when Hap and Sam weren't around to harass him. Didn't realize it'd be days." He didn't mention that he'd thought about the treasure himself. But she wasn't thinking about treasure—she was worrying about Win.

Lisa tilted her head, as if judging whether to believe him. Finally, she nodded and walked out to the tables to clear the last of the scattered glasses.

Frustrated that he didn't have any more answers about the map than he'd had a couple of weeks ago, and that the woman messing with his head didn't know anything either, he turned around and focused on finishing closedown.

"Trey?" she said softly, as if she was afraid to say anything. He glanced over his shoulder, but the expression on her face was one of worry.

"Yeah?"

"He'd never leave that here. Or throw it away. I'm sure of it." Her voice cracked. "Not because he is a treasure hunter." She shook her head. "But because he values family. He'd keep it because of who wrote it."

The silence stretched out as Trey lined up highball and wineglasses in the rack. "I know that." He glanced at her again. "That's why I've held it for him."

She climbed up on the first stool. "I'm worried."

Of course, she was. She was all about family, about caring and trust. That was so far from who he was. He couldn't believe in that kind of closeness—not now. Maybe never again.

Finished with the glasses, he walked to the register. Reaching in, he pulled out the map yet again and this time slid it across the bar to her. "Take it. See if you can figure it out. Maybe it'll help you find him." She didn't hesitate to pull it over and stare at it. "Does it make any sense to you?" he asked.

"I… I don't know." She leaned closer. Her brow furrowed, and he stood there watching her. Straight-armed, he leaned on the bar's edge, trying to keep his distance and perspective. Mesmerized, he couldn't take his eyes off her. Twice, she reached up and pushed her long pale blond bangs out of her face, slipping a stray piece behind her ear. She kept her fingers there, against her ear, forcefully holding the recalcitrant hair back.

Her nails, trimmed short and round, were a pale pink color, painted with a glittery polish. He envisioned her painting them, knowing she'd put all her focus onto the task—just as she was studying the hand-drawn map lying on the bar's surface.

"Oh, my gosh!" Lisa looked up at him, and the intensity and excitement in her eyes was like a kick that knocked his breath out of his lungs.

"What?"

"I… I think I know where this is. No. It can't be." She turned the worn paper toward him. "Here. That's the falls."

"The falls?"

"At the cabin Grandpa owns. My family has owned the ranchland it sits on for generations."

Trey froze. "The cabin?" Memories he didn't want to remember rushed to the front of his mind.

"Have you been there?" she asked.

"Yeah. My grandfather and I used to come up here and stay at the cabin." He frowned, running his mind back to the place. The last time he'd been there—nearly three years ago—he and his grandfather hadn't wandered around much. They hadn't been hunting, like they had in previous years. Granddad had been struggling to move then. He hadn't said anything, but his health had clearly been declining. Trey was pretty sure the old man had known he was dying, but he hadn't bothered to tell anyone.

Shaking his head, Trey shoved the memories of the old man away and focused on the memories of the land that might be on the map.

"On the far end of that small ravine?"

"Yeah." He could envision it now. He reached for the map. "This makes sense. This is that huge aspen grove."

She was nodding. "What's this?" She pointed at a dark circle an inch down from the falls on the hand-drawn map. "Is that supposed to be where the cabin is?"

Trey moved around the bar, sidling up beside her so they were looking at the same view.

"No. I don't think so. The cabin would be more to this side." He put his finger on the spot nearer the falls. "Maybe the circle is where the treasure is."

"Treasure?" She glanced at him, then hastily averted her gaze back to the map. "Is... isn't that supposed to be an *X*?"

He laughed, her comment shaking his concentration on her. "You've watched too many pirate movies."

Her cheeks warmed, and she rolled her eyes at herself. "Okay, that was a stupid comment."

"No. Not stupid." He laughed again. "Entertaining, though."

"Funny." She pulled the map closer again. "Do you think that's where he is? Didn't Grandpa disappear right after this map showed up?"

Trey nodded. Maybe she was onto something. The determined look on her face hinted at a plan forming behind those pretty eyes. "No, Lisa. You can't go up there now. There's at least two feet of snow in that backcountry— with more forecast to come."

The resolve on her face told him she didn't care. Her words confirmed it. "He's been gone too long. What if he's hurt, or sick? I have to help him."

CHAPTER EIGHT

MAYBE TREY HAD a point about the snow.

His comments swirled around in Lisa's head as she unlocked the kitchen door to Grandpa's house that night.

The drifts were deep even here in town, with more flakes gently falling even now. It'd be worse up in the backcountry. If a storm came in before she reached the cabin, it could be disastrous. There were no cleared roads up there this time of year, and while she had experience outdoors, she was a city girl at heart.

But what about Grandpa?

Sam was doing everything he could to find him. She trusted the sheriff, knew he was good at his job. And if Grandpa was at the cabin, it was well stocked and safe. But still...

Shaking her head, Lisa tried to dislodge her worry. The middle of the night was *not* the time to make decisions, even if it did seem to be when she did most of her thinking these days.

So, she continued through the house, checking every nook and cranny before she could sleep. Just like every other night, she flipped on light switches in every room and checked inside.

While she'd reconciled herself to the fact the intruder was unlikely to come back, she had to be sure. She didn't want to jump at every creak and pop the old house made.

It helped a little when she glanced out the window at the landing and saw a patrol car slowly going by. She smiled. Sam was still keeping an eye on her, and she liked that.

When she reached the tiny bedroom upstairs that had been converted into a small office, she stopped. She'd seldom come in here, and these past few days she'd only glanced in to make sure no one was there.

This time, she stepped to the middle of the room, turning around slowly, taking it all in—the old desk and easily-as-old wooden chair. A chipped coffee mug with a dozen pens inside. A picture of Grandma beside the desk lamp.

A small stack of file folders sat in the center of the desk. Had they been there before? She couldn't remember. Why were they out of the drawer?

Lisa glanced at the big metal file cabinet that had always sat in this room. Old, steel-gray, it was something Grandpa had bought at an army surplus sale ages ago. The top drawer was open, just an inch but—had it been open before? She couldn't recall.

Lisa stepped closer to the desk and reached for the top file. She turned on the desk lamp, the pool of gold spilling over the files. She flipped open the one on top. A stack of old black-and-white photos were neatly settled against the fold. Were these originals? They looked like they'd been printed back in the 1960s.

Who were these people? Family? She thought about the old telegram and map that were downstairs in her purse. Had she ever seen an image of her great-uncle Duncan?

She didn't recognize any of the people in these pictures. Turning the photos over, she didn't find any notes or indication of who they were.

She examined the background. Maybe that would give her a clue. The first image was of four young men. They were wearing pale versions of what her grandfather called a Hawaiian shirt. All the men were smiling so broadly she could almost hear deep, joyful laughter. They held beers in old-fashioned cans, lifting them toward the photographer in a long-silent toast.

The background was vague. A bar? Wood paneling covered the wall behind them. It looked like someone's old basement.

Who were these men? What were they celebrating?

She pulled out more photos. They were all of the same people. Just not people she could identify.

She put the pictures back and settled the file back where she'd found it. Then she picked up the next one. This one had pictures in it as well, but these people she recognized. Her grandmother looked so young and pretty. Lisa found one of her grandparents sharing a kiss. Someone had snuck up on them. It was cute.

"Oh, Grandma. I miss you," she whispered. There were two more files of family photos she'd seen over the years.

Then she found one that made her gasp. A man, who looked a lot like Grandpa, in a military uniform. This time when she turned the picture over, a name was written on the back. *Duncan.* Grandpa's brother who'd died in Vietnam. Her great-uncle. The man who'd sent the telegram and drawn the map.

How long ago that was. He seemed so young and full of life in this image. Like the smile on his face was something he was familiar with wearing. There were several pictures; none of the others were labeled, but they were all of Duncan. A couple were with Grandpa, and some with people she recognized as her great-grandparents.

What a treasure trove of family history. She'd have to remember these were here.

Wait. Was Duncan in any of the other pictures? She pulled out the group shot she'd been staring at before. It was blurry, but she thought the guy on the end was Duncan.

Lisa glanced at the file cabinet again. Why had the files been taken out? What else was in there?

Not usually nosey when it came to her grandparents, Lisa hesitated before she reached out and pulled on the heavy metal drawer's handle. It opened easily, smoothly. Files, neatly labeled and color-coded, stared back at her.

Grandpa's life was in here. The first file was the year he'd graduated from high school. Every year after was neatly typed, each decade's labels a different color. A beautiful rainbow. He'd put a lot of effort into this.

And if he could do this, how come he couldn't clean the kitchen counter? Waving away that thought, Lisa yawned. It was time to go to bed.

She planned to get up early tomorrow and talk with Sam about the cabin. Maybe she'd ask him about these pictures. He'd known her grandfather and her family for years. Maybe it was worth asking her mother, too.

A name on a file label caught her eye—and made her freeze. Duncan. That must be where the files belonged. What else was there? She reached out.

A dozen letters were carefully placed inside the front file. She pulled one envelope out. It was postmarked overseas; she couldn't read anything but *November* on the stamp. Around Thanksgiving.

These had to be from her uncle Duncan. They were addressed to various family members. Some to Grandpa, but not all. Of course, a soldier far from home had written to everyone. There hadn't been any cell phones or email back then.

She vaguely wondered if they'd written to him, too, and what had happened to those letters.

Carefully, gently, she lifted the first page from its envelope. A single sheet of inexpensive, ruled paper had been folded into a square. The handwriting was neat, but definitely heavy and masculine.

He'd written from the middle of the hot

jungle, from a place she didn't recognize. He missed home. Missed all of them. Wanted to know what everyone was doing. He seemed to ask more questions than tell of his experience. Of course, he wouldn't want to talk about a war, about a place he didn't want to be. At least, she assumed he didn't want to be there.

Lisa sat down at the desk, bringing the file of letters with her. She couldn't abandon Duncan now that she'd found him. And maybe there'd be something that went with the telegram. Maybe a clue to today's mystery of where Grandpa had gone.

She'd read five letters before she came across a paragraph that made her stop and reread it. Twice.

Duncan wrote about some of the men in his unit who had been out on a mission. He didn't say what the mission was, but they'd nearly been killed. One man had been injured and was in the infirmary. Duncan had been worried. And reading between the lines, he was scared. He'd written the other men's names. Doug Swanson. Bill Ryan. Kit Kline. And Pal Haymaker.

Haymaker. How many people had that last name?

Sleep suddenly seemed very far away.

THE NEXT MORNING, Trey trudged down the street. At the corner, he stopped, and, despite the cold wind whipping down the narrow street, he took his time and gazed up at the mountainside.

It had snowed again last night. Even from here, he could see the skiers racing down the slopes, tails of powder flying up behind them. He'd like to be up there right now.

But he wasn't going to get any runs in today. Not a chance. He was headed over to the sheriff's office and, he hoped, to meet up with Hap and Sam.

Before Lisa got there.

When he'd called Sam to ask about the cabin, the older man had finally admitted that he and Hap had been working on some ideas about where Win might have disappeared to. But they didn't want to talk to Lisa yet and get her hopes up.

And Trey wanted to talk to Sam about Lisa's plans to check out the cabin, if Sam hadn't already done it.

The traffic light changed, and Trey stepped off the curb. Why was he getting involved? He was being sucked into other people's problems—something he'd sworn he'd never do again.

The sheriff's office was at the edge of

town, which meant it was only a couple of blocks from the bar. Stepping inside, Trey found Hap already settled at the conference table that occupied half the front room. An old metal desk and a small waiting area took up the rest.

"You bring a bottle with you, by chance?" he asked Trey.

"Uh, how would it look taking alcohol into the sheriff's office? You trying to get me arrested?" Trey only half joked.

Hap did laugh, though. "It was worth a try. Besides, don't I own all those bottles, technically?"

"Technically."

Sam came through a set of doors in the back, carrying a cardboard box. He thumped it down on the table between Hap and Trey.

"Whatcha doing with my box?" Hap asked.

"I'm trying to find Win." Sam leaned against the big tabletop, shoving the box toward Hap. "Your wife gave me the one you found that telegram in."

"Why'd she do that?"

"'Cuz I asked her to." Sam grinned like he'd gotten the best of his friend and relished it. Trey had seen dozens of such interactions at the bar. "Actually," Sam leaned forward again, "I thought there might be more information in here. What in here is yours, and what was Win's dad's?"

Hap pushed awkwardly to his feet, using his rickety fists to hold himself up. He pulled the box closer and pawed through it. "None of it's mine." He pulled out an old wrench. "This ain't familiar. Looks old."

"Doesn't mean it ain't yours," Sam mumbled. "No more telegrams?"

"Naw. Just junk." Hap plopped back down in his seat. "You're welcome to take a look yourself."

Trey didn't wait. He stood and leaned over to examine the contents of the box. Yeah, junk—old papers, leftover office supplies, even a few pens—but he sorted through it anyway.

Finally, he glanced up at Sam. "How is this helping?"

Sam shrugged. "It was an idea." He walked back to his desk and faced a big map of the county that hung on the wall. "We were thinking." He tilted his head toward Hap. "Maybe Win's out hunting that treasure."

"Treasure?" Trey mentally cursed. Was everyone looking for it? Was there even anything *to* look for? Wild-goose chase came to mind.

Trey leaned back in the chair and waited a

long minute. They might as well hear it from him. "Lisa has the map, so don't go getting any ideas." He paused, making sure they were both paying attention. They were. "I didn't toss it out. I put it in the register for safe-keeping, and she found it."

"What'd you do that for?"

"It's hers, numbskull." Sam punched his friend's shoulder.

"How do you figure? I found it. Win didn't want it."

"Win didn't need it," Trey interrupted.

"What?" Both older men faced him, wide-eyed.

"Lisa recognized the landmarks on the map. If she knew them, Win obviously did, too."

"But—"

"He told her about the treasure?" Hap asked.

"No." Trey shook his head. "That map is of the property up on the mountain. The family ranch. You know, the old hunting cabin he rents out? She spotted the landmarks."

Sam looked at the map on the wall again, absently tapping the area around the cabin and nodding.

"You didn't notice those landmarks, Trey? You been up there enough," Hap asked.

Trey fought back a grin. "Like you showed

me the map when you were in the bar? I was readin' upside down, remember?"

Both men nodded. "Bet you must have pored over it plenty since we left it there," Sam said.

"Uh, yeah. Some." Trey gazed at Hap. This wasn't about him. "I've been working." Sure, he'd looked at the map, but until Lisa gave him one piece of the puzzle, it hadn't made sense to him.

"Gotta give the boy that." Hap sagely nodded. "My deposits have been up since he and Lisa been working there."

Sam nodded slowly, thoughtfully, as he continued to stare at the map.

Trey broke the silence. "Lisa wants to go up to the cabin to see if Win is there." Sam glanced over his shoulder with a frown. "Any reason she shouldn't?"

"Other than nearly three feet of unplowed snow?" Sam shrugged. "No."

Trey wanted Sam to argue with him, to say that search and rescue or his deputies had been up to check the place out. "Your guys been to the cabin, Sam?"

"Yeah. As far as we dared." Sam tapped the map. "The road wasn't plowed, or used, not since the first blizzard. No tracks that we saw. Couldn't go much farther."

"What about search and rescue?"

Sam shook his head. "We don't call them out unless there's a credible reason to risk it. No one knows where Win went, and we haven't found any sign to indicate where to look."

"Hell, he could be sitting in Vegas at a slot machine," Hap said.

"He'd have told someone about that," Sam snapped.

"Maybe." Hap wasn't going to be easily convinced. "Maybe not."

The three men sat there for a long minute. Trey wasn't thrilled at where this conversation was going. He asked, "You plan to send a deputy up to check the cabin now?"

Sam didn't answer right away. "Do you really believe he's there?" He returned Trey's stare. "Or is this just Lisa's wishful thinking?"

Trey couldn't answer him. Finally, he stood. "Let me talk to her again. She's working tonight. Then I'll let you know."

"Sounds fair." Sam took the cardboard box off the table and headed down the hall.

"Where you goin' with my box?" Hap yelled.

"Putting it into evidence. Just in case."

"In case of what?"

But Sam didn't answer him, simply kept walking through the big metal doors with the sign Authorized Personnel Only tacked onto them.

Trey watched him go, then, without another word to the men, he left and headed toward the bar. Lisa was working tonight, and so was he.

He had answers to get.

FINALLY, THE BAR was empty. It'd been a busy night and Trey was exhausted. Lisa sat at the bar, her feet dangling from where she sat on the high barstool.

Music drifted from the jukebox, but not the pounding beat that had been going all night long. Someone had stuffed a half-dozen quarters in and hit the buttons for the quiet love songs, though he or she hadn't stuck around long enough to hear the songs.

"I can unplug the thing if you want," he offered with a tilt of his head toward the jukebox.

"No. It's kinda nice for a change." She threw him a tired smile then returned to counting receipts.

Trey had told Sam he'd talk to Lisa, but he didn't have the heart to push her right now. She didn't look up to it.

Staring at the rows of alcohol bottles, illuminated by the light beneath, he marveled at the glow showing through the various colors of glass. Just like every other night, he poured himself that single shot. Remembering she was there, he glanced over his shoulder at her. "You, uh, want a glass of wine or something?" he asked.

Her laughter didn't hold even a drop of amusement. "You plan on carrying me home?" She shook her head. "I don't think so. I'm too tired. Thanks."

She sounded as worn out as he felt. He wasn't sure if it was from working, or the worry she kept carrying around.

Finally, pushing the neatly stacked receipts across the bar, Lisa took a deep breath. Slowly, she reached into the pocket of her apron and pulled out an envelope. She stared at it.

"I was looking through some of Grandpa's things last night. I was hoping I'd find some clue…" Her voice faded, and she set the envelope on the smooth bar top. "I found this." She slid it toward him.

The paper wasn't old, like the ones with the telegram and map, but the way she held it told him it was something just as surprising.

"What is it?" Trey reached for it, curious about the contents and about her interest.

"Look and see."

He pulled out a sheet of paper first. Unfolding it, he found a letter. He scanned the words, then saw exactly what had caught her attention. Was that why she was so stressed?

He didn't wait for her to ask. "Yeah, that's my grandfather." He slid the letter back to her. "We never talked about it, but I always wondered if that's how he knew Win and his family. They must have become friends when my grandfather kept renting out the cabin."

She let out a heavy sigh. "There's a picture in the envelope."

He pulled the picture out. Four men. He almost smiled, before he remembered what a jerk his grandfather could be. He couldn't remember when he'd seen his grandfather smile like that—like he was actually happy and having fun—if he ever had.

"Which one is your grandfather?"

He turned the photo around so it was right-side up for her. "This one." He pointed to the tall gangly guy on the end. "He must have been about twenty in that picture, maybe younger."

She nodded. "This is Uncle Duncan." She put her finger on the face of the man next to Pal. "The guy who sent the telegram and drew the map."

"Really?" He leaned closer, angling the picture back around to get a better look. "I see the resemblance now that you point it out." They both fell silent as the soft refrain of the song filled the room.

"Trey, he was so young," she finally said.

"Was he older than Win?"

"Yeah. By almost ten years. My aunts were in between."

Somehow, he knew she needed to talk. One thing he'd learned tending bar was how to read people. "That offer for a drink still stands."

She laughed, though there wasn't much joy in the sound. "I'd probably just fall asleep."

Trey couldn't help but wonder what she was thinking. The turmoil rolling off her almost answered him. Finally, she looked up and met his stare. "Maybe I will have that drink."

He tried to hide his surprise. Laws made it illegal to sell liquor after two in the morning. Nothing prevented Trey from pouring himself and her a drink, though.

"What would you like?"

She stared pointedly at the untouched shot sitting on the bar between them. "You gonna drink this? Whiskey, right?" She tilted her head to the nearly abandoned glass.

Trey met her gaze, realizing for the first time how deep the worry went in her eyes, how far he could see into her aching soul. He didn't ask the million questions in his mind.

He shook his head. Slowly Lisa reached out and curled her fingers around the glass. They shook, and a ripple marred the amber surface.

"You don't have to," he told her.

"I know," she whispered. Lifting the glass, she put it to her lips, took a sip—and grimaced. He laughed, the sound echoing around the deserted room. He almost expected her to say *Yuck*, and wrinkle her nose. She was silent, but her expression showed her dislike.

"The offer of a glass of wine still stands."

She shook her head. "Nope. I'm doing this." Her determination made him smile. She took another sip then looked up at him, her eyes awash in damp. He wasn't sure if it was the drink or her pain. "Your turn," she said.

"We're taking turns, are we?"

She stared down at the barely touched drink sitting in front of her.

"I'll wait." He met her gaze. "I'm not sipping any whiskey." Their gazes locked. Finally, she glanced back down at the glass.

This time, when she picked it up, the drink

sloshed over the rim and her fingers. "You'd better drink it before you waste it," he said.

She lifted the glass. And took another sip.

"Not like that, woman." He shook his head. "Like this." Before he could have second thoughts, he reached for the shot glass, brought it to his lips and tilted his head back. The full shot burned...his lips...his tongue...his throat...his gut in a blazing firestorm.

He slammed the glass down and let loose a fiery breath.

"Wow." She stared up at him. "That was—Where'd you learn to do that?"

He laughed, but this time it was as bitter as hers. He pointed at the picture still on the bar and tapped the faces. "My grandfather taught me."

Her eyes grew wide. "You're kidding."

"Nope." He reached up and grabbed the top-shelf whiskey. He laughed as he poured another shot. The bottle was half-empty, and he'd managed to not drink a single drop. Until tonight.

"Your turn."

Lisa didn't take her drink, though. She leaned back in the too-big chair and stared at him. "You know you're not getting away with that comment without giving me more." She crossed her arms on the bar and leaned forward again. "Tell me about him." She tapped the picture much as he had.

Trey shook his head, wishing he could walk away from her, from this moment. But he couldn't. He wouldn't. He'd already given in. Already taken that forbidden drink. In his mind, he saw his grandfather's snickering grin. "This ain't for you, old man," he said, this time staring at the face in the photo.

"Tell me," Lisa whispered again.

Maybe it was the whiskey, the memory of it that made his mind fill with words he wanted to share with her. Maybe it was knowing that she needed to be distracted from her pain and worry. Maybe it was the open, welcoming expression on her face.

Or maybe he was just a damned fool. But the words formed and demanded escape. "He was a class A jerk," he said. "A Vietnam vet. A man who had nothing to do but order us around."

Trey could see Pal standing there as if the old man were still alive and waiting for Trey to pour him his nightly shot. "It was a tradition on the ranch that the men all gathered each night and had a shot." He tapped the bottle, the ting of the glass against his finger loud.

"He poured my first one on my twenty-first birthday. A rite of passage, he said."

Lisa reached out and put her hand over his fist, a fist he hadn't even realized he'd made until then. Her fingers were so soft and cool against his. He barely resisted the urge to open his fingers and engulf her hand in his.

"Did you like the drink?"

Trey laughed. "I liked being considered an adult. I liked being included. But the whiskey?" He met her gaze again. "Was horrible."

Her laughter erupted with her surprise. The sound wrapped around him, and he closed his eyes for an instant, savoring it. He nearly sighed aloud. Instead, he pulled his hand from hers and the temptation she represented.

He heard Lisa's deep intake of breath. "Okay," she said, staring down at the glass still sitting in front of her and squaring her shoulders.

"You don't have to," he said.

The glare she sent him made him take a step away. "Don't even." Then, as if she were reaching for a bottle of nasty-tasting cough syrup, instead of warm, smooth whiskey, she imitated his action.

He watched, mesmerized, as her head tilted back, her hair tumbling in ribbons nearly to her waist. She closed her eyes, and he saw the movement of her throat beneath the smooth pale skin of her neck as she took the shot.

She imitated his action of slamming the heavy glass down to the wood. And gazed up. Her eyes were bright with the burn and filled with tears—from the whiskey, and something else—that trickled over her lashes then down her cheeks.

He was lost.

CHAPTER NINE

AT HER TEARS, something inside Trey twisted. "Hey. You okay?"

"I'm sorry." She grabbed a couple of bar napkins and mopped at her eyes. "I'm being silly. You're right." She met his gaze. "It tastes awful."

That wasn't what he'd expected her to say. Was he supposed to argue? Laugh? Ignore the fact that she was avoiding what she was really thinking? Convince her she was okay? He had no idea what to say or do. Thankfully, she didn't seem to expect anything.

She stood and pulled off her apron. "I should head to the house. Tomorrow, I'm talking to Sam."

"About?" Though he was afraid he already knew what she intended.

"About whether they've checked the cabin."

Trey nodded and took his time putting the whiskey bottle in its rightful spot.

"I talked with him today." He didn't look

directly at her; instead he focused on finishing up the cleanup.

"Did you ask whether someone's been out to the cabin?" She gripped the apron tight.

"I brought it up. They checked the road, but not into the backcountry. Said there wasn't any indication anyone went up there."

She sighed heavily.

"I see those wheels turning." He met her gaze. "It's dangerous to go up there this time of year. That cabin's too remote."

He knew the minute those last words were out that he'd made a mistake. She straightened her shoulders. "All the more reason to investigate. It's not safe there for him if that's where he is."

"It's well stocked and he'll be fine as long as he stays put. He's old, but not an idiot. He's very familiar with this country."

"If he's out looking for that treasure, he's not staying put." Neither of them said anything for a bit. Finally, she flopped down on the barstool. "I'm worried, Trey. It's been over a week. No one knows where he is. No one's found a single clue." Her voice shook, and Trey couldn't stay behind the bar anymore. He walked around, and, as the first sob broke loose, he reached out and put his arms around her.

And immediately realized it was a mistake. But what else could he do? What else should he do? She was hurting, and he couldn't ignore someone in pain.

Lisa let him hold her. Let him stand there, his mind filling with nothing but the sense of her. Words failed him, and she didn't say anything, either. The music wound around them. He closed his eyes and listened. To the melody, to the rhythm. To the beat of his own heart.

Felt the beat of hers.

Suddenly, the music ended, and the silence settled in low and thick. He didn't move. She didn't, either. Not for a long minute.

Finally, she took a deep breath, one of those shaky sighs that came after a bout of tears. "I—" She looked up then.

Her eyes were a deeper green in the bar's dim lights with the layer of tears still clinging to them. "I'm sorry," she whispered and took a step back.

It wasn't much of a step, though, and she was still in his embrace. Slowly, she lifted her gaze and met his stare straight on. "Thanks," she whispered.

Trey swallowed hard. He needed to let her go, but his arms wouldn't cooperate. "No problem." He didn't move. He wasn't sure he had the ability. He had to clear his thoughts. Had to remind himself that he was technically her boss, that they were not, either of them, in a good place now for a relationship.

But common sense and reason had completely abandoned him. "Lisa?" His voice came out softer than he'd intended. She lifted her chin then, her lips parting just a bit. Her breath washed over his chin. Over his lips…

Those lips were so close. And then the space between them vanished.

She tasted sweet and warm. Soft. He hadn't meant to kiss her—at least that's what his brain said. The rest of him…yeah, it'd been waiting since lunch the other day. Maybe longer. Wanting to hold her. Needing her with him.

Lisa leaned closer, her palms flattened against his chest, and her fingers curled into the fabric of his shirt. Holding on tight.

He reached up and palmed the back of her head. Her hair was soft against his hand, stray strands winding around his fingers.

Hunger for her, for what she was so sweetly offering raced through him. And he gladly accepted all of it. All of her.

TREY TASTED OF whiskey and warmth. His arms were solid, but Lisa knew she could easily move out of them. She didn't want to move away. She wanted to be closer.

She wasn't sure when she'd closed her eyes, but the darkness only made it seem as if they were the only people in the world. She leaned in to the solid wall of his chest. A sense of safety washed over her.

When was the last time she'd felt protected and supported? Safe?

Trey's arms slid down, and before she could think about what he intended, he lifted her, settling her up on top of the bar. She giggled and swallowed back the sound.

They were eye-to-eye now, and she couldn't break the hold his gaze had on hers. His hand, rough and big, settled along her chin and slid up, pushing her hair out of her face. "Beautiful," he whispered, and found her lips again.

Lisa wrapped her arms around his wide shoulders, buried her fingers in his hair and leaned into him. He didn't budge, even as she rested more of herself against him.

Suddenly, ringing shattered the silence of the bar.

Thinking for an instant it was the bar phone, she shut it out. Then something flickered in her memory. That ringtone...

She pulled back and realized how tightly she was holding on to him. She hastily jumped down and ran around the bar. She dug under the counter for her purse. The glow of her phone seemed overly bright, and she blinked several times to focus on the screen. "H…hello?"

"Lisa?"

"Grandpa?" She hastily looked up at Trey. "Where are you?"

"I'm fine…" Static filled her ear. "Don't worry…me."

"I am worried. You need to come home."

"Not yet." He said more, but she could only understand half a word here and there.

"You're breaking up. I can't hear you." She moved toward the window, hoping that would help. But she didn't really think it was on her end.

"Hear…now?"

"No." She knew her anxiety was painted all over her face, and Trey, bless him, put a hand on her shoulder. Supportive—though with a bit more distance than before. When he'd held her and… She pulled her thoughts back.

"Where are you?"

"Don't worry," Grandpa repeated, then more static. She glared at the darkness beyond the windows, toward the mountainside. Stupid mountains.

"Grandpa?" More garbled words. "Are you

still there?" Nothing. Her phone beeped and she looked at the screen. Call dropped.

Her hand shaking, she tried to call him back. But all she got was the voice mail she'd helped him set up all those months ago. Lisa nearly threw her phone in frustration.

"That was Win?" Trey stepped closer to her as she pulled the phone away from her ear and stared at the screen again.

"Yeah." Her voice shook. She couldn't break down now. Not here. Trey would feel the need to comfort and protect her. That would be wonderful. Delicious. And so wrong.

She swallowed hard, focusing on anything else. "He's alive." Though her mind filled with all kinds of possibilities—alive didn't necessarily mean well, or safe. Just...alive.

"Were you afraid he wasn't?"

Trey still seemed a little shell-shocked. Had the kiss shaken him as much as it had her? "Kinda," she admitted. "Look." She stuffed her phone into her purse. "I...well, uh, that uh...between us shouldn't have happened." She waved her hand back and forth between them. "I'm sorry."

Trey moved to his station behind the bar where he resumed putting the clean glasses into the racks. "Yeah. Must have just been the moment." Was that an edge to his voice?

Why did she feel as if something very special and bright had just faded to black?

With her purse in hand, she headed toward the back door. "I may not be here tomorrow."

"Why?" Trey frowned. "It's not a good idea to go up to that cabin." Anger was the edge in his voice this time.

She paused, knowing that he wasn't necessarily angry with her. Himself maybe? His inability to fix everything? His frustration that once again a staff member was calling off? She cleared her throat. "One kiss doesn't mean you can boss me around." That didn't even sound convincing to her.

He laughed, and the roughness of it told her he wasn't totally buying it, but it had hit a nerve.

"The two are not connected, and you know that." He grabbed everything on the bar and strode past her to the office. He tossed it all onto the desk, then followed her to the back door.

She didn't say anything, simply pulled on her coat. He slipped his on, too, then grabbed his Stetson and settled it on his head. "What are you doing?" she asked.

"Walking you home. Your car's not in the lot."

"You don't have to do that. It's just a few blocks."

The look he gave her said he wasn't going to argue—or give in. "Doesn't matter."

She could either let him escort her, or she could stand here and lose more sleep arguing with him. She headed down the alley and toward the street. He fell into step with her.

They didn't talk. The only sounds were the crunch of the snow under their feet and their breathing, in and out. Even though it was the middle of the night, the snow reflected enough light to easily see by. The white clouds of their breath floated behind them.

Finally, they turned the corner and she could see the house. It'd been daytime when she'd rushed out, and she hadn't left any lights on. The house looked dark, and just a little bit sad.

"I'm fine from here."

"Not a chance. I'll go in first and check everything."

"A bit macho all of a sudden?" She almost laughed at him, but the scowl on his face stopped her.

"Maybe." He stopped at the edge of the lawn hidden beneath the snow. "But something's going on, and neither of us knows what it is. Someone broke into this house. Your grandfather's missing, and then out of the blue, he calls? How did he even know you were looking for him?"

"I've called and left several messages." She'd been expecting him to call.

"And he's just calling now? At two a.m.?"

Okay, that was a bit odd. She shivered, and it wasn't from the cold.

Trey barely waited for her to process that before he headed up the walk. "Give me your key."

She didn't hand it to him, but instead, reached past him and unlocked the door. He pushed it open and stepped in ahead of her. He didn't tell her to wait outside, as she half expected him to.

Just like she did every night, he flipped on light switches as he went. She followed. And just like every other night, they didn't find anything.

"Everything's good." He was back at the door, ready to step out into the night.

And even though she wasn't sure she'd needed him to make sure everything was okay, she appreciated his concern. "Thanks."

"No problem." He put his hand on the door

latch, then stopped. "Look, I know you're determined to go up to the cabin."

"Yeah, I am." He wasn't going to dissuade her. She lifted her chin defiantly, as if that would add to her determination and get him to agree.

He sighed. "I'll take you."

Had she heard right? Wait...what? "I... I can't ask you to do that."

"You aren't." He faced her. "I'm offering. I know how to get there almost better than anyone, except your grandfather."

"Probably. I doubt I could find it on my own." Relief and something else—anticipation—washed over her. "I'd appreciate it."

He stood there, his arms crossed over his chest—arms that she very distinctly remembered being around her. She swallowed back the urge to step closer and see if he'd do it again.

"You ever do any snowshoeing?"

"What?" That hadn't been where her brain had gone. "Oh, uh, maybe once?" She'd been a kid. Did that even count?

"I'll get the equipment when Dell opens up the sporting goods store in the morning. We can drive about halfway to the cabin. But that last section isn't passable with anything else except maybe a Sno-Cat."

"Don't suppose we could rent one of those, could we?" She smiled.

"Maybe." He smiled back. "Let's see if there's a reason to, first."

"Okay." She stepped toward him, fully aware it was a bad idea, but not really caring. She leaned up on her tiptoes and put a soft, chaste kiss on his rough cheek. "Thank you," she whispered and hastily stepped back before she did something stupid.

HE'D BEEN FINE until that last kiss. It had just been a thank-you, but man had it turned him inside out.

Trey stomped through the snowy streets back to his apartment, even as he wanted to grab Lisa and hold her in his arms again.

The instant he'd realized she intended to walk home, he'd thought of the men the other night. Telluride was normally a safe town, but no place was ever truly safe.

And with what was going on with Win?

Was Trey even safe walking the streets at night? Oh, he could protect himself, but he really didn't want to have to. And he'd used everything he had just resisting Lisa.

He'd just reached his apartment when big

white snowflakes started coming down. The streetlights' pale white glow glistened off each crystal, and he looked up at the kaleidoscope of snow and light.

Growing up in Texas, he'd only ever seen snow when he went other places, like here in Telluride, to find it. His grandfather had been the first person to show him the sports of winter—sledding, snowmobiling, skiing. He'd tried, and loved, them all.

From here, with the streetlights reflecting off the clouds, he could see the slopes that hovered high up on the mountainside. The low-hanging clouds not only held the light close, but muffled the sounds. The quiet seemed almost unnatural, and several minutes passed as he stood there and let the peace balance out the anger he still carried around with him.

His phone beeped—just a faint sound, but it broke the night all apart. Thinking—hoping?—it was Lisa, he pulled the phone out of his pocket and thumbed on the screen.

Not Lisa. A text message from earlier. He recognized the area code.

Texas.

Home.

He didn't open it, though his finger hovered over the keypad for just that brief instant. Should he?

Shaking his head, he stuffed the phone back into his pocket and headed inside.

He'd offered to take Lisa to the cabin. What had he been thinking? That she needed it. That he was man enough to ignore the memories that lived up there. And for all he knew, Win could use his help. He couldn't back down now. Trey respected Win. He'd known him almost his whole life. Each year he and his grandfather came to the cabin, Win would join them for at least one night. Sit with Pal by the fire, chatting, telling stories.

Trey remembered falling asleep to the sound of their voices fading into the night.

What had they talked about into the wee hours of those long-ago mornings? He tried to remember, but back then he'd been too excited to have time with his grandfather, to be here, hunting and playing. He'd been a boy.

A spoiled-rotten boy.

He curled his hand into a fist. Granddad had helped make him that spoiled kid. And then he'd betrayed him.

Had the old man even thought about the consequences to Trey, or had he just been his usual pigheaded, do-as-I-damned-well-please self when he'd given Trey's car to an arsonist? Trey could have gone to jail when the man had started a deadly wildfire.

Trey would never get answers now since the old man was dead and gone. There weren't any out in the freezing snow.

Tomorrow, he'd take Lisa to the cabin. He'd help her find Win, but he'd shut Pal Haymaker deep in the recesses of his mind. This was not about him. The past was dead and gone, and he intended to leave it that way.

CHAPTER TEN

IT WAS JUST past ten the next morning when Lisa heard heavy footsteps outside. Glancing out the window, she spotted Trey's familiar frame standing on the porch. The sun was high today, though wispy clouds blew across the sky. That brightness made his hair look lighter, but she was disappointed that sunglasses hid his eyes.

She opened the door and smiled when she saw the equipment he was carrying. "You weren't kidding." They really were going snowshoeing.

"Nope." He stepped inside and put the load down. "It's the only way we're going to get through that last section."

"Okay." She glanced outside and saw the big red Jeep at the curb. "For a minute there, I thought maybe we were walking the whole way. Why did you bring the snowshoes in here?"

He turned around and smiled, pulling his sunglasses off. She couldn't look away from him for a moment. All the emotions she'd wrestled with last night, the wanting to follow him home, the missing the safety she felt with his arms around her, the ache to be with him again, rushed in. She took a deep breath and hoped he didn't notice.

"Because you're going to practice. I want to make sure you can manage on the snowshoes before I take you into the backcountry."

She might have been offended if she didn't understand the risk he was taking for her. She nodded. "What do I need to do?" She tried to sound all business.

"First off, relax." He smiled again. "I'll get you there, Lisa. I promise. But I want to do it safely."

Her throat tightened. He was being good to her. Protecting them both. She nodded again but couldn't say anything.

"Let's make sure you have the right clothes first. Is that your only winter coat?"

The pretty wool coat was great for keeping out the cold—in the city. She already knew it wouldn't work for this. "I think my grandmother had a ski jacket. I'll bet it's still in their bedroom closet. Should I get it?"

"Yeah. And check for wool socks, too. You'll want those. If you don't have them, we can get some over at the sporting goods store. I didn't want to buy any until I knew you needed them."

She headed upstairs and was relieved to find both the ski jacket and a couple pairs of socks. "Thanks, Grandma," she whispered to the room and grabbed them. She also found a warm sweater she remembered her grandmother wearing. Hugging it, she smiled, feeling like she was embracing the old woman again. Nice.

"I think I've got everything." She stepped into the kitchen. Trey was sitting at the table, a snowshoe in his hand. He was clipping off tags, and when he looked up, their eyes met. Time stopped.

Lisa stood there, holding the sweater tight to her chest. "How long will it take to get there?" She had to focus on something, anything but Trey.

"We'll drive as far as possible. I think to the river. Then snowshoe from there. It'll take a couple of hours, this way, to reach the cabin. We can't get there and back in a day." He shook his head and focused again on the equipment. "We'll have to stay the night at the cabin, but I remember that the place has a couple of beds."

"Who's watching the bar?"

Trey smiled, but not in the broad way he

did when he was happy. This was almost a grimace. "Rick's tending bar, and Gabe and Kerry swear they'll cover."

"You believe them?" How many times had they all called off and left him to pick up the slack?

"Uh, I have to." He finished clipping the tags off the snowshoes. "We'll get these ready, and I want you to test them out in the yard. Then we'll stop at the grocery and get provisions."

Moving to the table, she put her own supplies next to his pile. Scrutinizing all the items scattered on the old, familiar kitchen table, she realized how out of her element she was—and what he was doing for her. "How much do I owe you?"

Trey shook his head. "Nothing. We'll put it on Win's tab." He laughed and stood. "Okay, let's see how this works." He looked down at her feet. "Love the boots."

She followed his gaze. "Grandpa made sure I had a pair here when I visited." She stared down at the pale pink boots. "I was a bit of an…opinionated kid. Guess he still thinks I am." She shifted her foot back and forth, as if the boot were a high-fashion stiletto. "I wasn't sure they'd still be here. They were under the bed, just where I left them."

Shaking his head, Trey led the way to the back door. "Come on."

The yard was a wide expanse of snow. She couldn't discern where the small garden was, where the flower beds were or anything. Just deep, white snow. Trey handed her one of the snowshoes. She laughed as she examined it. "I never would have thought putting tennis rackets on your feet was such a good way to walk in the snow." Trey's laugh echoed around the yard and she felt it, warm and smooth.

Trey knelt to show her how to put the simple bindings on over her boots. It looked easy enough, but she had to lift one foot to do so. Putting her hand on his shoulder to keep her balance, her heart rate picked up.

Hard solid muscle shifted beneath her hand as he moved his arm to help her. Once both snowshoes were in place, though, he hastily stepped away. It took him half the time to put on his.

"Okay." He breathed in deep and put his hands on his poles. She mimicked his movements. "Let's give this a try. It's pretty easy, actually. Watch me." He took several steps across the snow.

"Ah! You don't really sink into the snow. You're walking on top. That doesn't seem too hard." She marveled and took a few tentative steps. Her right snowshoe caught on her left, and she landed flat on her backside. "Okay, maybe I spoke too soon."

Trey moved over to her, smiling down at her. "Spread your legs a little wider apart," he suggested.

"Oh, yeah. Okay."

Trey took a step back. "But it's good that you've fallen. Now I can show you how to get up again." He stood there, his hands on his hips, grinning down at her.

"Oh." She sighed and had to tilt her head way back to look up at him. "My backside's getting wet, thank you very much."

What was he waiting for? Finally, he knelt down beside her. "The snowshoes keep you on top of the snow, but when you fall, you're going to break through the surface. This isn't very deep."

He didn't have to tell her it would be much deeper in the backcountry.

"Use your poles. Plant them on one side." He pointed to her right. "Push uphill and work to get the shoes in front of you."

It wasn't difficult, but she could see how if done wrong, she'd simply dig herself in deeper. Finally, she was on her feet again, facing him.

The rush of accomplishment made her smile. "I did it!"

Trey smiled back at her. "Yeah. Good job." He moved closer. "Now, brush off the snow the best you can so you stay as dry as possible." He reached out and brushed snow off her shoulders and back.

The caring gesture sent a rush of warmth through her. She swallowed, trying to focus on her feet and walking.

"It's easier than I expected," she admitted after she'd tramped over most of the yard. "I think I'm ready." She'd have to change clothes before they left, however.

"I agree. Let's go." Trey walked back to the edge of the lawn and took off his snowshoes. She followed and mimicked his actions of knocking off the snow.

Once inside, he gathered her snowshoes and the rest of the equipment, then hauled it all out to the Jeep. "No sense getting the house wet," he explained, though she got the impression he was trying to get away from her as much as the snow.

While he packed the car, she changed into dry clothes and hung the wet ones up on the line in the laundry room. Gathering the last of her things, she took one last look for some extra wool socks and mittens. What had

Grandpa taken with him? Granted, this was all old stuff, so he could have done what Trey did and bought new. But she wanted to be sure they had enough.

Just before noon, they parked in front of the grocery store. Trey had a list already made. She added a couple of things, and they soon had everything stowed in the backpacks he'd put in the Jeep.

Behind the wheel, he turned to her. "You ready for this?"

"I am." She reached out and took the risk of putting her hand over his. "I appreciate how much you're doing for me. Thank you."

"Good. So, you'll follow my ground rules?"

Now he brought up ground rules? "Uh… what exactly are they?" She frowned.

He grinned. "I'm in charge. Not because I'm the big macho male." He winked at her. "Though that helps. But because I know what we're doing, and where we're going. You're the newbie."

"But—"

"Nope. You follow my directions until we get to the cabin. You have to trust me, Lisa. I won't let you get hurt."

"I do trust you." And she did. "But why didn't you say all this earlier?"

"What if you'd been a total airhead about

snowshoeing? Then there wouldn't be any need."

She smacked his arm. "You knew I wasn't an airhead."

"Yeah, I did." He started the Jeep. "Just hedging my bets." They both laughed, and she liked the camaraderie between them. This felt good. Felt right. She sat back and smiled.

FRESH POWDER WAS a gift up on the slopes. Here in the backcountry trees—not so much. Even if Win had come through here, all the new snow would have covered any tracks. Trey pushed the straps of his backpack up again, easing the weight for just an instant. "You okay?" He looked over his shoulder at Lisa.

She was only a few feet behind, but if he didn't watch closely, that gap would widen. She was tiring, but danged if she'd admit it. "I'm fine," she said, confirming his thoughts.

"Uh-huh." He slowed his pace.

Tromping the path through the snow, along the trail he was following from a faded memory, was a great workout, but even he was feeling the strain. He'd been in Telluride for nearly a year, so while he'd adjusted to the altitude, he still felt it. Reaching into his pack, he pulled out a water bottle and took a deep swallow. He stopped and waited for her to catch up, then extended the bottle to her.

"What's the matter?" she asked.

"Nothing. Have a drink."

"I'm—"

"Don't argue. Just drink."

She glared at him but did as he instructed. Her breath came in and out harshly, telling him she was more worn-out than she'd admit. He waited.

"How much farther?"

He gazed across the field that was the last expanse between here and the steeper climb. "A couple of miles." He wasn't telling her the last half mile was a 7-to-10-percent grade climb. He'd save that for later. When she got there. "When was the last time you were at the cabin?" Maybe she remembered.

"Not for a few years." She lifted her hand and glanced the way he just had. "I think I re-call the trail being steeper than this, though."

Yeah, he had to come clean. "It gets that way just on the other side of this field."

The last time he'd been up here, it'd been late summer. Gramps hadn't been able to hike, and they'd come up on horseback.

She sighed. "Well, then let's get going be-fore I change my mind."

Trey briefly wondered if the woman had

ever changed her mind about anything. He doubted it. She was about the most determined and single-minded person he'd ever met. She impressed him, which was surprising. He watched as she adjusted her pack, just as he had, then faced him. "Ready," she announced.

The sun took that instant to step out from behind the cloud and peek at them. It shone on the snow and reflected like a million diamonds. Lisa's skin glowed pink with the cold and exercise, and her hair had started falling out from where she'd stuffed it into her fur-trimmed hood. Half a dozen hanks hung in curls around her face.

"Are we going?" She met his gaze and he had to force his mind to function.

"Uh, yeah." Ripping his mind back to the task at hand, Trey continued on, tromping the snow down in a narrow path for her to follow. She'd offered, early on, to take her turn at creating the path, but he'd adamantly denied her the opportunity.

Not because he was a macho jerk who had to be in control, or the lead. But because he had more experience and could accomplish it without either of them being overly exhausted. He understood she needed this.

It only took about fifteen minutes to reach

the other side but it felt like an hour. He was drenched in sweat and needed another swig of water before the climb. She'd managed to keep up with him, which pleased and surprised him.

In the silence of the backcountry, the only sound was his own breath rushing in and out of his lungs and the crunch of Lisa's snowshoes as she tromped behind him.

"What's the matter?" she asked as she stopped beside him.

"Nothing's the matter." He stabbed the end of his pole in the snow. They didn't have much farther to go, but despite the cold, and exertion, he wasn't in any hurry to get there. He was enjoying this.

"Then why'd you stop?" She glanced around the fur-trimmed edge of her hood to look at him. Her cheeks were bright red from the cold and her breath fogged in the air between them.

"Maybe I'm tired." He tried to lie, but he'd never been very good at it.

She laughed, the warm, sweet sound echoing through the cold air. "You aren't tired." She took a deep breath. "Okay, maybe you are. But that wouldn't stop you."

"It would if I keeled over from exhaustion," he said and tried to appear shocked at her words. All she did was laugh and tromp a few more steps forward.

"Come on." She waved her mittened hand. "We're almost there."

Grumbling, he hurried after her. Suddenly, a movement caught his eye at the edge of the clearing. "Lisa," he called.

When a moose, tall and wide, separated from the shadows, he hurried his steps. Fear that the big animal would spook and go after her made him move even faster. "Lisa," he urgently called again, this time getting her attention. She stopped, looking over at him, her hood falling back and letting her long hair tumble down over her shoulders.

He pointed at the big animal. She stopped and waited for Trey to catch up to her.

While the moose was beautiful, they needed to get out of its path. "Let's take it slow," he suggested, keeping even with her. "Don't surprise it." They slowly made their way across the rest of the clearing and up the first section of slope.

Thankfully, the moose, while watching them with a bit of interest, didn't move toward them. But until they reached the thick trees on the other side of the clearing, Trey wouldn't breathe easily. "Come on." He glanced over his shoulder, thankful the animal hadn't moved any closer.

Here in the trees, the snow was much shallower. There were even spots of bare earth. Rocks and fallen tree trunks created shelves of snow and purchase for drifts.

"I can see the trail." Lisa's voice seemed loud in the silence they'd created as they hiked.

"That'll make it easier." Trey turned toward the faint trail, and several yards in, he stopped. He examined the bare dirt. "Doesn't Win have a horse?" The tracks were familiar to any good cowboy.

"He does—several, actually. They stay with Sam's horse, Biscuit. Grandpa rides up here occasionally." She came to stand beside Trey and followed his gaze. "I guess I didn't think about him taking a horse."

Trey knelt down, checking the tracks. Only one set, which was a good sign. "He could have, before these last snows. Looks like just one person."

Lisa simply nodded, scrutinizing the trail. "That's good, right? Maybe Sam came up here to look for him?"

Trey shook his head. "He said he didn't. Besides, these are older tracks. See, they're under the snow." He straightened and gazed around. "Come on. Let's get moving." Clouds were gathering on the horizon, and up here, sunshine could turn to a blizzard in an instant.

"Wouldn't Sam mention if one of the horses was missing?" She kept pace with him now.

"Maybe. If one was missing. But maybe not if someone borrowed one. Besides, there's nothing to prove this is any of those. Could be anyone."

They'd just reached the last ridge, where he could see the cabin nestled against the cliff's base, when the snowflakes started to fall.

Memories reached out to him and tried to distract him. How many times had he come here? He hadn't been up to the cabin since his grandfather's betrayal—and since his death. The remembered laughter and companionship felt like a sharp knife to an old wound.

Forcing himself to focus on the here and now, Trey was glad for the impending storm. It gave him something to focus on. Getting Lisa to the cabin and keeping her safe became his number one goal.

By the time they reached the ancient cabin, the wind was howling, and he could barely see a foot in front of his face. He noticed Lisa shiver and waved for her to hurry as much as he dared. She knew how to get up if she fell, but he didn't want to risk her getting any wetter or colder.

She didn't need much urging as the bitter wind bit through their skin, icy and sharp.

Win kept the place locked up, as much to keep the place secure from critters as humans. But the remote setting made it impossible for a locksmith to help if he locked himself out.

The snow was thick, with more coming down as they'd climbed, but the wooden key box under the steps was just where it had always been.

"He hasn't changed the combination?" Trey called to Lisa over the rush of the wind.

Lisa shook her head. "Still Grandma's birthday, as far as I know." Her smile was melancholy. He ignored the tug to comfort her and focused on the combination.

He had his own demons to deal with being here. Right now, they swamped him. He'd always been the one to dig out the key. *Hurry up, boy*, he heard his grandfather's whisper in the howling wind.

Pulling off his glove, Trey palmed the key and took off his snowshoes. He tossed them through the rails and up onto the covered deck. Lisa mimicked his movements and moved to stand beside him.

Telling himself it was to keep track of her and make sure they both got inside safely, he waited for her. He took her gloved hand in his and didn't intend to let go until they reached the solid, wooden cabin door.

CHAPTER ELEVEN

THE CABIN FELT SMALLER than Lisa remembered. Stepping through the rough wood front door into the great room, she let her gaze take it in. So familiar. And yet there was a difference—she just wasn't quite sure what it was. Maybe it was more that she'd changed than the place.

Dominating one entire wall, the old stone fireplace shot clear to the second story. Lisa had heard the tale dozens of times of how her great-grandfather had built it. The yawning hearth was dark now, but she remembered bright fires, the flames filling the gap, warming her clear through.

Trey closed the door and shut out the weather. The cold followed them inside, though, and stayed.

"He's not here," she said. Disappointment settled beneath the chill.

"Doesn't mean he hasn't been." Trey's footsteps seemed loud in the deserted room. "Here, let me take that." Trey reached for her backpack and helped her pull it off her shoulders. She hadn't realized how heavy it had gotten.

Trey moved through to the kitchen area, pulling out the provisions from both their backpacks and setting them on the counter. He was quiet and focused on the task.

What was he thinking?

The closer they'd gotten to the cabin, the more withdrawn and quiet he'd become. She'd put it off to exhaustion earlier, but now—watching him—was that all of it?

He had memories of this place, too. But where hers were filled with fun and laughter, she wasn't sure what his were. He'd hinted that he was estranged from his family.

"You came up here a lot?" she asked as much out of curiosity as in hopes of gauging his mood.

He paused. "A dozen times, at least. We came nearly every year after I turned ten. Hunting's good up in these hills."

She nodded. Her grandfather wasn't a hunter, but he'd rented the cabin out each year to several groups. Her grandparents had taken a vacation each year on the profits. She remembered Grandma serving some of the game their renters shared with them.

"I never hunted." She shuddered. The idea made her cringe.

"Ain't a Texas boy worth his salt who can't hunt," Trey said, his drawl deep and rich.

"Your accent's faded," she commented.

"That's my goal." The Southern drawl in his voice vanished again. "Hopefully, someday, no one will be able to tell where I came from."

Lisa watched Trey's face and knew the memories were hitting him hard. They flashed painfully through his eyes. "I'm sorry."

She wasn't sure what to say, but felt the need to say something. After what he'd shared at the bar the other night, she wondered if his coming here was a mistake.

"No problem." He brushed it off and shrugged out of his damp jacket. "I'll get a fire started." He headed to the hearth. "You should get out of those damp clothes and warm up." He didn't look at her, and she got the feeling that was on purpose.

"So should you." She waved a hand toward his soaked jeans. "Do you want the loft? Or shall I take it?"

He glanced over his shoulder at her. The lines were deep around his eyes. "I'll take it."

He nodded toward the short hall. "Take the master. A bit more private."

Over the years, she hadn't slept here often. Most of the time she'd come here with her grandfather, it had been to prepare the place for a renter. On the few occasions they had stayed, her grandparents had slept down here, and she and whichever cousin who'd come with them had headed up to the loft. It was the perfect place for kids to hide out.

Taking her things into the master bedroom, she set them on the bed and her heart sank further. If Grandpa was staying here, he hadn't left any evidence behind.

What had she hoped? That she'd find him, his feet kicked up, reading a book before the fire? Okay, she'd lost her mind if that was the case. But why couldn't there at least be some sign that he was staying here?

If he wasn't here, where was he? She glanced to the window. In the mountains, the sun set fast and hard. Already, the last rays of light were melting away.

When she flipped on the bedside light, her own reflection stared back at her in the glass. She could feel the cold air slipping through the panes. She shivered. Was Grandpa out there? Freezing in the storm? Dying?

Or was he someplace else entirely and this was a waste of time?

Footsteps made her spin around. She knew it wasn't Grandpa, knew he wasn't here, but still her heart rate picked up in hope. No, it was just Trey heading upstairs.

When she returned to the main room, her damp jeans traded for a warm, dry pair of leggings, Trey had a fire blazing in the big stone hearth. She moved over to it, stretching her hands out to its warmth. "Don't make it too big or you'll never sleep tonight. It'll be hot up there." She nodded toward the loft.

"Yeah." He smiled, but it didn't reach his eyes. "I remember." He didn't look away from the loft for a long time.

Finally, he smiled at her. It was a forced smile, but she appreciated the effort. "All settled?" he asked as he walked closer, not stopping until he stood beside her. "You okay?"

"Yeah." She glanced over her shoulder at the front window. Still nothing beyond. "It doesn't look like he's been here."

Trey shook his head.

"I can't help worrying. I didn't really believe he'd be here," she finished. She glanced down, avoiding Trey's astute gaze. "But I hoped."

"I know." Trey put a hand on her shoulder.

"You're human. He's your family." Why did a grimace sift through his eyes? Was he thinking about his family? How bad could they really be? He seemed to understand what a family should be. If they were so bad, where had he learned that?

"Come on. Let's get something to eat. Then we'll discuss what to do next."

Though they'd brought provisions, the cabin was fully stocked. Trey knew that from when he and his grandfather used to rent the cabin, and she'd helped her grandfather prepare the cabin dozens of times. They both opened cabinets to check out their options for dinner.

"Comfort food." He pulled out a can of tomato soup, then reached for a pan hanging on the rack above the stove. "We brought bread and cheese." He nodded toward the small refrigerator.

He gave directions, and she did as he told her. Not because he was dictating or bossing—like he did at work—but because she couldn't function otherwise. If he weren't here, she'd probably still be staring out into the night, looking for someone who wasn't coming.

Pulling out an old griddle from under the stove, Trey put the grilled-cheese sandwiches together. "I can do that," she offered, forcing herself to shake this stupid lethargy. "I need to do something."

The simple task did as she hoped, pushing her to reconnect. "Sorry I'm such bad company."

"You're not bad company." He stirred the soup. "I'm enjoying the peace and quiet. Beats making drinks."

"Or serving them." They laughed, and the kitchen warmed just a bit.

Trey took a full plate of sandwiches and his cup of soup to sit on the couch by the fire.

Lisa followed and sat down on the edge of the hearth. She was still chilled, and the fire on her back helped. Besides, sitting on the couch near Trey was *not* a good idea.

He dug into his food, his concentration on eating, his big hands dwarfing the sandwich. She couldn't look away.

It was bad enough being alone with him at the bar, where a customer could come in at any moment. No one was going to show up here.

They were alone.

Lisa focused on her sandwich. At least that's what she intended. The furtive glances she kept giving him were simply her being polite and acknowledging his presence. Yeah. That.

Finally, Trey set his empty dishes on the worn coffee table. "That hit the spot."

"It did, didn't it?" She stood and reached for his dishes.

"I'll take them." He didn't move. "Eventually."

She laughed. "It's not a problem. Not like it's a ton of dishes." She headed to the kitchen, thankful for an excuse to put some space between them. "Sit and relax. If we're here tomorrow…" Her thoughts froze for an instant. "Uh," she cleared her throat, "you get dish duty."

"Mmm-hmm."

She glanced over her shoulder. He was leaning back, his eyes closed, his feet up on the coffee table. He'd taken off his boots at the door, and the jeans he'd changed into were worn and dry.

Her gaze wandered, and even though she knew she shouldn't, she let it take in the length of that denim. Faded and frayed in a few places, the jeans fit the image she carried of him in her mind. A rough-and-tumble cowboy who didn't spend a whole lot of time primping. He wore a long-sleeved blue shirt that hung loose on his rangy frame when he stood, but sitting like he was, the fabric fell at just the right angle to show her the muscular lines of his chest, the bulges of his biceps.

His arms were crossed over his chest, and she didn't look away when she saw him move. She instead shifted her gaze to his face, to his strong jaw, the tanned skin from the hours he spent on the slopes—and found him staring back at her. Intense and unflinching.

For the first time all night, he grinned. "Like what you see?" His drawl was thick and deep again.

She didn't dare answer. Spinning on her heel, Lisa headed to the sink and hit the faucet handle. Too bad there weren't more dishes. She needed a moment to recover.

Lisa didn't hear him move, but the feel of warmth behind her told her he was there.

"Sorry. Didn't mean to tease you."

"Yes, you did." Her cheeks warmed, and she was sure her face was beet red. Risking a glance at him, she found him standing there, grinning, not a drop of remorse in his face. She grabbed the towel on the counter and smacked him with it. "Now you're gonna help me with the dishes." She tried to glare at him, but that smile made it impossible.

"How often did *you* come up here?" Trey asked, drying the first plate, enjoying the smile that bloomed on her face.

"Not much, really." She looked around. "But enough to enjoy the place."

"Guess when you visited, you stayed in Telluride and skied."

She nodded. "I grew up on skis." Her enthusiasm was definitely lacking.

"But?" he asked. "Not much excitement there."

"Nope." She handed him another plate. "I like the sport. Somehow, they need to make it warmer."

He laughed. "I don't think that would work very well."

She shrugged and smiled, as if it didn't really matter. Her face lit up with that smile, and for a long moment, Trey couldn't look away.

Clearing his throat, he turned to put the dishes in the cupboard. The goal of coming up here had been to find out if Win was here—which he wasn't. The only reason they were spending the night was because of the weather and distance.

Nothing else.

He had to keep reminding himself of that. And he definitely wasn't thinking about holding her as he'd done the other night. No, definitely not that.

"You do have some good memories of your

grandfather, though, don't you?" Lisa asked, rinsing the bowls under the steaming water and forcing him to focus on actions, not the thoughts in his head.

"Yeah. Somewhere." He heard the grimace in his voice. Focusing on the task, he took the bowl from her and dried it—taking his time putting it away. "I went and played on the slopes or hiked. I didn't realize until later that my grandfather was with his mistress."

Trey heard the bitterness thick in his voice. His family was a convoluted mess. "My father grew up as an only child—not even knowing that he had a sister until a couple of years ago."

He assumed they were finding their way in building a relationship, but he hadn't a clue—he'd left home and all of that behind.

"Oh, Trey, I'm so sorry."

He knew she wanted to reach out and touch him. She was a toucher, he'd found. But that would be a mistake. "Don't be. I don't need your pity."

"Empathy is not pity." She turned back to scrubbing the last pan. Silence settled between them as they finished the task, and the kitchen was put to rights.

The awkwardness returned. Trey took

a deep breath, and, as he thought better of being so close to her, he headed for the couch.

The fire had settled down low in the hearth, and Lisa grabbed the thick, crocheted blanket off the back of the couch and wrapped it around her shoulders. "Grandma made this. It's the warmest thing I've ever known." She snuggled down on the end of the couch. "As a kid, I loved to curl up in it at her house."

Trey frowned. How long had it been here at the cabin? He remembered it always being right there on the back of the couch. Familiar. Almost like home.

"You cold? I can add to the fire."

"No. That'll make sleeping up there miserable. The blankets will keep me warm." She looked up then and their gazes met. And locked.

He had to escape before he revealed even more to this woman. And fell even harder.

TREY SHOT TO his feet and made for the kitchen. Lisa frowned. Why did he bolt whenever she started asking more about his past?

"Here." Trey's arm appeared in front of her a few moments later, a thick stone mug in his hand.

"I'm not really thirsty."

"My mom says there's always time for a

cup of warmth. Here. It'll help take the chill off."

She curled both hands around the mug. The heat melted into her, reaching through her fingers and up her arms. She sighed. Heaven.

He walked around the couch, and instead of settling beside her, he took the big over-stuffed chair. He had a matching cup in his hand, the steam rising in front of his face. She stared at him for a long minute—until he turned his gaze to her. Their eyes caught again and held.

She was the first to look away, staring down into the drink. She frowned. She smelled chocolate and something else. She took a tentative sip as much to taste as to distract herself from wondering what he was thinking, what was behind his eyes.

The drink was delicious. And not like anything she'd ever had. "What did you put in here?" She didn't hide the suspicion in her voice.

He laughed. "Arsenic?" At her wide-eyed glare, he laughed even harder. "Some touches my mom used to add. Brandy. And a little cream."

Recovering, barely, she took another, bigger, sip. It was delicious. "Don't put this in the morning coffee," she warned him. "Or I'll never get anything done."

She took her time finishing her beverage. The warmth of the drink was partially to blame for her growing lethargy, as was the alcohol he'd added to it. Finished, she set the cup on the scarred end table. A comfortable drowsiness settled in, and she didn't even bother to stop her gaze from roaming to him.

"Why are you here, Trey?" she asked before she could stop herself.

"Uh, we're looking for your grandfather, remember?" He was laughing at her again.

"No." She leaned forward, the blanket slipping down off her shoulder. The room was comfortable now, and she was no longer cold. "In Telluride. Why did you come here? You're not from here."

"What gave it away? The boots?" He grinned at her, stacking his feet on the old coffee table. His boots were across the room, and she glanced over at them, noting the scuffed leather. Well worn, the dark brown boots had seen better days.

"That—and the accent. You said Texas, right?"

"Yeah." He still had some drink left, and he stared down into it. Was he wondering how much to tell her? If he should lie? "I came here to build a life for myself. Away from my family." His words were soft, and yet she didn't miss the harshness.

She watched as the firelight danced, creating and erasing shadows over his features. She shouldn't notice, but—the man was fine. She almost laughed at herself. Then gulped, hoping she hadn't said her thoughts out loud. When he didn't react, she breathed a sigh of relief.

"But why here? Why not...any place else?"

He looked at her then, and it wasn't trauma staring back at her. Or anger. Or anything she expected. She saw hurt there. Deep, unrelenting pain. "I'm sorry." She hadn't meant to dig up something painful for him. She was curious and just a tiny bit tipsy. "You don't owe me an explanation."

Trey shook his head, and as if he couldn't sit any longer, he shot to his feet. He bent and set the now-empty mug where his feet had been. He turned to stare down into the fire while leaning against the mantel with a forearm. His eyes were distant, and she knew he wasn't seeing the flames.

"My grandfather was nothing like yours. He was a real jerk." The snap and pop of the fire was all that filled the long silence. She waited, knowing he had to be the one to speak, knowing that there were hard words coming.

"About a year ago, the old coot killed someone." His voice faded and as she watched his profile, he swallowed. Hard. "He nearly framed me for that murder."

Lisa had never heard a sentence spoken with so much pain. And betrayal. Heartbreaking betrayal.

He covered it well, but suddenly some of his behavior the last few days made sense. His distance. The reluctance he'd displayed. They were all portions of that emotion.

"Oh, Trey." She set her own cup aside and walked over to where he stood by the fire. "It didn't work, though, right?"

Stony silence settled over them. Finally, Trey stood and gathered their cups. "Now you know why I'm losing the accent. Telluride was familiar." He shrugged. "I figured that'd give me a better start."

She wanted to hold him, to touch him and ease the hurt she saw in his eyes.

She settled for touching his arm. This time when he looked at her, the hurt was faded and something else had taken its place.

"Lisa," he whispered. The restraint in his voice was aimed straight at her. She ignored it and didn't bother to resist the urge to reach up and touch him.

His jaw was rough under her hand, with the day's growth of whiskers. She ran her thumb over his lips, unable to stop herself. "I'm sorry for bringing you here. I know you don't have happy memories here."

Trey tried to smile, but all that did was move his lips against her hand. An unintentional caress.

"Maybe it's time to face them. And let go." He held her gaze. The fire snapped, and she jumped, then laughed. Instead of joining in, Trey leaned in closer, his eyes darkening. "You're very distracting."

"Is that a good thing?"

"Oh, yeah."

Leaning in even closer, Trey put his lips on hers and everything vanished except for the feel of him. His strong arms encircled her, and it didn't take but an instant for her to slip her arms up around his neck. His hair hung just past his collar and teased her fingers as she slid them up.

Closing her eyes, Lisa saw and felt nothing but his overwhelming presence. She couldn't remember ever getting so lost in someone else. It felt wonderful, and she hoped it never ended.

But it did.

Trey stepped away, clearing his throat and putting his big hands on her shoulders. He took several deep breaths before looking at her again. "That's not why I came up here."

Mortified, she stepped away, putting space between them and feeling like a fool.

"No." Trey reached out and took her hand, pulling her back into the space they'd just shared. "Don't misunderstand me." He cupped her chin with his big hand, tilting her face up. "I want to hold you," he whispered, his breath slipping over her lips. "But I'm afraid if I do… I won't ever let you go." And then his lips came down on hers again.

This was no soft, sweet kiss. Not this time. Maybe never again. This was deep and hungry and more than she'd expected. She drank him in, hoping he'd never stop.

But he did. Again. Barely pulling away, he put just a bit of distance between them. He waited until she opened her eyes. "Do you understand?"

She nodded slowly, and he stepped back. She felt cold despite the flames just inches away.

Trey shoved his fingers through his hair, and she could see the indecision on his face.

He walked around the couch, putting it between them. "I think I'll turn in."

Only the clatter of the cups he set in the sink and his steps as he climbed the stairs broke the quiet. And then he was gone.

"'Night," she whispered, pretty sure he'd heard her. He didn't reply.

CHAPTER TWELVE

FRUSTRATED, AND WIDE-AWAKE despite the brandy in the drink, Lisa stared up at the bedroom ceiling. The flames in the hearth were low, but the dancing light still slipped around the partially closed door and blinked around the small room. Moonlight shone off the snow outside and fell through the fabric of the old curtains.

It was nearly as bright as the city.

She snuggled down in the big, four-poster log bed in the main-level bedroom, fighting with sleep and the sheets that kept wrapping around her.

Trey was upstairs in the loft. Even though they'd kept the fire low, it had to be warm up there. She remembered sleeping up there on nights they'd had a fire. She used to shove open the window, which only made things worse, drawing the heat upward, though as a kid she hadn't realized that. She'd sat there on the old chest, for what had seemed like hours, staring up at the starry sky.

Closing her eyes now, she could almost feel the cold air washing in the window, cooling her overheated skin.

Just like back then, sleep eluded her now. She didn't dare get up. Trey would hear her, and caretaker that he was, he would get up to check that she was okay. That would be a disaster. Especially after…

Her cheeks warmed at how he'd caught her staring at him. At that kiss… They'd tried to ignore the tension and attraction between them, but that didn't mean any of it had dissipated. Those moments by the fire were seared into her memory.

He wasn't sleeping, either. She could hear the old bed upstairs creak as he tossed and turned. He was as restless as she was, which didn't help at all.

She cursed. Throwing back the covers, Lisa walked over to the window. At least she'd get it open and let some of the cool in.

The curtains were the same ones that had always been here. She pushed them aside and wrestled with the latch on the window. These hadn't ever been replaced, either. She shoved hard against the old aluminum and grumbled as it resisted. Finally, it gave, and icy-cold air rushed through the ancient screen, washing over her. She leaned toward the screen, gulping it in.

Snow had drifted in the back, mounding toward the tree line at the edge of the property. Lodgepole pines stood thick and dark against the white. The night was strong overhead and stars shone bright here. She'd missed that in the city. Why didn't she come here more often?

Something moved at the edge of the yard. She gasped and stepped back. What was out there? This place was remote enough that they'd had bears visit before. And lots of deer. Even a moose or two had come through, like the one they'd seen this afternoon. Grandpa had lots of stories about the critters who'd passed through.

And Trey and his grandfather had surely seen plenty, since they'd come here to hunt.

She recalled what Trey had told her before about his grandfather killing someone. He hadn't elaborated. Surely, he hadn't shot anyone—

There was that movement again. Just on the edge of the clearing, between the trees. That wasn't a deer or a moose. Maybe a bear on its hind legs, not on all fours?

That wasn't an animal. She swallowed back her next gasp and reached up to close the window. Was that a person? Who would be out in this cold, this time of night? Of course, the old window frame stuck, and she nearly cursed aloud again. She bit her lip to stop the sound. It would echo loud and far in the still, snowy night.

Finally, she got the window closed and locked tight, but not without making noise. Whatever—whoever—was out there couldn't have missed the sound.

What should she do? What was going on? Who was out there—and why?

TREY HAD SPENT more nights than he could count sleeping up here in the cabin's loft. As he'd told Lisa earlier, he'd been something like ten the first time he and his grandfather had come here on a hunting trip. To Trey, the man had seemed to walk on water back then. Trey scowled into the darkness.

They'd come here every year until his grandfather's death. Sometimes to hunt, but as the old man had grown frail, they'd just come to experience the outdoors and solitude.

Looking back through the warped lens of time, Trey saw everything so differently.

Staring up at the ceiling, the moonlight slipping around the old blinds, painting bars of light on the pinewood walls, Trey scrubbed his face with his hands. He wasn't going to sleep tonight.

If he were back in town, he'd head downstairs to the closed bar and have a drink. Something short and cold and lethal. The brandy in the cocoa hadn't done a bit of good.

But going downstairs now would be a huge mistake. He didn't want to wake Lisa.

In just that instant, he heard something move downstairs. The loft was open, so there was nothing to stop him from hearing any sound from below.

Was Lisa having trouble sleeping, too?

But what if it wasn't her?

Slowly, carefully, he swung his legs over the edge of the bed and yanked on his jeans. Hearing the sound again, he crept across the bare wood floor. The tracking skills he'd learned in these mountains served him well as he moved silently.

He reached the rail, then leaned over, hoping to see what was going on. If Lisa was having as much trouble sleeping as he was, he didn't want to scare her. The shades downstairs were at half-mast, so the reflection of the moonlight came in and lit the great room with a pale glow.

A figure moved. *Crap.* That was *not* Lisa. But Lisa was down there. He could see the corner of the bedroom door. The intruder hadn't gotten there yet. And Lisa thankfully wasn't investigating.

In his younger days, he'd have been dumb enough to leap that rail and try to land on the man. He knew now all he'd do was hurt himself. Instead, he reached for a weapon. There wasn't anything. But the short ladder stairs ended at the edge of the kitchen—right next to the block of knives on the counter.

How many times had he slid down those rails as a kid? Plenty—and that skill hadn't abandoned him. He hit the parallel rails and was at the bottom in an instant. The landing wasn't loud, but it wasn't quiet, either. That didn't matter. He had the butcher knife in his hand in the next instant.

LACK OF SLEEP was starting to become Lisa's norm. She hadn't done much of it since coming to Telluride. Between her grandfather's antics, the late nights at the bar—and now being here at the cabin with Trey, she was beginning to think sleep was a thing of the past.

Looking out the window again, she didn't see anything. Had she imagined it?

Then she heard a sound. Something—someone—was moving around inside the cabin. She froze, not even breathing, not wanting to be heard, not wanting to miss the sound if it came again.

A thud, not of someone falling, but of a step?

Had Trey heard it? Was he asleep and oblivious? Was he making the noise?

Slowly, Lisa moved toward the door. The air was cold since the fire had died down. The wood was ice beneath her feet. She held her breath and prayed the board didn't squeak. First step was good. Then the other. Still silent.

She'd left the bedroom door ajar, hoping to let the firelight and warmth in. Another creak sounded.

Without a weapon she wasn't going to be able to defend herself. But she wasn't keen on the idea of being a sitting duck, either. She glanced around. Something. Anything. Her hairbrush was the only thing she found. It was better than nothing. At least it made her feel that way.

Moving silently to the door, she peered out through the gap between the door and its frame. Nothing. Just the dim light from the embers. Wait. A shadow? She waited, not wanting to be seen if it was someone intent on hurting them.

What if it was Trey? Wouldn't that be good

for their growing relationship if she brained him with her hairbrush?

She barely moved, but whoever was out there must have heard her. She wasn't sure who moved first, but the door flew open, and she barely moved back in time to avoid being hit. She screamed. The high pitch of it echoed off the rafters and startled even her.

"WHAT THE…" The man's voice was rough in the wake of Lisa's scream.

Trey recognized him first because she heard him say, "Win? Jeez!" He hit the switch and the dim light above the kitchen sink illuminated the room. "What the blazes are you doing?"

The old man stood there, looking as startled as she and Trey.

She hurried to her grandfather. "Grandpa?" she finally asked.

"Lisa?"

Everyone talked at once, which delayed her realization that she was staring at the barrel of her grandfather's old shotgun. She gulped.

"Put the gun down, Win." Trey's voice was closer now, reassuring, and she breathed a huge sigh of relief when her grandfather moved the gun away. She gulped in cold air and tried to slow her pounding heart.

"What are you doing here?" Grandpa grumbled and moved back across the room. He cracked the gun and tilted it to spit out the shells. At least it wasn't loaded now. He set it beside the stone fireplace and then hunkered down to stir the embers and add a couple of split logs. "Dang, it's cold out there. This feels good."

Only then did Trey put the knife back in the block with a resounding thunk of wood on wood.

No one said anything more until the flames had caught the wood, and light and heat washed over the room. Unfrozen now, Lisa moved closer to the fire, and her grandfather. She wanted to reach out and hug him, wanted to call her mother and tell her he was okay, wanted to smack him for scaring them half to death.

"You didn't answer my question." The old man straightened and the glare he gave her didn't invite her to hug him. "What are you doin' here?"

"Looking for you."

"Well, you found me. You can go home now."

"Really?" She parked her hands on her hips, suddenly realizing she was wearing her nightgown. Luckily, it was large, bulky and flannel. "It's the middle of the night. If you haven't noticed—" She glanced at the door. "And it's snowing." She crossed her arms over her chest and moved closer to the fire to keep herself from shivering. "And I'm not leaving until you answer my questions."

"What questions?" He frowned.

"I'm not calling Mom until you answer where you've been and what you've been up to."

For the first time since he'd scared her, he smiled. The welcome sound of his chuckle filled the room. "Yep, your mom would want those answers. That's my girl. She's tough."

"Tough?" Lisa stared at him. "Relentless is a better word."

He laughed again. "I taught her well."

"That still doesn't tell me where you've been for two weeks."

His smile and laughter vanished, and he stared into the growing flames. "I don't know if I should say."

"You better give us something, old man." Trey cut in. "We didn't come all the way up here, half freezing to death, to turn around and go back for nothing."

Win's gaze darted between them. "Maybe I should be asking the questions. How did you manage to connect with my granddaughter?" He looked over at Lisa. "Should I be concerned?"

"Stop trying to distract us." Lisa turned and walked into the bedroom, stomping a bit to warm up her feet and to burn off some of the adrenaline that wouldn't quite go away. She grabbed an old robe and yanked on a pair of socks. It helped, but she still shivered.

Opening her backpack, she pulled out the papers she'd been carrying with her for nearly two weeks. Maybe this would help.

Trey had started a pot of coffee and made them each a cup while she'd been gone. He handed her grandfather one and set hers on the coffee table. She didn't take it, didn't do anything except walk over to where her grandfather sat and slapped the hand-drawn map on the table in front of him. "Explain."

He stared at the paper, and his eyes glistened in the dim light. He shook his head before reaching out to pick up the page.

Her grandfather had some serious explaining to do. Lisa glanced at the clock. It was nearly two in the morning. "What are you doing here? Where have you been? We've been worried."

The old man moved slowly to stand and, avoiding her, stirred the fire again. He tossed another log on the embers, staring down at it as the flames grew. He stretched his hands out toward the heat.

Lisa looked at Trey then, and she saw her concern reflected in his eyes.

"You okay, Win?" Trey moved closer to the old man. "Where have you been?"

Win took a deep breath and settled down on the hearth, staring into the fire.

Lisa scrutinized her grandfather. The light over the sink and the flicker of the flames was the only illumination. The lines on Grandpa's face seemed deeper. His hair looked thinner, and she wondered when he'd combed it last. She bit her tongue as the questions poured into her thoughts.

"Drink some of that." She pointed at the cup. "It'll help warm you up."

"I'm fine. The fire'll do the trick." He softened his tone, as if realizing he'd snapped at her. He did wrap his hands around the warm cup for a long moment before he finally took a sip. The big white mug provided his face cover, and he took his time drinking.

"Normally, I'm serving you whiskey." Trey settled on the couch, leaning forward, his elbows on his knees across the table from Win.

"Yeah." Win lifted the mug in a salute. "This is better right now."

They sat in silence for a while, waiting.

"Okay," Trey sat straighter. "We've been patient. Now you owe us—or at least Lisa—an explanation. She's been worried about you."

Win chuckled. "You don't need to worry about me, girl. I been taking care of myself almost seventy years now."

"No, Grandma was taking care of you until last year," she petulantly pointed out. "Where have you been?" Her patience faded. "What are you doing here tonight?"

He shook his head. "I thought you were claim jumpers," he growled.

"What?" Why would he assume that? "Oh. The treasure."

"Now, Lisa—" Grandpa lifted a hand, as if to stay her words. That wasn't going to work.

"Don't you 'now, Lisa,' me. I've been worried about you, and you're running around on a wild-goose chase."

"It ain't a wild-goose chase," he snapped, and set the mug down with a thud. "But right now, I'm not at liberty to tell anyone."

"At liberty?" She glared at him. "What does that mean?"

Grandpa simply shook his head. They let him sit for a long minute.

Then Trey leaned forward again. "You're

not going to be able to brush her off. You *have* met your stubborn granddaughter, right?"

Win sighed and rubbed a hand over his face. The rasp of his whiskers against his rough hand seemed loud. He looked every one of his years, and guilt washed over her. The expression on his face was one she hated. The one he got whenever Mom berated him or nagged him about something. She'd always sworn she wouldn't do that to him, to anyone. She backed off.

"You're exhausted and cold." Lisa touched Grandpa's arm. "I'm sorry. I'm just concerned." She stood and walked over to the couch. "We can talk tomorrow. I shouldn't be so pushy."

"No. You got a right to be concerned." He stood and moved over to stand in front of her. He left the mug sitting on the tabletop. "I— uh—know you've been in town for a while." He had the sense to appear chagrined. "I should have let you know I was okay, but I didn't dare."

"What? Why?"

The old man sighed. "There's a lot you don't understand. And I don't have the energy to go into it tonight. Tomorrow's soon enough."

Disappointment took over, and she resisted

the urge to push him. "Okay." She gave in, but reluctantly. "We all need some sleep." Both Grandpa and Trey looked as tired as she felt. "You can have the bedroom." She tilted her head toward the master. "I fit better here on the couch."

"Oh, no." Grandpa laughed. "Your grandma would come back and smack the heck out of me for doing that. I'll be fine out here."

Lisa hesitated, realizing he wouldn't change his mind. She'd come by her stubbornness honestly. "Are you sure?"

He didn't answer, but grabbed the familiar afghan. "Get on to bed, kiddo. Morning's coming quick."

Lisa stood on her tiptoes to give him a kiss on that rough cheek. The adrenaline that had kept her humming at a fever's pitch for the past couple of weeks was quickly melting away. Her eyelids were heavy. Maybe now she could sleep.

Tomorrow was soon enough for answers, she reminded herself. At least he was home and safe.

TREY WASN'T QUITE ready to sleep. And he wasn't buying the old man's stalling technique. As he watched Lisa walk into the bedroom, he frowned. Why had she backed down? Concern for the old man? Exhaustion? Something else?

"You been taking care of her?" Win's voice was soft, and if Trey hadn't known him so well, he'd have resented the threat in it.

"Trying to." He turned around to face Win. "But it ain't easy when I have no idea what or who to protect her from." Would Win share information with him now that Lisa was in the other room? "How did you hear she's been in town?"

Trey waited. Win simply puttered around the old couch, making a bed out of the thing. He didn't speak or answer Trey's question. When he finally sat down, it was with an air of defeat.

"We aren't the enemy, Win."

"I know." Again, silence stretched out and the old man simply settled down to sleep.

With a sigh, Trey headed for the loft. He stopped at the bottom of the stairs. "You got anything to share?"

But Win only said, "Thanks for lookin' after her. I appreciate it." The fire snapped and crackled, but Win didn't continue.

Looked like Trey would have to wait, just like Lisa, until tomorrow.

But when morning came, the afghan was neatly placed just where it had always been

on the back of the couch. And Win was nowhere to be found.

Again.

CHAPTER THIRTEEN

"I'M GOING TO kill him. Plain and simple, once I find him again, I'm going to kill him." Lisa smacked the old frying pan on the burner.

Trey leaned against the counter, wisely keeping his distance. He'd never seen her in quite this temper before. It was an interesting display. He couldn't help but smile.

She looked amazing with the color high in her cheeks and the fire in her eyes.

"Don't you laugh at me." She shook the spatula at him. "Or I might kill you, too."

"Yes, ma'am." Trey turned away and opened the cabinet with the plates. Since she was making breakfast, the least he could do was set the table. Besides, it put distance between them, and distance was safest in the current situation.

Under normal circumstances, they'd be racing after Win, but two things kept them here. One, they had no idea where to even look, and two, Win had left a note. Brief, and to the point, it told them he was safe, and he'd be home when he finished his business. Instead of "Love, Grandpa" or "Sincerely" he'd simply signed it, "Go home."

Lisa was not happy with any of it.

The bacon snapped and popped in the cast-iron skillet, and the eggs she was frying sizzled enticingly. Several minutes later, she sighed. "Why is it that I only make you breakfast food?"

"We made soup and sandwiches last night."

"True." She competently filled plates with the grease-laden feast. "But you did that one."

He tried to judge her mood, the one underneath her anger at her grandfather's desertion. Whatever it was, she was covering it well with bluster.

Lisa set their plates on the table and sat down. For a long minute, she stared at hers, poking at the bacon with her fork.

Trey gave her time and space to sort through her thoughts and decide if she was going to eat or not. After taking only a few bites, she set her fork down and settled for drinking her juice. "Can I ask you something?" he finally asked.

"Sure." She was almost too eager, as if she wanted to get out of her own head.

"You backed off last night. Why didn't you push him to answer you?"

Lisa stared at him for a long moment, then carefully set her empty glass down on the table. She kept her hand wrapped around it, though, as if she still needed something to hold on to.

"I—" She took a deep breath. "My mother is always pushing Grandpa—and everyone else for that matter." Her voice went soft on that last part. "She's always on his case about things. He gets this look on his face when she does it, like he resents her."

"He seemed proud of her for being tenacious last night."

Lisa nodded. "He says that, but—" She paused. "But when she's that way with him, he always seems…hurt. As if he wants her to trust him."

Trey waited for her to elaborate. He didn't have to wait long.

"He got that same expression on his face last night. I…" She stared at her empty glass, twisting it around on the tabletop. "I don't want him to see me like that. He's a grown man, and I admire him. I love him just the way he is—imperfections and all."

Trey nodded, any words he'd hoped to say lodged behind the lump in his throat.

Trey recognized that admiration—admiration that could be blind. He'd known Win since he was a kid, and the man had always been fair and decent to him. But Win was hiding something. Something big, and Trey couldn't escape his own distrust.

He'd admired his grandfather like that. Once. He wouldn't make that mistake again. Not with anyone.

LISA WATCHED TREY put the last of his things into his backpack. There wasn't much, so it didn't take long. After breakfast, while she'd cleaned up the last of the dishes, he'd gone out to prepare their equipment.

If they left now, they'd be in town by lunch.

Carrying her pack out to the step, she couldn't help but take in the view. The breeze was brisk, and while no new snow was falling, flakes danced around everywhere, glistening in the bright sun. She pulled her hood up, thankful for its warmth.

There were footprints all around the area. She knew some of them were hers and Trey's. She could see the trail they'd made coming up the hill.

Another pathway was clear from the front porch back toward the falls. She frowned. That had to be her grandfather—didn't it? "Trey?"

He looked up from securing his snowshoes to his boots. "Yeah?"

"Those tracks." She pointed. "Are those Grandpa's?"

Trey straightened and followed the direction of her pointed finger. He took a step. "Yeah. They have to be."

Glaring, as much against the reflected sunlight as from her own thoughts, she glanced back at him. "What if we followed that path? Do you think we'd find him?"

Long seconds of silence ticked away as he gazed at the trail, then up at the sky, then finally at her again. "Probably. We won't make it back to town today, if we do." He met her eager gaze. "You game?"

"I—" She couldn't ask him to do that for her. "Don't you have to work at the bar?"

Trey shrugged. "I told Gabe I wasn't totally sure when I'd be back. He'll cover until I am." He took a couple more steps. "Come on. Let's give it a shot."

"Oh, Trey. Thank you!" In her excitement, Lisa rushed over to him, and even with her bulky ski jacket on, she was able to give him a hug.

They both froze, and not from the cold. Lisa looked up, unsure what she'd see on Trey's face.

Tenderness and something else—longing? Her breath caught in her throat, and she couldn't look away. She didn't want to.

And neither, apparently, did Trey. Slowly, his eyes wide open as he stared down at her, he leaned down, closer, his lips grazing hers. Softly at first, then as if judging her response, and finding the silent invitation, he leaned in closer, deepening the kiss.

His arms came around her. The whisper of his nylon jacket against hers was loud and echoed across the yard. He held her tight.

The taste of him—rough and delicious— mingled with the icy flavor of the snowy air. Crisp winter and warm man were a delicious contrast she couldn't resist. She put her arms up around his neck, returning his kiss.

Lisa completely lost track of time. In the distance she felt the cold air, but Trey kept her warm. She leaned in to him, letting herself get lost in sensation.

In him.

Her sigh floated away on the breeze and while a small part of her mind knew this wasn't why she was here, the rest of her ached to hold Trey for days.

"Lisa," Trey whispered, pulling back just a few inches. She looked at him, and he stared down at her.

"Mmm?"

"If we want to track your grandfather, we need to go before the wind covers the tracks." He didn't let go, however, and certainly didn't move away.

He was right. "I, uh, I guess so." She reluctantly broke the embrace.

Before she could move too far away, Trey reached out and gently grasped her chin. His fingers were cold against her skin, but she liked his touch.

"I meant what I said last night. This isn't the end." He kissed her forehead, his lips hot. "Not by a long shot."

But for now, it had to be. After they'd both put their snowshoes on, Trey led the way, just as he had when they'd come here.

Grandpa's tracks were easy to follow in the snow, but half a mile later, they hit a high meadow where the wind had swept most of the snow into drifts against the hills.

The short mountain grasses and rough stone made tracking difficult. But not impossible. Trey concentrated on the ground for a long while, hoping to find something soon.

He was surprised to see several sets of horse tracks, though. "Remember when we saw that hoofprint yesterday?" he asked after he'd crisscrossed the same area several times.

"Yeah?"

"Do you think your grandfather did bring a horse?" Why hadn't he considered that earlier? If Win was on horseback, he could be a lot farther away than Trey had originally guessed. He looked around. The meadow seemed to go on forever.

"He might. He does have the four of them. This is one of the high pastures where he lets them spend the summer."

That would also explain some of the tracks, especially since none of these looked new. "I remember borrowing the horses once." Memories of a hunting trip that his father had actually come on filled his mind. He hadn't thought about that trip in a long time. It had been a good one.

"Wasn't one of them named Chisolm? Beautiful horse." He remembered the dark brown beauty.

"Yeah, he still has him. Along with King, Cassie and Beau. Beau's my favorite." She smiled, and Trey liked watching the joy on her face.

He thought about the horses on the ranch at home. They'd had dozens of them, none of them truly his. Horses were equipment to his grandfather. Not pets. Not friends. But

Trey had still had a fondness for one of them, Devil's Gold.

"Did you have a horse in Texas?" she asked.

Trey nodded. "Yeah. Several." He knew she didn't want to hear about what a callous jerk his grandfather was again, so he held that information back. "Devil's Gold was the son of my father's horse, Silver Devil."

"They sound pretty intense."

"Just their names. They're both beautiful and good-natured horses." Silence settled between them, the only sound the rush of the wind. Then he said, "You said your grandfather's horses spend summers here. I assume they work hunting season, in the fall? Where are they now, for the winter?"

"At the stable in town with Sam's horse."

Trey looked out over the beautiful, wild country. It was open, like back home in Texas, but in no other way the same. This land was rougher, more jagged around the edges. A wave of homesickness hit him by surprise. He hadn't missed the ranch since he'd gotten here.

Trey kept walking, watching the ground, hoping to see something new, something different. Lisa kept up with him. "How much of this land belongs to your grandfather?" He asked the question as much for curiosity as for conversation.

"I'm not sure. A lot. My great-grandfather started the ranch and the next generation added to it. I'm not sure how many acres. But I do know everything you can see here is his."

She sounded so matter-of-fact, and he recognized just a bit of himself in that observation. He'd never really thought about all the land his grandfather, and now his father, owned. Hundreds—thousands—of acres. It was just the norm.

"My great-grandparents used to actually ranch all this land. I vaguely remember herds of cattle. Grandpa never did, though."

"I wonder why." They walked for a while without talking. She seemed lost in her thoughts.

"I'm not sure. Grandpa was a mechanic, and he enjoyed running the garage. Guess I'll have to ask him why he didn't ranch." She paused. "If I get to." Her concern was loud even though her voice was soft.

"Hey, he was fine last night. I'm sure he still is. He's just—" He was what? What was he supposed to say? The old man was hiding and had run away from one of the people in the world who cared about him most. Something was going on. "Don't worry yet. We'll find him."

She forced a smile and nodded. "He's probably hiding because he knows I'm ready to shoot him," she grumbled, some of her earlier anger coming through.

"There you go. Think positive."

She laughed and the sound carried like soft bells on the wind. He decided it was one of his favorite sounds. He couldn't help but join her.

After a few more feet, Trey stopped and knelt down. He took several minutes examining the ground to make sure he was right. Finally, he pointed to a spot. "Here."

Lisa hurried over to his side and he traced a small indentation. The shape of a bootheel.

CHAPTER FOURTEEN

NEARLY AN HOUR LATER, cold, musty air wafted up toward her. It didn't fit. Standing here in this meadow, the air should be clear and crisp. She looked over at Trey. He was frowning too, but he was staring intently at the ground.

"What is it?"

"The tracks stop."

"What do you mean 'stop'?"

"They stop. Right here." He moved around, kicking at the rocks and dirt. His frown deepened. "Hmmm, what do you know?" He hunkered down and brushed rocks and dirt away from a spot at the bottom of the bluff.

"It's a covering. Help me move it." His voice was impatient, and harsh enough to shake her out of the spiral her overworried mind had gotten trapped in.

"Oh!" She saw it now. A piece of plywood had been put down on the ground and very carefully, artfully even, covered with rocks and dirt. She tried to move some of the stones and found they were stuck to the wood. What the heck?

"Here. Clear these." He pointed to where he stood. "It's the edge." He brushed away pieces that covered the wood. She knelt beside him and helped him push more of it away.

Finally, they had enough moved that Trey could get his hands beneath the plank. He pulled up. "Jeez, that's a heavy…" He took a deep breath and put his full weight behind it.

Lisa stood back, worried about getting in his way as much as to watch. He gave the plywood a hard shove. They both stood there, staring at a small hole in the ground. Not much bigger than a manhole, it wasn't something any man had dug.

"It looks like a crevice of some sort." Trey put his arm out in front of her—as if he could stop her.

"Hold it right there!" A dear, familiar voice came out of the darkness, along with the business end of that same shotgun she'd stared at last night.

"Grandpa!" she cried, her relief and frustration with the old man so overwhelming she took a step forward. Only Trey's strong arm kept her from falling into the hole. Maybe he wasn't totally crazy after all.

"Really, old man?" Trey growled. "The gun, again? Put it away."

"Lisa?" The shotgun disappeared and her grandfather's face appeared in the bit of sunlight that was slipping past the edge of the plywood. "What the he…uh…heck are you doing here? I told you to go home." He didn't sound happy at all to see her, but he still couldn't bring himself to curse in front of a woman.

"Still trying to find you, apparently." She stepped back, her hands on her hips, expecting her grandfather to come up to the surface. When he didn't, her relief shifted into anger. "What are you doing down there?"

"Ah, crap." The old man's face disappeared from the light. "You might as well come on down and see. 'Cept you gotta promise to keep it a secret."

The upper rungs of an old metal ladder appeared, clattering loudly against the rock edge of the hole.

"Ladies first." Trey waved toward the ladder and the hole. "You, I'm sure he won't shoot."

"Don't count on that, boy," Grandpa grumbled. "You haven't known her as long as I have."

Trey laughed as Lisa stepped onto the ladder, hoping it was on stable ground below.

OUT OF THE WIND, the tunnel was actually warmer than outside. She was still glad she had on the thick jeans and her heavy shoes, though. Begrudgingly, she admitted, yet again, that Trey had been right about her needing the extra clothes. Her feet finally reached the bottom, where her grandfather held the ladder steady on the uneven ground.

As soon as her feet hit the dirt, she turned and threw her arms around him. "You scared me half to death—again." She failed to hide her tears of relief.

Awkwardly, he patted her shoulder and let her hug him. Finally, he pulled back. "We'd better make sure Trey gets down here safe." His voice was rough, and she knew he was moved by her display of affection.

"Okay," she whispered and moved to the other side of the ladder. They both helped steady it as Trey descended.

Finally, he reached the bottom and then faced them. "Well, old man. You going to explain now?" He didn't seem angry, but his frown hadn't disappeared.

"I'll have to show you. Might as well come on in."

That's when Lisa noticed the flashlight her grandfather had propped on a ledge. She frowned. "Where are we?"

"You'll see." He didn't say any more, but climbed up the ladder, nimbler than she expected. The plywood they'd worked so hard to move away scraped over the stones, and he settled it in place again. "Ain't taking any more chances. That's why I made that cover in the first place." He climbed back down and left the shotgun leaning up against the wall of the...where were they? A cave? A mine?

"Follow me. Watch your step and stay close," he instructed as he headed down what looked like a tunnel.

"This isn't man-made," Trey said as they followed Grandpa.

"Nope. This is pure God." Grandpa's voice was soft. "Careful here." The tunnel turned, and the ceiling was nearly too low to stand up fully. She could, but both men had to stoop over. Finally, Grandpa halted, spreading his arms out to stop them. What was with everyone thinking they could stop moving objects with their arms?

But she did as he silently asked. Trey was close behind her, his body's warmth a welcome touch in the cool cave. But why were they here? And why was her grandfather hiding it? "I'm still confused."

"Patience, kiddo."

At the sound of his pet name for her, she smiled. She'd missed him so much, and was glad he was safe and sound. Except she wondered how sound his mind was, having apparently snuck away from his home and spent at least a week camping out in a cave.

"Are you hiding here for a reason? Is someone after you?" She thought about the break-in at his house. All the scenarios she'd come up with over the past weeks nearly came bubbling up.

Trey put his hand on her shoulder, and she glanced back at him. He simply shook his head. She frowned as her grandfather rummaged around in the semidarkness. "Just wait."

Why was Trey so patient? She wanted answers, and all she was getting was a walk through a really creepy, dark cave. How far underground were they? She looked up at the stone ceiling, a wave of claustrophobia suddenly washing over her.

She leaned toward Trey, and he let her.

It wasn't long before she heard a click, and then light from a lantern shot out in front of them. And upward. And around. And down.

Lisa stared, blinking rapidly at the suddenly bright light and unbelievingly at the world before her. Was that echoing sound her gasp?

They stood at the end of the tunnel, on a ledge that hung out over an enormous cavern. A piece of rope, thick and old, had been anchored into the wall. It was all that kept someone from stepping off the ledge.

She couldn't resist the urge to peer down, and immediately regretted it. Her stomach flipped, and she leaned back again. Trey's solid chest, and his strong arm slipping around her waist, stabilized her.

She couldn't see the bottom. Turning her gaze, she found a wonder and awe she'd never felt before. The ceiling glistened with some type of crystal, looking almost like stars trapped in the stone.

On the walls around them, a rainbow of color was layered in the stones. She'd seen layers of sandstone along the highways, but nothing that resembled this. Glittering pastel colors refracted around and over them. Pink. Purple. Green? Was that possible? Her eyes didn't lie.

"It's beautiful," she whispered, and then laughed at the pure wonder and beauty.

"Win?" Trey spoke softly, his voice filled with the same awe. "What is this place?"

Grandpa was silent for a moment. "We need to talk." He switched off the lamp, and all that was left was the beam of the flashlight again. "Come on. I've got a camp a bit farther on. We'll talk there."

This time, her grandfather's tread was slower, softer, as if he really wasn't sure what he was doing. If he'd been here these past couple of weeks, wouldn't he be sure of his steps? She slowed her pace, though, just in case. The depth of that cavern remained in her mind. The idea of falling to her death deep in the earth where no one would ever find her made her shiver.

Finally, the walls closed in again, and they followed another tunnel. The flashlight's beam soon found the edge of a blanket. They turned a corner and stepped into a dimly lit room.

"Wait here," Win said. They stopped and he moved forward. This time when he turned up the lamp, it was a much smaller opening that they saw. There wasn't any endless drop to avoid, but when she looked up, there was nothing above them. Were they inside the entire mountain?

No bright colors or sparkles here, though.

Just flat ground and rough stone walls. A sleeping bag was stretched out against one wall near boxes of what appeared to be supplies. A set of snowshoes, much like hers, only older and worn, lay nearby. That had to be how he'd gotten here this time.

"Is this where you've been staying?" she asked.

Grandpa nodded. "Yeah. It's nothin' new. Done it dozens of times before."

"We saw horseshoe tracks." There wasn't any horse in here.

"Yeah in the summer it's a nice ride up here and I can leave 'em in the pasture. Don't work so well in the snow."

That made sense, and she felt relief that no animal was out in the elements.

"Here, have a seat, Lisa," Trey offered, guiding her to a flat rock that seemed to be made for sitting on. Trey stepped past her and found another rock to perch on. Win took his time setting the flashlight up and lighting yet another Coleman lantern. Finally, he pulled an old metal-and-web lawn chair forward and took a seat.

"Welcome to The Parlor." The old man grinned like a little boy with a secret he could barely keep any longer.

They waited patiently. Lisa couldn't help

but appreciate her grandfather's smile even as she struggled with a million questions running through her head.

Trey finally spoke, breaking the silence. "What is this place?"

Grandpa tipped his head back, staring up toward the unseen roof.

"You know, I been looking through these caves since I was a boy, and I still find something new to amaze me." He stared into the darkness.

"Since you were a boy?" Lisa was shocked. "Why didn't you tell anyone about this?" she asked, her soft voice echoing around the cavern. She'd never heard about the cave, and knew no one else had, either. The Telluride locals weren't that good at keeping quiet. "Why is it a secret?"

Grandpa turned back to them, and she wasn't sure he was going to answer her.

"Duncan found it." His voice grew faint, distant. "When he was just a kid. Heck, he was always a kid. He never really got to grow up." He sat there, twisting his hands together. "I haven't shared this place with anyone. Except Duncan," he whispered, thick and rough. "Your grandmother never saw it."

Lisa gasped, then quickly swallowed the sound.

"I know." He nodded. "There shouldn't be secrets in a marriage. But I didn't consider it a secret. Heck, I went years without thinking about it myself. It's been here, forgotten, abandoned, alone for all that time."

She watched the pain in his eyes as he glanced around at the stone walls.

"Duncan's here for you." Trey's words were loud—and dead-on. Understanding filled them. He sat partially in the shadows, but the lamplight tried to reach him. She couldn't see his expression clearly, though.

Grandpa nodded. "He loved this place. I bet he explored every inch of it." He shook his head. "Our folks had no clue. Not that they'd have stopped him. Parents didn't do that kind of stuff back then." His voice grew wistful. "We ran wild all over these hills. The only time we went home was when the sun went down, or we were hungry." A smile spread over his face. "He loved bein' down here and I loved followin' my big brother." He kicked a rock with the toe of his boot. "Used to tease him about bein' a mole or something in a different life." His laughter was warm.

"I wish I could have met him." She really did.

"You'd have liked him. You remind me of him. Single-minded and stubborn."

"Thanks. I think."

The silence wasn't heavy this time. If nothing else, it was warm, and the fact that Grandpa was finally explaining made it welcoming. She wanted to ask a dozen questions about her uncle, but hesitated, not sure the memories were what her grandfather wanted to visit right now.

"Why are you here, now, Win?" Trey asked, pushing as Lisa wasn't ready to do yet.

The smile faded from her grandfather's face, and she almost stepped in to say he didn't have to answer, but he spoke before she could. Then she realized Trey was doing the right thing.

"Until that telegram showed up, I never felt right claiming this place." Grandpa pushed to his feet, moving over to a crate on top of the stack. He lifted the lid and pulled out a small, old-fashioned box.

"I found this here." He handed it to her. "It ain't Duncan's, but I don't know whose it is."

She lifted the lid on the old box. There wasn't much inside, and she picked up each item and examined it. A scout knife. Arrowheads. A matchbook. Trinkets from boyhood. "I'm confused. You're sure these aren't Uncle Duncan's?"

"Positive." Grandpa reached out and took

the box back. "My brother had a box like this. We all did. They sold them down at the drug-store when we were kids. All of us bought 'em and kept our secrets in 'em." He laughed. "But this ain't mine, or Duncan's. I have them both at home."

Trey met Grandpa's eye and the old man nodded. Confused, Lisa gazed between the two men. "What—?"

Trey looked back at her. "That means someone else discovered this place."

"But I don't know who." Grandpa paced. "When that map showed up, things changed."

"How?" Trey prodded.

"For one, it helped knowing Duncan had told our folks about the cave, and he knew he might not come home. That made it easier for me to…" His voice faded, and he cleared his throat. "Made it easier for me to think about maybe letting other people in on our secret."

"You mentioned claim jumpers last night. Want to elaborate?" Trey asked.

Grandpa nodded. "You remember that fool, Lance Westgate?"

"Yeah," Trey answered.

"He wants this land. Wants to build on it."

"Is he trying to get the mineral rights?" Trey asked.

Grandpa shook his head. "He doesn't have

a clue about the cave. At least I don't think so." He nodded toward the area behind him. "He wants to develop the land. And he's been trying to force me to sell. I won't. This land's been in my family for generations, and while I never ran cattle on it as my father did, it's been profitable to rent to people like you and your grandfather. Hunters love it up here. Hikers. Plus, renting out the pastures to my neighbors helps them thrive and stay in business."

Trey nodded, as if understanding the love of that land. "I get that. It was a great place for me." Memories cloaked his words, and Lisa ached to know more. He didn't share, though, and instead asked another question. "So, what's bothering you?"

"A few weeks ago, a couple of guys came to the house. They wanted to chat, they said. I let them in. I never shoulda done that." Grandpa's pace picked up in agitation.

Finally, he stopped just inches from where they sat. He slowly pulled up his flannel shirt, exposing his ribs that were covered in healing bruises.

"Grandpa!" Lisa leaped down from her perch to get a closer look.

He stepped back. "I'm fine now." He let

his shirt fall down into place. "Hurt at first, but it's better."

Then she remembered. "Is that all they did? I... I saw blood on the kitchen floor."

"Thought I cleaned it all up. That wasn't them exactly. I was trying to fix dinner and since my side hurt, I couldn't get a good grip on a knife." He held up his hand where he had a bandage around his thumb.

Somehow, that wasn't very reassuring.

"Any other threats?" Trey asked. "Did you tell anyone else?"

"Just Sam."

That surprised her, and Lisa looked over to see the same surprise on Trey's face. "Sam knows you're here?" she asked.

Grandpa shook his head. "No. He might have an idea, but he don't know for sure. And I never mentioned this place to him."

They sat in silence for a bit. Lisa let the information soak in, not really sure what to do next. "Are you going to sell the land?"

"Not to Westgate, if I can help it. He finds this place—and they will if they start digging for a development—he'll either destroy it, or screw up any chance of preserving it."

Lisa walked around a bit. Picking up the flashlight, she shone it up toward what she thought might be the ceiling. The light beam went on forever, never finding anything. She angled it to a wall and just a few feet above their heads she saw layers of crystals and stones that shone back at her. The idea of this place being destroyed actually hurt.

"Can we save it?"

Grandpa didn't answer. Neither did Trey. Finally, she turned back around to look at them. The sadness on Grandpa's face nearly made her cry. "What?"

"It'd take either a pile of money—and possibly years—to get through the government red tape." He shook his head. "I'm not getting any younger. There's no one in the family who has the attachment to the land." His gaze, so familiar, suddenly filled with pain she'd never seen before. She'd like to deny what he was hinting at, but she couldn't.

Neither her mother, nor Uncle Phil, lived here and seldom visited. If Mom were given a choice, Grandpa would visit her in the city, not have her come here. They hadn't celebrated a Christmas in Telluride since Grandma had passed away. None of her cousins were any more attached to this place than she was, though she was growing more so by the minute.

"I'm afraid of what will happen when I'm gone."

"Don't talk like that." She moved closer to Grandpa.

"I'm not being morbid. I'm being realistic, kiddo."

"He's right. If Lance has resorted to thugs and break-ins—who knows what extremes he'll go to?"

The air of the cave was different than any other place she'd been. It was heavy and scented like the earth. "Wh…what can we do? What can Sam do?"

Grandpa shrugged. "He's doin' his job, I'm sure, but…"

Trey leaned forward, his muscular arms flexing as he leaned his elbows on his knees. He looked Win in the eye, and the silence that filled the small cavern was thick with a message she couldn't even begin to decipher. Was it a guy thing? A secret they shared? Whatever it was, she wasn't a part of it. She didn't appreciate being excluded.

"There is one solution." Trey's voice filled the chamber as he faced the older man.

"What?" Lisa asked and was surprised when her grandfather simply glanced at Trey—and nodded.

Trey stood, shoving his hands into his back pockets. He paced a step or two, just as Win had done moments before. "You know me, my background." He paused a long time, as if holding his breath before doing something risky like jumping off a diving board. "I love the land, as you do." He paused, then faced Grandpa. "Sell it to me."

Lisa gasped. That was *not* what she'd expected Trey to say, and she certainly wouldn't expect her grandfather to nod in agreement.

"What's going on?" She looked from her grandfather to Trey and back again. Where would a bartender get that kind of money?

"What would stop them from coming after you?" Fear for both of them put panic in her voice.

Trey leaned back against the stone wall. "I'm not seventy years old, for one." He glanced at her, and she could swear his eyes were filled with sadness—and something else. Something darker. "I'll be fine."

What was he talking about? Who was he? Suspicions she didn't like one bit hit her. Was this why Trey had offered to help her find Grandpa? Had he used her?

Had all the laughter, and those earth-shattering kisses, come with a hidden agenda?

CHAPTER FIFTEEN

THE THICK STONE walls of the cavern felt as if they were closing in on his head. Trey stared into the old man's eyes and saw understanding and—what else? Relief? Gratitude?

Glancing at Lisa, though, he realized she was hurting; it was painted all over her face. He owed her an explanation, but had no idea where to begin.

He stood, not sure how she'd react to any of it. "I've told you about my grandfather." He'd start there.

"Yeah?" She frowned, her stance stiff as if she were waiting for the walls to fall in on her, too.

"He's…he was…the head of Haymaker Holdings. HH." He waited for her to recognize the name. She just stared back. He wanted to curse. It'd be a whole lot easier if she already knew that piece.

"I thought you said he'd passed away."

"He did. Last year."

"And that you didn't have a good relationship with your family."

At least she'd been listening. "That, too."

"But what does that have to do with anything?" she snapped.

"Listen to him, Lisa," Win said sharply. "He can explain."

She crossed her arms over her chest and settled back on the rock where she'd been perched before. "I'm listening."

Trey took a deep breath. A big chunk of the future was riding on this moment. His. Win's. A part of hers. Everything.

"Haymaker Holdings is one of Texas's largest cattle ranches. My grandfather built it after he came home from Vietnam. Built it big."

She nodded, still staring hard at him.

"Over time, he expanded the business, and HH has properties all over the world. Heck I'm not sure anyone except the lawyers even know what all we own. What's one more?"

For a long moment, there wasn't any manmade sound in the cavern. In the distance, Trey heard water drip, slowly, tediously. But nothing else.

"And you're working as a bartender because…?" Lisa asked.

Of course, she aimed right for the heart of

the situation. He couldn't even explain half of it to himself. How was he going to make her understand without baring his soul? Not here, not now. Maybe never.

Trey glanced over at Win. He'd known Pal, and was aware of a lot of the details of why Trey moved here—but no one could grasp how he felt, how bad the taste was in his mouth at even thinking about going back to that life. To that place.

Lisa jumped off the seat. "If you're not going to explain—"

Win stood then, too. "Sit down and listen." That was the first time Trey had ever heard the man raise his voice, and from the look on her face, Lisa hadn't heard it much either.

"You want life to be easy," Win continued. "And I've given you the impression that it can be—I've always tried to help all you kids out. I've always supported you. But not everyone's had such a life. Remember that."

Lisa settled back down, and while she did as her grandfather asked, the storm in her eyes didn't calm. She did wait—though her left foot tapped softly, impatiently.

"I didn't lie to you. I'm not here for some secret mission," Trey said. He'd never been able to share his feelings well, but he had to give her something. "I left home to escape all that. To build my own life."

"And you came here? Where you knew about Grandpa and the land? Convenient that you got that job in his favorite bar. Sounds like you had the money to go anywhere to build a life, yet you just ended up here? Why?"

"I… I couldn't say." He'd asked himself the same question and come up with the same lack of answers dozens of times. "You can choose to believe me, or not. I don't care." He did care, but he wasn't going to beat himself up for her, for anyone. He could have stayed in Texas for that.

Trey could see the thoughts flying around in her head. He waited for her questions. But when she remained silent, he was surprised. Maybe even disappointed. Questions would be easier than her stony silence.

Even Win gave her a sideways glance as if he were surprised, too. Finally, Win broke the silence. "We ain't doing anything about it today." Win looked pointedly at Lisa and then back at Trey. "I'd rather work with Trey than Lance, any day, so yes, I'm open to discussing your offer." Win extended his hand. Trey took it.

That made it as official as they could get

right now. Trey nodded, knowing this wasn't the end. If anything, it was the beginning of one grand mess.

Lisa finally found her voice. "How can you be sure Trey's not working with Lance? They seem pretty friendly in the bar."

"Everyone's friendly in a bar." Win waved away her comment. "Careful where you go, girl."

Too late, Trey almost said.

It took nearly four hours to get down off the mountain, and Lisa's mind raced the entire journey. All the people, all the interactions. Everything Trey had talked about. It all looked so different now.

Tainted by her doubts of why he'd done it.

When they reached the ridge, Lisa and Trey—Win had been adamant he was staying in the cave—strapped on their snowshoes, and she had to focus on moving and not falling. By the time they reached the lower river where the Jeep was parked, Lisa was exhausted. And that same exhaustion showed on Trey's face.

But there was also a piece of heartache. Like a shard of her broken heart had dug in deep and was slowly killing her. He wasn't who she'd thought he was—and on that realization's tail came the knowledge that everything in her world was changing.

This felt too much like Robert's deceit. She was back to being jobless. They couldn't work together at the bar after this.

Grandpa's mortality was real to her now, and the legacy she'd never given much thought to was gone just when she'd come to appreciate it.

She couldn't think about the kisses. She didn't dare.

Trey was as silent as she was, and the closed expression on his face revealed nothing. Was he angry for her outburst? Was he hurting, too? Did he even care? She couldn't tell, and that fact made her more upset.

Once in the car, Trey drove down the hill in silence, and she had no intention of breaking that silence. He'd said plenty when they'd been talking with Grandpa—none of it had alleviated the sense of betrayal she felt.

Though she stared straight ahead out the windshield, she could see Trey's profile in the corner of her eye. He was focusing on driving, his eyes never wavering from the snow-packed road, his big hands easily steering the vehicle over the bumps and ice.

Finally, the sun low in the sky, they reached the outskirts of town. The traffic and people milling in the streets were jarring after two days in near solitude. She flinched away from the sensory overload.

Trey pulled the Jeep to the curb in front of Grandpa's house and hastily hopped out. He opened the back and lifted out her gear. She jumped out, too, careful not to slip on the mounded snow along the sidewalk as he set her backpack, snowshoes and poles on the cleared sidewalk.

Silently, she shouldered the pack and grabbed the gear. She needed to say something. But she didn't want to fight with him. Not now. Not here. "Thanks for taking me up." She forced the words through her tight lips. "I appreciate it."

Icy wind whipped over her, catching her hair and sprinkling it over her face. She shoved it away with an impatient hand.

"Lisa." Trey took a step toward her and her reflexive step backward made him stop. He cleared his throat. "I want to explain…" The look on his face, distant, closed, didn't say that, though.

"Why?" She moved up to the cleared walk. "I think I get it." She tilted her head toward the mountain. "It was pretty clear."

His jaw clenched. "I made an offer. An

honest business offer to help your grandfather solve his situation. It's a fair deal."

"A deal you certainly benefit from." Her anger was returning, and she didn't want to feel this way. She hurt too much to add anything more to it. Slowly, she backed away. "Not now," she whispered and spun around. "Just go. Maybe later," she whispered more to herself, fairly sure he couldn't hear her.

She hurried along the walk. The house was dark and empty. Grandpa wasn't coming back to town yet, though he'd said he would soon. Now that they were all aware about the true threats, his hiding was fruitless.

"Lisa?" Trey called after her.

She froze, not ready to face him, but knowing she had to. She settled for glancing over her shoulder. "Yeah?" He wasn't getting back into the Jeep, wasn't getting ready to leave. Instead, he leaned against the Jeep's side, his hands in his jacket pockets. Casual and relaxed.

How did he do that? How could he be so calm and normal? She felt like every molecule in her body was being shattered by the hurt.

"I'm not leaving you here alone."

"I'll be fine."

"Yeah." He nodded. "Sam is sending a deputy. I won't leave until he gets here."

She sighed. Manners told her she should invite him in. It was freezing out here, but she couldn't. She just couldn't. She needed to be alone. Needed to reevaluate everything.

Instead of voicing the polite words a good hostess would utter, she simply nodded and continued on toward the front door. She unlocked it and stepped inside, pulling the door closed tightly behind her.

Silence engulfed her. No traffic sounds. No voices. Nothing. Until the refrigerator made that soft hum, and the clock in the hall clicked off a minute. And then another.

She dropped the backpack. Heard the clatter of the snowshoe equipment as it hit the wood floor. A few more clicks of the clock and the resounding chimes called out the hour. One. Two. Three. Four. Five.

Time for the day to end. Time to figure out dinner. Time to move on.

Closing her eyes, Lisa leaned against the door. She was shaking. Was it the cold? A reaction to all the turmoil? Her anger? Loss? What? She didn't know. She didn't care.

Her eyes burned. Her throat ached with the tears that were trapped there. "Why?"

she asked the empty house. No answer came back.

Instead, her brain taunted her with memories of the last couple of days. Of the warm fire at the cabin, the kisses and laughter she and Trey had shared, of her hopes that had quickly been dashed.

She cursed, half expecting to see the white cloud of her breath that she'd grown so used to up there on the mountain.

Even that failed her.

WHAT HAD HE just done?

Trey tromped through the snow. The deputy who had shown up was the same one who'd nailed the boards over the broken window. He was familiar with the place, with the situation. Sam trusted him, so Trey headed back to the bar.

He needed space, needed time to wrap his brain around the repercussions of the offer he'd made.

Rick was already behind the bar. The younger guy looked relieved when Trey told him to finish the shift. "I'll work on paperwork tonight." He had to get the deposits done anyway. Hap would be expecting them.

But once the office door was closed, Trey

simply stared at the pile of receipts and money.

His body was tired, achy even, from the exercise. But his brain spun fast and furious.

There was no stopping it now. Leaning back in the old, creaky chair, he closed his eyes. He knew what he had to do. Who he had to call.

Who he *should* call.

Like a giant eraser, he wiped that thought out of his head. His father was not on the list. Even though Pal Senior was gone, the fact that Pal Junior hadn't stopped him from his maniacal behavior still didn't sit well with Trey. His father had been absent too many times.

No, this was a business deal. Family wasn't a part of it.

He pulled out his phone and wasn't even surprised that the battery was nearly gone. Five percent wasn't going to suffice for this call. He hadn't taken a charger to the mountains, knowing it'd be a waste.

Reaching for the bar's landline, he thumbed the cell phone to his contact list and found the one person he was sure he could trust. Maybe.

Trey dialed. And waited. He wasn't leaving a message, so he hoped Jason picked up.

Jason Hawkins had been a friend since they

were kids. His family had owned the ranch next to Pal's, and while he had lived in Austin, Texas, with his mother, he'd spent summers at the ranch. The Hawkins brothers had fit right in with Trey and the other kids.

The fact that Jason had married Trey's newly discovered aunt made Jason family. Lord, his family was a mess. But Jason was family too, and he'd taken on a big chunk of the legal work when Granddad had died.

"Hello?" Jason's voice was sharp and clipped. That didn't bother Trey. Just like all the other Hawkins boys, his intensity was what made him successful.

"You busy?"

"Trey? That you?" The sharpness dropped and surprise came through the line.

"Yeah. But don't go planning any family reunions. I'm calling about business."

There was a long silence. "Okay. Fair enough." The sound of movement on the other end of the line told Trey Jason had sat down. "What's going on?"

"You got some time? This could take a bit."

Jason laughed, though not with a lot of humor. "I'll make time. You've been gone too long, my friend."

"I know, and this won't change that." Trey took a chunk of silence. "I don't want you telling my folks about this call. I'm… I'm not ready for that."

"Can't say I agree with your decision, but okay. Tell me what's going on."

Trey closed his eyes and tried to figure out where to start. "You remember the ranch where Granddad and I used to go hunting? Up in Colorado?"

"Vaguely."

"Well, the old guy who owns it might be selling. I've offered to buy it."

"Really?"

"Don't sound so surprised. I've always loved the place." Though some of the memories were tainted, that love had never diminished, he realized, though he wouldn't admit that to anyone.

"You think it'd be a good acquisition for HH?"

"No." Trey shook his head even though Jason couldn't see it. "This is me. All mine. It's what I came here looking for."

Until that moment, he hadn't realized it. But it rang true. He'd wanted a place of his own. And the place he'd always felt welcome, always enjoyed, was here.

At that ranch. In that cabin and with these people.

All these people.

Glancing out the small window of the office, he saw the snow falling down gently again. The backlight glistened off the flakes, big, fat and fluffy.

An image came to mind, of Lisa, snow falling down around her, that gorgeous hair tumbling from beneath the hood of her coat. A smile wide on her lips and bright in her eyes.

He certainly hadn't come looking for her. But somehow she'd found him.

Shaking his head, he dispelled the image. No. Not now. He wasn't ready for anything like that in his life. He might be the heir to Haymaker Holdings, but he'd already let everyone know he didn't want it.

He didn't have anything to offer her, or any more answers to give her to the angry questions he'd seen in her eyes. Not yet. But Jason could fix that.

"There's a lot going on here—" Jason said, and Trey cut him off.

"All I called about was this deal. I left that all behind on purpose." He could hear movement. Jason must have risen and started walking. Probably headed to court or something. "Look, I know you're busy. I'll get you the specifics and go from there. I just need to get the ball rolling on the money."

"How much we talking?"

"Probably most, if not all, of the trust fund."

"What if it's more? You could partner with HH."

"No." The single word came out harsh and cold. "If it takes that—" Was he ready for this? Was this the answer? "Sell my shares."

This silence was complete, no sound of movement on Jason's end of the line now. "You're serious."

"Yep."

Jason cursed, and Trey wondered if anyone heard him. That fancy lawyer's office of his probably wasn't used to such colorful language. Then he remembered who he was talking to. He smiled. They were used to it.

"You ever comin' home?" Jason softly asked.

"I don't know." And he didn't. "I'm not sure why I would." This was not a conversation he wanted to have, so he forced them both to focus on business. "Do what you need to. I'll get you the particulars as soon as I can, and I'll call you the first of next week."

He didn't even say goodbye, simply put the old-fashioned receiver back on its cradle and sat staring out the window.

The snow was falling harder now and the wind whipped up, stirring the flakes to block the view. A storm was coming.

And there wasn't a blessed thing he could do about it and hoped everything came out okay on the other side.

CHAPTER SIXTEEN

THE LEAST LISA could do was to let her mother know Grandpa was okay. The phone rang several times, and for a moment, Lisa wasn't sure if her mother would answer.

Finally, she did. "Hello?"

"Mom?"

"Oh, Lisa. I've been wondering what was going on up there."

"Good news. I found him. He's fine."

"Thank goodness. What in the world has he been doing? Did you tell him how worried we've all been?"

"I did say that, yes." Lisa paused. She actually had no idea how her mother would react to what she was going to say next. "He's talking to someone about selling the ranch." The land that had been in the family for generations.

"Oh, thank heavens. Your uncle and I have been trying to get him to consider that for years."

"What? Why?" Though she'd already answered herself, days ago, it still surprised her when spoken aloud. The family never came here to Telluride, not to mention visiting the cabin or the ranch. Okay, up until these last couple weeks, she hadn't been much better.

"What are we going to do with it?" her mother asked. "No one's going to run the ranch or wants to take care of that old cabin. It's just not practical for the rest of us."

"But—" Practical? What did practical have to do with family and history? And legacy?

"No, we've been talking to him about it for a while. If he doesn't sell it now, we'll probably do so when he's gone."

"Oh." That could be years away.

"I'm so glad he's finally agreed to meet with Lance Westgate. That would be an easy way to solve this whole mess."

"You know about him?"

"Of course. I went to school with his mother. He contacted me several months ago. I told him I'd support a sale. He seemed fairly certain he could get it done quickly."

Disappointment about everything settled heavy on Lisa's shoulders. Disappointment that Trey seemed to have ulterior motives. Disappointment that her mother didn't value her birthright. And just a bit of disappointment that her mother and Uncle Phil were going to dismiss her, and her cousins', possible interest. They hadn't even asked, and Lisa felt the mantle of childhood settle back in place. Would her mother ever see her as an adult with opinions and ideas worth listening to?

"What if I'd have wanted the land?" she asked.

"Why would you want that? You can't afford it anyway. It's high-dollar property. No, this is a much better way to handle all of this."

Someone knocked on the door just then, and Lisa moved to check out the window. Sam stood on the front step. "Look, Mom. I gotta go. I'll keep you posted."

"You do that. Tell your grandfather I'll be chatting with him soon. I'm anxious to hear the details of the sale."

As they said their goodbyes, Lisa opened the door and waved Sam in. He finished closing the door for her.

"Dang, it's cold out there." The big man rubbed his hands together.

"You knew where Grandpa was the whole time." She rounded on him, hands on her hips.

He had the decency to look embarrassed. "Yeah. He told me he was heading up to the cabin. That's why I didn't send my guys up to check." He pulled his gloves off and tossed them on the kitchen table. "Mind if I make some coffee?"

"Do you know where Grandpa keeps it? I've searched but couldn't find it anywhere. Then you can answer my questions."

Sam laughed and nodded as he headed to the freezer. "Someone told your grandmother it stayed fresher in here. No idea if that's true, but it makes it easier to find." He reached clear into the back.

"Only if you know it's there." She had questions for Sam and decided that sharing a cup of coffee might be the easiest way to get answers.

He pulled a plastic container out and the warm aroma of coffee wafted in the air as he brewed a pot.

Sam set the cup in front of her and settled across the old table.

"Sam, what's going on?"

"With your grandfather?" At her nod, Sam shrugged. "He's not talking much, but said he's got a lot of thinking to do. He said the cabin was the best place to do that." He took a drink of the coffee. The mug looked small in his big hand.

Lisa curled her hands around her mug. The heat felt good. She didn't believe Sam knew about the caves. She almost asked but bit her tongue. That was Grandpa's secret to share.

"Have you figured out anything about the break-in? Is there anything else you aren't telling me?" She made sure she met his gaze and held it.

He didn't look away as he shook his head. "We found a bunch of fingerprints. Heck, mine and Hap's were in the mix."

"Grandpa said something about Lance Westgate wanting to buy the ranch. Mom was just on the phone saying he contacted her a while back. Were his prints 'in the mix'?"

She thought about their meeting in the hotel, about his conversation with Trey the night she'd ducked behind the bar. He hadn't seemed aggressive, just overly enthusiastic. Then Grandpa's bruises came to mind, and his conviction that the men worked for Lance.

Sam frowned. "I don't know offhand. I'll check with the guys." He stared into his empty cup. "You saw the person running away. Did it look like Lance?"

She thought back, trying to picture the person. It had been too long ago. "I couldn't say. I was too surprised." She closed her eyes, hoping that would bring back something. "Nope." She opened her eyes. "I'm pretty sure it was a guy, but it was getting dark and his clothing was dark. If he hadn't broken the window, I'm not sure I'd have even discovered him. Do you have any idea what they were looking for?" She waited a minute. "The map?" she ventured.

Sam glanced up then, covering his startled expression all too quickly. But she still saw it. "Yeah, I know about it."

"Trey said you did." He nodded. "You and Win talk about it while you were at the cabin?"

What was he fishing for? Information about the case, or information to get rich quick? It hurt her head to think of all the people she knew and loved...

Loved? She looked at Sam. She loved him like the good family friend that he was. Like everyone else who had been a part of her life for as long as she could remember, she held a deep affection for them all. It wounded her to believe they'd do something to harm her or her grandfather.

Everyone except Trey. She'd only just met him—and yet? She felt something for him. Did he feel something for her? Or was he just like the rest? He wanted something from her family.

Where did he fit into that whole everyone-she-loved thought? She wasn't sure. But the fact that he crossed her mind made her pause. But right now, she was afraid to look too deep.

"We did." She forced herself to focus and recall Sam's question. "He shared a little, but there's more he's yet to say. He'll tell me when we have time to sit and talk." She watched for a reaction, any sign that he was overly interested in the map or the secret it went with. She didn't detect anything but the usual Sam in business mode.

Sam nodded. "Win called a while ago. He's coming back to town tomorrow." He stood and put his cup in the sink. "Let's take you over to the hotel for tonight."

"What? No." The possibility of running into Lance wasn't acceptable. She quickly shut down the thoughts of the bar next door. The bar and Trey. "I'll stay here."

"Da…dang it, Lisa." He turned around to face her. "I don't have the manpower to watch you until Win gets home."

"I don't need watching." She knew there was a deputy outside right now. Trey had left when he'd gotten here. "I'm an adult who lives on her own in Denver. I'm not fourteen anymore, Sam." She hated to admit that Mom's treating her like a kid didn't help.

"That's not my point, and you know it."

Lisa stood and took her own cup to the

sink. "You can't keep worrying about me. I promise, I'll lock the place up tight." A shiver of apprehension slid up her spine. So, she'd be sleeping with every door and window locked and her phone in her hand. Normally, that would mean a sleepless night, but she was so tired from the hike into the mountains, and the emotions swirling through her, that she was sure she'd be sound asleep despite the coffee.

"Fine," Sam grumbled as he stomped over to the cabinet beside the sink.

"What are you doing?"

"Borrowing one of Win's thermal cups. If Thompson is gonna sit his butt outside all night, he's gonna need something warm."

Sam was not going to guilt her into going to the hotel. "You can make another pot, if you need to." She headed toward her room, but stopped when someone pounded on the door.

Through the curtain she saw two shadows and her heart hitched, thankful Sam was still here.

"You stay right there." Sam pointed at her. He walked to the door and pulled it open. They both breathed a sigh of relief.

"Found him heading to the door," Deputy

Thompson waved at Hap. "Figured I'd better help before he broke a hip or something."

"I'm perfectly capable of keeping myself safe, young man." Hap shoved his walker through the door, and the sound of the metal thing rattled loud in the kitchen. "Do I smell coffee?"

Sam grabbed a cup and they settled in like they were staying instead of her. Throwing up her hands, Lisa returned to her seat. "What do you know about the map and the break-in here?" What the heck? She didn't have anything to lose.

"I found the map when I was going through old boxes we stored out on the porch." Hap rubbed his chin as Sam set a fresh cup of coffee down in front of him. "Wonder how long it's been in that box."

Too long. "You ever see it before?"

"Nope. Hadn't checked in that box since I packed it until a few weeks ago." He lifted his steaming mug. "You make a mighty fine cup of joe, there, Sam. Maybe you can get a job at the bar if the whole sheriff thing don't pan out."

"Like I'd work for you. I'm curious, too, Hap." Sam leaned back in the chair, casual, but Lisa saw the spark in his eyes that was anything but casual. He was as keen on Hap's answer as she was. "Why'd you give the map to Win? You've always been a greedy SOB."

"I thought you were my friend." The accusation might have stung, if Hap hadn't been grinning. "Greedy, my…" He looked over at Lisa and didn't finish the sentence. "It didn't belong to me—I knew that. Besides, my *good* friends would share their fortune with me."

"Uh-huh. You just wanted Win to do all the work if there was any," Sam said.

Lisa laughed. They knew each other too well. And if Grandpa were here, he'd have joined right in. She wished he'd come down the mountain with them. She frowned. "When is Grandpa getting back tomorrow?" She turned that frown to Sam.

Hap started to laugh. "If he's at the cabin, depends on how long it takes him to snowshoe out to wherever he parked his truck."

"Where would that be?" She stared at them both. She hadn't seen any other vehicles parked near the Jeep, but she hadn't been looking for one, either.

"There's easily half a dozen trailheads in that area," Sam explained. "You gotta snowshoe into your granddad's place but the rest of the mountain is a big tourist draw, especially in the summer."

And then it dawned on her. She focused

on her now-cold coffee to hide her expression. That's why Grandpa had kept it isolated, why he'd limited the number of people who traipsed around the property. The tourists would have found the caves.

While she'd believed Grandpa when he'd said he hadn't told anyone, she hadn't really believed these guys knew nothing. Now, either they should get awards for acting, or they hadn't a clue. Since Hap loved to brag about everything, she was pretty sure it was the latter.

"You remember that Westgate kid who used to steal candy from the convenience store your brother used to own?" Sam asked, not looking away from Hap.

Where had that come from? She might not like Lance, but this wasn't helping. He'd been a thief?

"Little brat," Hap grouched. "Neil wanted to strangle him on a daily basis."

Sam nodded. "I hauled his butt in a few times. I was pretty convinced he'd end up in jail one day, but he seems to have turned himself around. He's the developer on that retirement project."

Hap glanced up, a deep-creased frown between his eyes. "I thought I recognized that name. Shoot. I was starting to agree with my wife that it was a nice place, too."

"Still could be a nice place. He's been talking to Win about buying the ranch to expand."

"What?" Hap's coffee cup hit the table hard. And loud. "That little…" He took a deep breath. "I assumed Trey would be the one going after that."

That shocked Lisa. "You… Wait…why would you think your bartender could afford a million-dollar ranch?" Trey had barely shared his past with her. Surely, Hap hadn't known he was rich when he hired him.

"Bartender?" Hap laughed. "He's just playing at that. His granddaddy and daddy are loaded. I figured it was just a matter of time before he made a move on that land. It's a valuable place, and Win ain't getting any younger. None of us are."

"You knew his grandfather?"

"Everyone in town did. He spent a lot of time here, and if there was one thing ole Pal was good at, it was partying and schmoozing."

She looked over at Sam, who nodded. Why was she the only one who'd never heard of Trey and his grandfather? Then again, she'd lived in Denver and only come up to Telluride occasionally. Slowly, carefully, she set her cup down, knowing that if she let her frustration out, she'd slam it down instead.

"I give up," she whispered as she stood. "I'm going to bed. You can let yourselves out."

THE NEXT DAY, Trey carried the last box from the day's delivery into the bar area. Gabe was thrilled that his pantry and freezer were full, and Hap hadn't complained much about the bill. It was good to have the bar fully stocked. Not that Trey had turned anyone away, but he was starting to think he'd have to get real creative with some of the drinks.

The front door opened. Crouched down as he was, he couldn't see anyone, but when he heard the sound of heavy boots, he knew it wasn't Lisa. Was that disappointment he felt?

Mentally kicking himself, he focused on getting the last bottle out of the box and greeting the customer. After that, maybe he'd burn off some of his frustration breaking down all the boxes by the Dumpster.

"Can I help—"

"Anyone here?" a voice said from the other side of the bar at the same time.

Trey froze. Rising slowly from behind the bar, he came face-to-face with Jason Hawkins's grinning face. While he was surprised, he couldn't say he was shocked. What *did* shock him was the person standing beside him. Jason's brother, Wyatt.

Both men looked like they always had. Stetsons, jeans and worn boots. Texas had come to Colorado, Trey thought and shook his head. Darn. "I knew calling you was a bad idea." Trey tossed the empty box up on top of the bar.

Jason laughed, and the two men climbed up onto barstools. Wyatt set a white box on the counter in front of them.

"Came to get a drink, didn't we, Wyatt?" Jason looked over at his older brother, who nodded. They shared a grin.

"Yeah. Seemed like a good idea."

Both men had been Trey's friends since high school. He knew what they drank but just to prove he could keep his distance, he went into bartender mode. "What can I get-cha then?"

Wyatt laughed. "I'd say the usual, but I gather we're new here and not supposed to have a usual?"

"Kinda takes the value out of leaving all of you behind."

"About that…" Wyatt leaned forward. "You got some explaining to do."

"Not if you want a drink, I don't." The two men stared at each other for a long minute.

"Good enough for now." Wyatt nodded and ordered his usual Wild Turkey. Jason nodded, ordering the same. As Trey pulled the bottle and two shot glasses out, Wyatt pushed the box smoothly across the wood. "Addie sent you these."

Addie. Wyatt's sister was known for the world's best cookies. A little taste of home.

After filling both shot glasses and setting them in front of the men, Trey grabbed the box. The scent of peanut butter and chocolate wafted up toward him. Heaven. Trey pulled out a cookie and took a big bite. Around the sweet deliciousness he'd missed, he said, "Tell Addie thanks. And no, you don't get any." He shoved the box under the counter where no one could reach it.

The other men laughed, and after lifting their glasses in a silent toast, took their drinks. An uncomfortable silence settled around the bar for a long minute. It was early, and Trey didn't think anyone would come in—unless Lisa decided she could still work for him. He tried not to think about the fact that she was already ten minutes late.

The Hawkins brothers shared a look, and Jason glanced around as if assessing the chances of an interruption. "Can we talk? Maybe someplace more private?"

Trey shrugged. "This is as good as it gets." He could call Rick, but he wasn't going to. Instead, he leaned against the back counter and waited. "Go ahead. Try and talk me out of it."

The brothers shared another one of those looks, but this time there was something more in it. Wyatt spoke first. "That's not what we came here for."

"Yeah." Jason leaned forward to match his brother. "Honestly, we need to talk."

Anyone else, Trey would have dismissed, but he knew these two men well. He nodded and stepped into the kitchen. Gabe wasn't a bartender, but he could watch things for a few minutes.

Trey called Gabe over, and the other man agreed to watch the bar, though he couldn't promise he'd make anything other than a beer. "Call me if you need me," Trey called over his shoulder as he led the two brothers down the short hall.

The office usually worked well for what he needed, but there wasn't much space. They made it work.

Jason looked at Wyatt. Younger brother to older, they'd always done that.

"We aren't here to talk you out of anything," Wyatt began, settling on the corner of the old desk. "You haven't taken any of the calls from home recently." It wasn't a question. They knew the situation.

"And that's the way it's going to stay."

Again, that look. "You should call your mom," Jason said, softly.

The hairs on the back of Trey's neck rose. "What's going on?"

Wyatt took a deep breath and met Trey's gaze. "It's your dad. He took a nasty fall with Silver Devil. They were out in a storm searching for a couple of lost calves when they fell into a ravine. The horse had to be put down."

Trey felt the blood rush out of his face and the icy coldness of fear settle in. "Is he…"

"Alive, but it fractured his pelvis and a few vertebrae." Jason frowned. "Doc says he'll be back up on his feet eventually, but he was in that ravine for several hours. It was bad."

"Why in heaven didn't anyone tell me?" Anger at himself, at his grandfather, at the entire situation made his question come out rough and loud.

"Like anyone knew where you were?" Jason bit out. "I just figured it out from your call yesterday. Your mom's been taking the brunt of all this. The girls are helping as much as they can, but they aren't her family." He paused. "They aren't you."

He should have been there. No. Trey stood, mentally cursing the tiny space. He needed to move. Needed to escape this pain. This guilt. This…

No. He ached to pace again. His parents were part of the problem. Pal was gone, but neither his mother nor his father had ever done anything to save him from the old man's tyranny. They'd never stepped up to stop him.

Once again, the brothers shared a look. "Cut that out," Trey snapped. "Say what you're thinking."

"Go home." Jason stood as well, facing Trey across the desk. "She needs your help. The ranch is running, but it won't for long without someone guiding the business. Someone has to make the decisions."

"Is Dad that far gone?" Was the man unconscious? Mentally incapacitated? The ball of dread settled in Trey's chest, and he wondered how he was even able to breathe.

"No. He's as with-it as ever. But he has to focus on healing, on getting through each day of therapy and medicine—not worrying about a thousand head of cattle and a bunch of cowhands that can't manage to stay out of a fistfight."

288 A COWBOY AT HEART

Trey didn't ask about the rest of the businesses. The lawyers managed most of that. The ranch was personal. It was where his family lived.

"Like the hands would listen to me?" Trey did not want to go back there. He couldn't. He just couldn't.

"They'll listen to whoever is cutting their paychecks." Wyatt said. "It isn't like you're on your own. Everyone's there. Even Chet came out of retirement to help. He and Juanita are splitting their time between your ranch and my place while Emily gives your mom a break."

Everyone was stepping up. The neighbors. Probably the whole community. And Trey could hear it in their voices. Felt the expectations closing in on him.

Outside the office door, quick, light footsteps seemed especially loud. "Sorry I'm late," Lisa called out. "Had a flat tire, and the deputy is slower than anyone I've ever met helping me change it."

The warmth and lightness of her voice contrasted so drastically with the dark weight of the air in the room that he nearly expected to see bright blinding light around the closed door. He envisioned her. From the sound of her steps, she was wearing those boots... Was she wearing jeans or that dress she'd had on last week? He closed his eyes, holding the image of her close. Watching it fade into the distance.

When he opened his eyes, he stared down at the desk. He almost laughed. Receipts and cash were still scattered on the top of it from the deposit he'd half finished. No one had even noticed. He certainly hadn't. He didn't even care right now.

The brothers were right. He needed to go home. But if he did—there was no coming back here. No returning to the solitude and anonymity he'd actually begun to take for granted.

Scary part was, he wasn't sure if that was a good thing or not.

CHAPTER SEVENTEEN

GABE WAS BEHIND the bar. That was *not* a good sign. "Where is he?" Lisa asked.

"Trey?" Gabe tilted his head toward the short hallway she'd just come through.

"In the office?"

"Yeah. He's got visitors. I don't recognize 'em." Gabe didn't look up at her. He was too busy flipping through a bartender's guide from under the counter. She was pretty sure he had no idea how to be a bartender, but he was a good cook. He could figure it out.

The office door was closed, just as it had been when she'd arrived. She could only hear the tone of male voices, not words. Unless she put her ear to the door, she wasn't going to hear much of anything.

She couldn't quite bring herself to do that—though it was tempting. Heading back into the barroom, she focused on getting ready for the rush. She glanced at the clock. It was late, so some of the ski runs would be closing soon. Skiers would trickle in then, filling the tables and booths for the next four to five hours.

She kept watching the hall as she worked. Who was in there with Trey? What were they talking about?

Finally, she heard heavy footsteps coming closer. She scurried down to the other end of the bar. She hadn't been listening, though she couldn't deny that she hadn't been trying—if someone happened to ask.

Lisa couldn't help but stare at the two tall cowboys who came toward her. Was that what people meant when they talked about a tall drink of water? Wow! And these guys were *real* cowboys, not the city-slicker wannabes that normally came to the slopes.

They wore cowboy hats that sat snug over their brows, and their jeans were faded all the way down over their boots—boots she half expected to hear jangle with spurs with each step.

"Drive careful down that mountain," Trey told them. They each shook his hand before making their way to the exit.

The taller of the two turned back around before he stepped outside. "See you soon, Trey." His words were thick with expectation and a Southern accent.

"Yeah." Trey leaned against the doorway and watched until the men left. Then he walked slowly back to the office.

Lisa followed. "Friends of yours?" He seemed to fit in with them. The look, the familiarity, the feel.

Trey glanced up, seemingly surprised to see her. But since he didn't ask, she didn't repeat her earlier explanation about her flat tire.

"Uh, yeah. Old friends." His voice and gaze were a long way away.

"From Texas?"

"Yeah." He stared down at the desk. It was a mess, which was strange. Why was it in such disarray?

"Are they coming back?"

"No." Trey stood there for a moment, then slowly gathered up the scattered papers and cash on the desk. Was he trying to organize it? He frowned as if not really aware of what he was doing.

Finally, he stopped and just stared. Lisa moved to the desk. "Trey? Are you okay?"

"Yeah. Fine." He shook his head and looked around as if just waking up. Gazing at his fists full of receipts, he shoved them into the deposit bag and after zipping it closed, tossed the bag into the open safe. He didn't bother to close it.

Instead, he grabbed his own Stetson that

always hung above the desk, and pulled it low over his brow, just like those other men. He headed back around the desk and to the door.

"Are you leaving? Now?"

The man who turned around to look at her then wasn't anyone she'd ever met before. Trey's features were twisted with emotions she couldn't decipher, and the shadows in his eyes were dark.

"Uh…yeah." He stared at her then strode back to the desk. He pulled a sheet of paper from the top drawer. "Here. Call Rick. Ask him to cover."

"What? For how long?"

"Indefinitely. He needs the money right now. He'll do it." Again, Trey headed to the door.

"You're not coming back." Why did that realization hurt so much? It wasn't like he owed her an explanation, or they were a couple, or anything.

"Don't know." He reached for his jacket and slipped it on. "I doubt Hap will hold my job. He shouldn't. This place needs someone to run it."

"So, that's it? What about the offer on the ranch? Is that still good? Is that even real?" Was he like Robert? Was this job going away, too?

Okay, she'd known it wasn't permanent from the start. But she wanted to leave on her terms, not someone else's. In the middle of last night, she'd reminded herself that she'd never walked out on a job. Oh, she'd wanted to a few times, but she never had. She'd always given notice and worked the two weeks.

That's why she'd come in today. To give her notice. She had an apartment, and just enough money to pay her rent this month. She needed to find a new job anyway.

"It's a legit offer," he assured her. "I just have to take care of some…business first."

"Business?" Lisa heard the shrill tone in her voice, but dang it, he couldn't do that to her grandfather. He was hanging his hopes on the promise Trey made.

"Not business, exactly. Personal business."

She watched the pain flash in his eyes before he looked away. Her heart ached for him, and she stepped closer. "What happened?" She glanced back toward the hall. Had those men said something to him?

"Uh, yeah." Trey cleared his throat. "My dad was hurt in an accident." His voice faded on that last word. "The horse was put down."

She frowned, remembering the horses they'd discussed up on the mountain. Was it the same horse? "I'm sorry," she whispered. "Is your dad okay?"

As if the questions shook him out of a reverie, Trey nodded. "He will be. In time. But Mom needs my help now."

"I see." And she did. Or thought she did. It was just like her coming here, when she lost her job, to help her family out. But she wasn't estranged from her family. "You said you weren't getting along with them." She knew she was being nosy, but things just didn't add up.

"Well, sometimes life doesn't care about that." His voice was bitter, angry and she could only stare. Slowly, he turned and walked out the back door.

MIDNIGHT CAME AND WENT. Last call loomed and the bar was empty. Only an hour until close. Trey had tried to sleep upstairs, but his mind spun so he'd come to the bar again.

Lisa. The cabin. Win and the caves. The Hawkins brothers. His father. He'd come down here to escape himself.

Lisa had left an hour ago, when the last customer had departed and the snow had started to fall—again.

"Head on home," Trey told Gabe. "I'll finish up. I've got some things to do in the office." Like *everything*. His flight left Denver tomorrow—today actually—at three.

At the kitchen doorway, Gabe stopped. "You leaving?" he asked.

Obviously, he'd heard enough to know what was going on. "Yeah."

"You comin' back?" The look in the man's eyes was more than curiosity but Trey didn't have time to figure out what.

"Hope to, but I can't promise." That was all Trey could say right now. He had no idea what his father's condition really was, and while he wanted to run away from his obligations, he couldn't.

If this situation had taught him nothing else, he'd at least figured that out.

Gabe nodded. "Then I'll say my goodbyes now. You've been a good boss. I appreciate it."

"Thanks." Hearing the appreciation made Trey smile and lifted his spirits just a bit. "I've enjoyed it, too. You've improved."

Gabe blushed. "Yeah, not as much partying. Put that in my file, will you? So the next guy don't fire me, 'kay."

"Will do." Trey smiled for the first time all day, and he made a mental note to do just that.

Gabe continued on into the kitchen and after a few minutes, and a few noises of pots and pans banging around, he heard the back door open and close. Gabe was gone.

Out of habit, and because of the swirling thoughts in his head, Trey reached up and pulled down the top-shelf whiskey. The bottle was new. He'd cracked it open for a customer a few days ago.

The rich, dark scent wafted up to him as he poured the familiar shot. When he was home, the men would expect the tradition to continue.

Could he do it?

Twisting the lid back on the bottle, Trey stared at the liquor an instant before putting it on the shelf again. Setting the full shot glass on the counter, where it could taunt and remind him, he glared at it. "I'm still not drinking with you, old man," he whispered. "I'll do it for the men." He cleared his throat and stepped back, leaving the shot untouched— for now.

Trey glanced up at the clock. He considered locking the doors early, but Hap would have a conniption if he heard about it—and he would. That man knew everyone and everything.

Five minutes later, Trey softly groaned as the door opened. *Should've closed early.* Seeing who came in, he mentally repeated that statement.

Two men came through the door in a hurry, shivering against the icy blast that came with them. A few steps behind, just before the door could fully close, Lance Westgate brought up the rear.

"It's five minutes until last call. Make your orders quick, gentlemen," Trey announced. "Unless you're here for a soda or coffee."

Lance was the only one who laughed, and Trey hadn't meant to be funny. "Ah, Trey. My friend. We'll take a round of your best draft beer. My men are just celebrating a successful evening's work." He led the way to one of the farthest tables and pulled out a chair. "Have a seat. Trey, come join us after you've closed up."

Trey didn't drink with customers. During or after hours, and especially when that customer was Lance. "Thanks," was all he said as he prepared the drinks.

From his vantage point from the bar, Trey could see the entire place. It was designed that way. Even when customers crowded around the bar, the raised floor gave the bartender a bird's-eye view. Over the tap, Trey watched the men.

Lance he was familiar with. The man was

clapping the others on the back and grinning from ear to ear. They were nodding and smiling in return, but not with quite as much enthusiasm. Trey frowned.

What had Lance said about a successful night's work? What did these guys do?

"Here you go, gents." Trey fisted the thick beer mug handles and carried them to the table.

"Where's your pretty waitress? Lisa." Lance took the mug.

"Light crowd tonight," was all the explanation Trey gave.

"Smart man." Lance lifted his mug toward Trey. "I always keep an eye out for men who know the value of a dollar and when to conserve resources."

Was Lance offering him a job? He looked a little closer. How sober were these guys? They'd said they'd just finished a job, but had they been drinking elsewhere before they came here? Luckily, they weren't so far gone that last call wouldn't solve that situation.

Without responding, Trey returned to the bar and started to count down the drawer. One last deposit to finish.

He kept an eye on the men and forced his brain not to eavesdrop on their conversation.

Finally, Lance stood and headed toward

Trey. A flash of memory made Trey stare. Though Lance had taken off his coat, Trey saw the black ski pants Lance was wearing. Looking over at the chair Lance had just vacated, he noticed a black ski jacket draped over the back.

The way he moved, the black clothes... Lance had been the guy on the slopes that day!

Chairs scraped against the floor, breaking into Trey's thoughts. He glanced away from Lance and watched the other men walk to the exit.

"Thanks for the drinks, boss." The taller man waved from the doorway as the shorter man held the door open. Another wave of recognition washed over Trey then. He saw their shadows passing an envelope in the alley.

What the hell was Lance up to?

Trey recalled Win's revelation about the two men who'd come to the house and beat him. Were these the same men? His blood ran cold, and it wasn't from the weather.

He needed to call Sam. It helped knowing there was a deputy at the house watching over Lisa, but what about Win?

Trey frowned as he looked back at Lance still standing on the other side of the bar. Maybe he could get more information for

Sam. "What exactly do those guys do for you?" he asked as casually as he could.

"Oh, a little of this, little of that." Lance set the empty beer mugs on the bar. "Tonight, they were able to bring me the last piece of information I needed to close a deal. I can move on to developing phase two." He walked back to the table and retrieved his coat. "Someday soon, this town is going to be a retirement mecca."

Trey frowned. That wasn't quite what he'd expected Lance to say. "Okay, I'm curious. Why would elderly people come here? It's the middle of the mountains. There's three feet of snow out there. They don't ski." Or hunt. Or even scoop snow if they don't have to, not to mention any of the other winter things this town was famous for and relied on for its income.

"Ah, my friend, you are just what's wrong with our society."

Trey frowned and watched Lance's smile turn into what he could only call a sneer.

"This town is more than winter. At least six months a year, it's beautiful and warm." He shook a finger at Trey. "But not hot like Florida or Arizona where most of them do the snowbird thing."

Trey still didn't understand, and it must

have shown on his face as Lance laughed and continued.

"Think about it." Lance leaned on the bar. "Wintertime, we continue to pull in the young skiers—and in the summer the seniors—with all that disposable income to fill the gap."

Comprehension dawned. It wasn't a bad idea. Except somehow, the fact that it was Lance suggesting it made Trey wonder what else Lance wasn't explaining.

Suddenly, Lance leaned back and laughed. "This town is gonna love me. You can be the first to congratulate me." He lifted his arms like he'd won an Olympic downhill race. "I might even buy this place and you can work for me, too."

Lance grabbed the shot glass still sitting, full, on the bar and lifted it. "To an awesome day." Before Trey could say anything more, Lance upended the shot and took the drink. He slammed the empty glass back down on the bar.

"Put that on my tab." Lance shrugged his black jacket on and followed his men out the door.

As Trey rushed to turn the lock before anyone else came in, he fished his phone out of his pocket. On the third ring he realized what time it was.

"Hello?" Lisa answered.

Relief nearly sent Trey to his knees. "You're okay?" He sat down on the first chair he came to.

"I was safely asleep, yes." Her voice was muffled, and he pictured her snuggling down into her pillow. "You, my friend, might not be so lucky."

"Sorry to wake you. But Lance was just here, and I got the distinct impression his thugs did some of their dirty work tonight."

Her silence added to his anxiety.

"You there, Lisa?"

"Uh, yeah. Do you think they hurt someone?" Her voice wasn't muffled now. She must be sitting up. "You were worried it was me?"

"Yeah." His voice was just above a whisper.

Again, more silence, but he could hear her moving around so he knew she was still there. "Thanks."

"No problem. Now go back to sleep. I'm going to call Sam."

"Like I can sleep now?" At least she laughed softly.

"Try, okay? 'Night, Lisa."

"'Night." Her voice was muffled again, and he closed his eyes to savor the sound of her warm—safe—voice.

Finally, he hung up and dialed the next number. Sam's hello wasn't nearly as friendly. "Sam, we've got a problem."

CHAPTER EIGHTEEN

"Sleep is overrated," Lisa mumbled into the pillow that five seconds ago had been so comfortable. Now it was flat and lumpy and totally wrong. With a sound that resembled a growl, she sat up and stared into the darkness.

Two in the morning.

Trey's words rattled around in her head. What had Lance's men done? Did he think by being vague that she'd just roll over and go back to sleep? He'd only made her brain race more.

And worry. Grandpa was still up on the mountain. Alone. He'd said two of Lance's men had been the ones who'd injured him. Had they found him and the caverns? Was he now hurt…or worse?

She stared at her phone, wanting to call Grandpa and make sure he was okay. Besides the fact that it was two in the morning, was there even any reception down in the caverns? She'd never sleep if she didn't call. She punched in the familiar number and waited. The only good thing about her call going straight to voice mail was hearing his familiar voice ask her to leave a message.

"I know you're probably asleep, but call me when you wake up." She paused. "Please."

Grabbing her robe, Lisa headed to the kitchen. Her worry and frustration chased the tiny bit of tiredness away. Maybe a glass of warm milk—or water, or something—would help. Should she call Sam? And tell him what? Trey had said he was going to do that anyway. He didn't answer when she punched in his number. At least someone was getting sleep.

The kitchen light was bright, and she blinked several times before her eyes adjusted. She'd barely opened the refrigerator when someone knocked on the door—and she jumped nearly a foot. She squealed too, though she clapped her hand over her mouth to stop it, so that didn't count as overreacting, she decided. "This better be good."

Reaching for the door handle, she suddenly froze. What if it was Lance's men? What if—

"Ms. Duprey?" Deputy Thompson's voice was familiar and soft, as if he didn't want to wake up the neighbors. "You okay?"

Should she open the door? She was fine,

but what if someone else was with him. How well did she know him?

And...maybe she'd watched too many thriller movies. "I'm fine," she called without opening the door. "Just having trouble sleeping. Sorry to bother you."

"No problem, ma'am. Sheriff Coleman called a few minutes ago to check on you. I'll report back."

Oh, good. Her sleeping habits were now going to be part of a police report. Sinking down to the wooden chair, she rested her chin in her hands. This entire situation was getting out of hand. She was fairly certain she was losing her mind.

When another fist, more insistent this time, pounded on the door a short while later, she somehow knew it was Trey. He didn't care about waking the neighbors, apparently.

"Lisa. Let me in."

"I'm asleep." She wished she were. She should have known from his call that he'd come over.

"Funny." He tapped on the door one more time.

Pushing to her feet, she went to the door and unlocked it. "Come on in." Was that a touch of sarcasm in her voice? She went back to the refrigerator and pulled out the milk.

"Did you bring any of that brandy with you? I could use some," she asked as he followed her.

"Uh, no." He stood in the doorway watching her. "Sam's on his way."

She glanced over her shoulder, then hastily turned back to focus on filling the mug. Until it was settled in the microwave, she didn't face him. Despite the long day and the late hour, Trey looked too good, too competent— his shoulders broad and strong. She could so easily let herself depend on him.

But he was leaving, and once Telluride was in his rearview mirror, she was certain there was no looking back. Why would he? He could go anywhere in the world. Be with anyone he wanted to be with.

"Want some?" She lifted the milk jug.

"No, thanks." The legs of the chair he pulled out scraped loud against the floor. He'd just sat down, when yet another knock came at the door.

"Grand Central station, how may I help you?" She yanked open the door and stomped back to the microwave. Its loud ding told her the drink was ready, though why she was bothering to try to sleep now, she hadn't a clue.

Sam looked like he'd crawled out of bed,

as well. His hair wasn't its usual smooth style and—she peered closer—was that a pajama shirt under his sheriff's jacket?

"Did you bring Hap with you?" She made a show of gazing past his shoulder. "A few more deputies?"

Sam laughed and shook his head as he took a seat at the table. "No, just me."

Drink in hand, Lisa sat and took a tentative sip of the heated milk. "So, why exactly are you two here?" She looked first at Trey, then at Sam. "I called Grandpa to see if he's okay, but all I got was voice mail. You didn't answer, either," she pointed out to Sam.

Sam lifted his phone. "I talked to him. Figured if we're all up, he should be, too." The big man shrugged. "He's fine. He said he hasn't run into anyone around the cabin today."

Every muscle in her body relaxed and she nearly wilted. At least that worry was gone. For now.

Then, maybe because she was finally waking up, or because her worry was out of the way, it dawned on her. "You're not here because you're worried about Grandpa. You think they'll come here? I'm the problem, aren't I?" She swallowed back her panic and let her indignation run the show.

Both men had the smarts to look sheepish. "Now, Lisa…" Sam started.

"Don't 'now, Lisa' me." She stood. "I'm not some foolish Gothic heroine who runs around chasing bad guys in the middle of the night in her night…uh…gown." She felt her cheeks warm. "Okay, bad example."

She reached over and put a hand on Sam's arm. She didn't dare touch Trey. She might never let go. "I'll be fine. I am a grown woman, and I take care of myself just fine in Denver."

"This isn't Denver," Trey offered, his voice soft and deep.

"You're right." She was angry now. "It's a small town I've visited all my life. I'm safe here. You've got a deputy outside, and I'll keep everything locked up tight."

Neither man appeared even slightly convinced. "Talk some sense into her." Sam stared pointedly at Trey and headed to the door. "I'll go brief my deputy."

The big man surprised her by putting an arm around her shoulders and giving her a brief hug. "It's not just about your grandpa. We care about you, too."

And then he was gone. The big old bear of a man, who'd kept her out of trouble as a kid, was doing the same thing now. Okay, she could forgive him for being a little over-bearing.

Once Sam was gone, Lisa breathed a sigh of relief and heard Trey do the same. She couldn't resist taking another look at him.

"What was Lance talking about?" she asked. "What information could he possibly have gotten from those two goons that made him think he was getting the land?"

Trey hadn't said anything, or moved, while Sam talked. Now he shrugged.

"I thought maybe you'd have some idea," he said.

She shook her head. Totally at a loss. She felt Trey's gaze on her, sensed the intensity. What was going on in his head?

TREY STARED. Lisa had no clue how amazing she looked right now. As she sat there, slowly sipping the warm drink, her hair mussed from sleep, her robe gaping open to show a pretty nightshirt beneath, her feet bare—with toe-nails painted a deep red. He couldn't tear his eyes away.

He didn't want to. She was safe. Sitting across from her reaffirmed that fact. The panic that had shot through him at Lance's words was fading, but the dregs still left him drained.

She'd become more important to him than he wanted to admit. Unnerved by that revelation, he sat there, silently waiting—for what?

She needed reassurance. And, unfortunately, so did he. The idea of heading to the airport later, leaving her on her own, didn't sit well with him. "I'll be back once my dad recovers."

She simply stared into her now-empty mug, slowly turning it back and forth. Finally, she looked up. "Will you? Why?"

Their gazes locked. "I—" Something in her stare told him that giving the business deal with her grandfather as the reason for returning wasn't a good idea. But was it the truth? Was that the only reason he would come back here?

Suddenly, Lisa stood, the chair scraping loudly across the floor. "Don't bother to answer. And you and Sam don't have to worry about me anymore after tomorrow." She walked over to the sink and turned on the water. "I'm heading back to Denver."

What was that note in her voice? Anger? Pain? He felt like he'd been dropped into the middle of a minefield.

He stood as well, but didn't move any closer. She dumped dish soap into the water and ran the sink full—to wash the single mug.

"I'm awake now, might as well clean up the kitchen for Grandpa—heaven knows he won't do it for himself." She wrung out the dishrag and started scrubbing the counters. "I might even have time to run the vacuum…"

Trey walked over to her and reached out, putting his hands over hers. After a brief, half-hearted struggle, he took the cloth from her hand and tossed it into the water with a splash.

"I'm coming back," he repeated, putting a finger beneath her chin and tilting her face up so she could see him, and he could see her. She tried to look away, but he tilted his head down, forcing her eyes to meet his.

"I won't be here," she whispered.

"I know where Denver is."

"It's a big place. Not that hard to find."

Trey laughed and pulled her into his arms. He ached to hold her and protect her, but he was also proud of her when she stood up for herself. She made him believe that Lance would regret ever tangling with her.

Holding her felt good, felt right, and he didn't have to wait long before she gave in and put her arms around him. She laid her head on his shoulder and hid her face against his neck.

He'd be happy to stay like this forever.

Then he would know she was safe, that no one would get to her.

He'd never been affected by a woman like this before. Thoughts of protecting her, wanting to be with her, never wanting to leave, swirled in his head.

He half expected her to ask him not to go. She didn't, and he was relieved. He wasn't sure he could tell her no.

And then she spoke, and his gut tightened in anticipation. "Trey?"

"Yeah?"

Lisa shifted, leaning back and looking up at him. Uh-oh. Here it came. He couldn't let her say it, couldn't hear her ask. Couldn't refuse her.

Slowly, Trey leaned toward her…close… closer still. Her breath hitched, and he saw her eyes widen, felt the hot rush of her breath on his skin. "Lisa—"

TREY HAD KISSED her before, but Lisa knew this time would be different. This time it would mean more. So she didn't let it happen.

"Thank you. For everything." Slowly, she pulled away, taking a step, and then another until there were several inches between them. "For hiring me, and for caring enough to take me into the backcountry. And…and for worrying about me."

She was babbling. She'd caught herself doing it a couple times tonight. Lack of sleep must be getting to her.

Trey stood there, not moving, frowning slightly, as if he wasn't sure what she was saying or doing. Finally, he leaned back against the kitchen counter and crossed his arms over that broad chest. "You're welcome." He gave the polite response. "It worked out well for both of us."

"Yeah. Guess it did." He'd gotten help at the bar and a great deal on some land. She ignored the resentment she'd felt earlier. Neither of them said anything more for a long time and she waited for him to head to the door. He didn't move.

Finally, he pushed away from the counter and she clasped her hands together, afraid she'd grab him and ask him to stay. He half turned, and her heart sank painfully in her chest.

She might never see him again. That hurt.

She was surprised when he didn't pass her, and even more surprised when he gently touched her chin. "Look at me," he said, softly, gently, sweetly.

Before she had a second thought, she lifted

her gaze. He was so close, close enough that she could see each individual eyelash that framed his eyes, and the pattern of his day's growth of beard. So close. So intimate.

"I'm not leaving yet. Not until—"

"Until?"

"Until this." Trey leaned in then and put his lips on hers. He slid his hand up the side of her face, cupping her jaw and gently urging her closer, deepening the kiss.

She'd known this time would be different, and she'd been right. His lips were hot, and insistent, asking her to return his feelings.

His arm slid around her waist, engulfing her.

Hoping to keep him here, Lisa wrapped her arms around his waist and held on tight. In the back of her mind, she knew he was still going to leave, knew they couldn't stay like this forever.

But oh, how she wanted to.

He pulled back just a fraction of an inch, gulping in a deep breath. She opened her eyes to find him looking into them, as if trying to see more than was there.

"Stay," she whispered, flinching only slightly at the pleading in that one simple word.

"Don't tempt me."

But she must have since he leaned in again and kissed her more, even deeper this time.

Time moved slowly as they explored the feel and taste of each other.

"You're beautiful." He traced the oval of her face, brushing his thumb over her lips. "So beautiful."

She wanted to laugh, knowing she looked rumpled and half-asleep, but his words made her feel beautiful in this moment. She happily took his word for it.

With the tip of his finger, Trey tickled the soft skin of her neck. Slowly, he leaned away and the expression on his face made her heart sink.

"What?" she asked.

"I gotta go." Regret painted itself all over his face. He actually looked like he was in physical pain. "I don't want to, but—" He took a step back. "It's better this way."

"For who?"

He laughed. "Definitely me." Before she could say any more, Trey moved away and grabbed his coat. He was at the door before her heart even slowed in her chest.

Just before he stepped outside, long enough to let a cold blast of winter inside, he stopped and looked over his shoulder. "I'll be back."

And then he was gone—taking her heart with him.

She watched him leave, saw him disappear into the night shadows.

She'd been right. That kiss had been different. Far different, because somewhere along the line she realized she'd fallen for him. Hard and deep.

"I don't believe you," she whispered to the cold and empty room. But, oh, how she wanted to.

CHAPTER NINETEEN

JUST AFTER DAWN, Grandpa walked into the kitchen, his boots loud on the old linoleum.

"You're home!" Lisa ran to him and he hugged her tight. It had only been a couple of days since they'd been at the cabin, but with all the worry and stress—and the fact that he hadn't been here—it felt like ages. "I've missed you."

"Ah, honey. I was fine. But thanks for comin' to check on me."

"Can I make you breakfast?" she offered.

He shook his head. "How about I take a rain check?" He looked closer at her. "You look as exhausted as I feel. How about we both get some shut-eye, and I'll take you out later."

"I *am* tired." Now that he was here and safe, she could barely keep her eyes open. "I can still make breakfast, but later sounds good."

"Deal." He headed to the stairs. "It'll sure feel good to sleep in my own bed."

Lisa waited until she heard the bedroom door upstairs close before heading to her room. As she settled under the covers, she breathed a sigh of relief.

The pillow felt comfortable now and the blankets soft. Warm. She so needed a good night's—*day's* sleep, she amended as she watched the rays of morning light filter in through the curtains.

But behind her eyelids, she saw more than the welcome darkness. She saw Trey. His smile. That blasted Stetson low over his brow, hiding his eyes from her. The wind-blown look of his skin and tousled blond hair after he'd been skiing.

A lump grew in her chest, aching. She missed him already. He wasn't even really gone. He was probably at his place, soundly sleeping.

He'd said he planned to head to the airport later. Would she even be awake when he left? Her eyes burned. She hadn't told him goodbye. She didn't want to tell him goodbye. She wanted—

Wanted what?

Tears clung to her eyelashes, and she squeezed her eyes closed to keep them from falling. *Sleep. Go to sleep.* She was exhausted. Why wasn't she out cold already?

Because somehow, someway she'd managed to fall in love with Trey Haymaker. And there wasn't a blessed thing she could do about it now.

He was already gone.

DENVER INTERNATIONAL AIRPORT was a long drive. That gave Trey too much time to think as he drove. He turned on the radio to distract himself, but as he was winding through the mountain roads, he mostly got static. Driving east, he was facing into the sun and between the two, his head ached.

It was going to be a long, painful day.

By the time he reached the city limits of Denver, he was ready to point the car in the opposite direction and go straight to the cabin. No one was there, and he craved the solitude he knew was nowhere in his future.

He glanced at the dashboard clock. Was Lisa asleep? Had Win come down off the mountain yet?

None of that was his concern anymore, he reminded himself. Despite his promise to her that he would be back, he wasn't sure he'd be able to keep the promise anytime soon. Not that he was expecting her to wait for him. But he couldn't help but wish...

A truck suddenly pulled in front of him,

and Trey slammed on the brakes. Thank goodness the road was dry, and not covered with snow or ice like at home. Home. That word echoed around his head.

He was able to swerve out of the way and get clear, but not without his heart lodging in his throat.

He couldn't stop along the highway, but he did pull over and slow the car. Driving the rest of the way to the long-term parking lot, he focused on the road and didn't let himself think about Lisa or Win or the cabin or anything.

He headed to the plane, and finally, once he was seated, his eyes grew heavy.

"Ladies and Gentlemen, welcome to Austin, Texas," was the next thing he heard.

Awake now, he felt the humidity, tasted the heaviness in the air. Groaning, he stretched and glanced out the window. The sun was low in the sky over the familiar landscape of Texas.

He stared at the horizon. Not a mountain in sight. He already missed Telluride, missed the life he'd started building.

Standing in the cramped cabin, he waited impatiently as the rows of travelers ahead of him struggled with their luggage and inched toward the door. His ear caught the sound of

Southern twang as he finally walked through the airport.

He thumbed his phone on when he felt the familiar buzz of messages loading. None from Lisa.

THE NEXT DAY, Lisa opened her apartment door and, for a long, painful moment, stared inside. Unlike at Grandpa's house, there was no feeling of homecoming. No inanimate welcome. Just empty sadness.

Maybe she should get a dog. Oh wait, no pets allowed. Maybe she should move. And where would she get money for a deposit? And other moving expenses? She could make this month's rent—but after that? Who knew? Stepping inside, she shoved the door closed with her foot and set her suitcase down.

She should unpack. That'd take at least five minutes. Then what? Watch TV? Go to bed early? Maybe she should read a book. Tomorrow she needed to seriously start her job search. Technically, she could start tonight since everything was done online these days.

She flopped down onto the futon and stared at the TV screen. It wasn't until the sun had gone down far enough in the sky to make the room fall into shadow that she realized time had passed.

Her stomach rumbled. She should have dinner. What the heck was she going to eat? One of Gabe's mushroom-and-Swiss burgers would taste good about now. Her mouth actually watered. "Now cut that out."

Lisa pushed to her feet and made herself flip on the lights. She was *not* going to let herself slip into useless depression. She had a life to rebuild.

Half an hour later, she had just finished putting her now empty suitcase in the hall closet, when her phone rang. What if it was Trey? She hurried to her purse, then stopped when she reached it. "Don't seem too eager," she reminded herself.

As if he'd know? She rolled her eyes just as the ringing stopped. "No!" She thumbed the screen on and saw a number she didn't recognize. Not Trey. She slumped back down on the couch. Drats. She'd wasted excitement over a robocall.

Tossing her phone into her purse again, Lisa headed to the kitchen. Did she even have any food? Opening the freezer, she found two frozen dinners. Lovely. Yum…not.

She heard her phone ding to indicate a message and frowned. Robocalls didn't usually leave messages. Curious, she grabbed one of the meals and shoved it into the microwave before heading back to get her phone.

She was surprised to hear Trudy's voice. In the past, the older woman had called from work. That number wasn't any good anymore. What was this number? Her cell? Lisa hit the button to retrieve her message.

Hey, Lisa, Trudy began. *You'll never guess where I'm calling from. My new job! I'm so excited. And today they asked if I knew of any event planners looking for a job. I told them about you.* The woman finally took a breath. *Get down here tomorrow, girl, and I'm sure you'll get the job.*

Trudy rattled off an address, and Lisa scrambled to find a pen and paper. Finally, she found everything, and after playing the message twice, captured the information.

See you soon. Trudy's voice echoed around the room.

Relief, excitement, trepidation and a tinge of disappointment washed over Lisa. It hadn't been Trey calling, but it was the chance at a new job doing what she loved. She wouldn't have to resort to taking another waitress job to survive.

She should be thrilled. She *was* thrilled... wasn't she? The microwave sounded, and she retrieved the meal. Sitting down on the couch, she watched the steam rise from the ziti-and-cheese dish-in-a-box.

For an instant, she let herself smile as she took a bite. She forced herself to swallow. She didn't have the luxury of wasting it. Hopefully, that was a temporary situation.

CRESTING THE LAST HILL, Trey glared at the place he'd lived for the first twenty years of his life. The house looked just like it always had. Too big for the small family, and too small for Pal Haymaker standards.

Despite all that, it still felt like home.

Easing off the accelerator, he steered the car to the final turnoff. Questions raced through his mind. Who was here? Who wasn't? It was ridiculous to think that way, but too late now.

From here, he saw the glimmer of the crystal clear waters of the river as it wound its way through the land that he'd once believed was his birthright.

The ranch was recovering from the fires his grandfather had had a hand in starting a couple years ago, but while the land had healed, the people were a different thing.

He thought about turning around for half an instant but he kept going. His anger and resentment at his grandfather were still strong.

When Jason had said his mother was struggling he'd tried not to let his concern show. He'd gotten good at that. Not caring. Not needing anyone. Not letting anyone in.

How many times had Trey nearly picked up his phone and called his mother? But Trey hadn't called. Had never reached out. He'd just tried to move on.

Slowly, he pulled into the drive that wound up to the big house. To the left a large pasture stretched beyond the white rail fence. Driving slowly, he noticed the paint needed a touch-up, and at least two of the posts tilted precariously.

Wyatt's comments that the ranch was desperate for a manager returned to haunt him.

Closer to the house, several horses ambled toward the fence and curiously watched him pass by. He counted four head. Silver Devil was gone. He smiled when he spotted Devil's Gold lifting his head, and swishing his tail as if saying hello.

Would Dad let him take the beautiful horse back to Colorado? Would he have a choice? Concern and just a bit of anticipation made Trey push a little harder on the accelerator.

The garage was open but Trey didn't pull into his usual spot. He didn't even look at it. Granddad had given Trey's prize car away and the car had been destroyed.

He knew it was just a thing, but the car represented so much more than just a means of transportation. It had been *his*. It had been a prized gift, a token of his place here.

No one came out of the barn or the garage to check on the visitor. No one came to the front door. Where was everyone?

He left everything in the car. Not that he'd brought much, but he wasn't sure where to put it. He still wasn't sure where he'd be staying.

At the front door, he paused. Should he knock? Should he just walk in? They didn't ever lock the front door, but he wasn't sure what the reception would be on the other side.

Slowly, he turned the knob and pushed the door open. He was surprised to hear a soft squeal of hinges. More signs of things not being kept up.

The wide-open great foyer was empty. He was relieved to see a fresh bouquet of flowers on the central table. Mom's domain was intact. That was reassuring.

"Hello?" he called, softly at first, then again, more loudly. "Mom?" No answer. Where was the housekeeper?

Disheartened, Trey walked across the hall and headed toward the rear wing where his parents' bedroom was located. About halfway down the hall, he heard soft voices. He smiled.

The door was open, and he could see the edge of the big four-poster bed that had been here as long as he could remember. His mother was sitting in a chair beside the bed, her back to him. He took a step, and she spun around.

"I didn't mean to startle you," he said.

Bess Haymaker was still vital and pretty, at least to Trey. For a long moment she simply stared, then hastily shot to her feet "Trey! Look, Pal, Trey's home." She hurried toward Trey, not even bothering to pause as she reached up and wrapped her arms around him.

Trey had to admit it felt good. Mom's hugs had always been the best, though rare and reserved for special occasions. After they'd said their hellos, Trey glanced around the room.

It looked like something out of one of those doctor TV shows. Monitors beeped, and an IV pole stood beside the bed. A wheelchair and the hospital bed sat in the middle of the big room. From where his father lay in the bed, he could survey the entire ranch through the big glass windows.

Trey scrutinized his father. Pal Haymaker Junior appeared nearly as old as Pal Senior had just before he'd died. His father was much thinner and frail. His steel-gray hair was matted down and there was a paleness to his skin, probably from being inside more than out.

"He's been up most of the day," Bess explained.

"Trey. Welcome home," Pal said, though Trey could hear the tiredness in his voice as he struggled to sit up straighter.

The concern and consternation on his mother's face made Trey smile. It was a common look for her and he couldn't help but appreciate it.

"Don't worry, Dad. I'm not going anywhere for a while. Get some rest, and I'll catch up with you later."

Trey knew his father wasn't doing well when he didn't argue.

"We'll be back, dear." Bess leaned over and kissed his father's cheek, just like Trey remembered her doing to him when he was sick as a kid. It was a long-forgotten memory and a lump caught hold in his chest. He missed the obliviousness of childhood.

Once they reached the front room, he settled on the couch while his mother took her usual wingback chair by the front window.

"How's Dad truly doing?" he asked her,

not really sure if she'd answer him. He wasn't sure about anything at this point.

Her chin wobbled and her eyes sparkled. She shook her head and reached for the box of tissues on the side table. She grabbed two for good measure. "Oh, Trey, it's bad." She looked up then, her tears tipping out of her eyes. "I'm not sure what I'll do if he doesn't recover."

Flashbacks of his childhood made him cringe. He loved his mother, but she had always turned on the emotions to get his father's and grandfather's attention. He almost snapped at her to stop the melodrama, but he couldn't quite do it. He hadn't seen his father since leaving, he hadn't talked to the doctors, hadn't done any of that because he hadn't been here. She had, and he could see the strain on her face. "He's here at home, isn't he? That's gotta mean something good."

"It only means he wasn't going to put up with all that poking and prodding that the hospital insisted on." She dabbed at her eyes. "He said if he was going to die, he wanted to do it in his own home."

"Ah." That sounded more like his father. "How about we take it one step at a time?"

"Yes, yes." She sniffed. "One step at a time. I'm so glad you're home."

"I'm glad I can help." And he was. The problem was he could see his mother's expression. She had expectations. "Mom?" He faced her. "I didn't come home to stay."

He saw the flash of her anger, which in a sick sort of way gave him hope.

"But sweetheart—"

"No, Mom." He held up a hand. "I'm not ever coming back here to stay. I can't." He thought for an instant that he should have softened the blow. "And if that's not okay with you, well, I can't change that."

She nodded and visibly straightened her shoulders and lifted her chin. "Very well, but don't tell your father that yet. He needs all the help he can get if he's going to recover."

He didn't like it, but he nodded. Seconds ticked by as they looked at each other and he wondered if she knew how close he was to turning around and walking out the door and heading north again.

A FEW DAYS LATER, the big ranch kitchen was silent, the only sound the occasional hum of some appliance or other. Trey sat at the table with a tepid cup of coffee in his hands, reading the newspaper that his mother had left scattered on the end of the big wooden table.

He scanned the headlines and skimmed the

stories that caught his attention. Not much had changed in this part of Texas. Not much at all.

Footsteps made him look up. His mother came in carrying the tray she'd taken in to Dad earlier. It didn't look much different today than it had any other day. But she did. The sadness in her eyes had deepened and her shoulders, the shoulders that had held up too much work over the years, slumped.

"He barely touched it," she whispered as she took the tray full of dishes to the sink.

Trey sat there, silence gathering between them. He didn't have a clue what to say or do. His father didn't seem to have any will to get better. His mother was trying, but it was wearing her down.

"What can I do, Mom?"

"Nothing anyone can do if he doesn't want to get on his feet again," she whispered. After a deep breath, she slammed the handle of the faucet and rinsed the dishes. They clattered when she put them into the dishwasher.

Once that task was done, she slowly dried her hands on the ever-present towel hanging from the handle on the stove. Finally, she turned around and leaned against the counter. "Why did you come home?"

Trey was surprised at her question nearly

as much as her tone. Mom was mad, and to be honest, he couldn't remember the last time he'd seen her that way.

How honest should he be? How honest *could* he be? He carefully set the coffee cup down before answering. "I came because the Hawkins brothers found me and told me Dad was hurt."

"Is that it?"

Trey had to think about his answer, as much to not upset her as to get the right words. "Pretty much."

She poured herself a cup of coffee and took her time fixing it to her liking with cream and sugar. Finally, she moved to the table and sat down. She met his gaze squarely. "So why are you staying? He's not doing anything different now that you're here. You're going to leave. Why not just get it over with?"

Her bitterness surprised him. "I'm here for you, too."

She set her cup down after taking just one sip. "Really? You do remember who you're talking to, don't you?"

She sat, silent, and Trey wasn't sure what to do or say next. He waited, like he always had as a kid. He leaned back in the chair, the wood groaning in protest. "Do you want me to leave?"

For a moment, she didn't say anything. The eyes that he'd inherited just stared at him. "I don't know. I just want you to *do* something."

He felt as helpless as she was depicting him. "Like what? The ranch is back on track but Dad's not interested in anything. He's given up, Mom."

She nodded and took her time taking a deep drink. "He has. And I don't really blame him."

What was she talking about? He bit his tongue at first. He loved his parents, but the bitterness he still carried with him at his grandfather's actions was too strong to ignore. "He gave up long ago." Trey almost bit back the words, but changed his mind as they spilled out.

"What is that supposed to mean?" Her "mom" glare was sharp.

"Oh, come on, Mom. Dad always gave in to Granddad's demands. The old man ran the show." Trey wanted to stand, but made himself stay put. Maybe it was time to clear the air.

"Is that really what you believe?" She was glaring at him now.

"It's what I saw, Mom." He didn't glare back. He couldn't glare at her. She'd been as much a part of the problem as Dad. The only excuse she had was the fact that Pal Hay-maker hadn't been her blood, hadn't been her direct responsibility.

The silence filled with anger and pain and a whole lot of what-ifs. Trey finished his coffee and stood to put his cup in the dishwasher. He had to do something. He hadn't come here to hurt anyone, especially not his mother, but his hurt was too strong to keep bottled up.

CHAPTER TWENTY

THE NEXT MORNING when Lisa opened the door of the West Media Team's office, Trudy sat at the front desk just like she had at the previous place, the quintessential receptionist. She wore a headset and grinned at Lisa as the younger woman pushed open the glass doors. When Trudy had successfully transferred the call, she came rushing around the counter, so full of energy.

She engulfed Lisa in a warm hug, then tapped the headset and answered another call. After two more calls, she was finally able to talk.

"It's so good to see you." The older woman beamed.

"What is this place?" Lisa looked around the cavernous lobby. Lined in dark marble and edged with brass—this was not like the catering company they'd worked for previously.

"It's a marketing firm." Trudy reached under the desk and pulled out a glossy, multipage pamphlet. "Look!" Trudy gestured Lisa to a set of leather chairs a few feet away. "Take a seat for a second and I'll let Martha know you're here."

"Martha?"

"The owner. Jeannie, the HR director, was probably who set up your interview. Martha hires everyone. I told her you'd be coming in."

How confident had Trudy been that she'd be here? Was she that predictable? Despite her growing trepidation, she settled in the chair and flipped the pages. Wow! This place had some amazing clients. Some of the biggest firms in the country.

After a few minutes, she couldn't sit any longer. She stood and paced. The short hallway to the right was lined with beautiful paintings and she couldn't stop herself from getting up to examine them.

They were Western themed. The first was a beautiful landscape of a high mountain ranch. She swallowed the ache in her throat. It could have been the place she'd just left behind. Her grandfather and Trey could easily be painted into the middle of that high mountain meadow.

"Ms. Duprey?" A woman's voice called her and she spun around, her cheeks warming as she felt like a child wandering out of class.

The woman standing there was probably the same age as her mother. But where her mother always looked like she'd been out digging in the garden, Lisa wasn't sure this woman had ever seen a garden. Her smile, though, was warm and welcoming.

"Uh. Yes." Lisa stepped forward and offered her hand.

"Martha Kline." The woman shook her hand, firm and very much the shake of a woman who was used to working in a man's world. "I see you've found our clients' gallery."

"Clients' gallery?"

"Yes." The woman fell into step with her. "I know Trudy's filled you in some. We're an advertising marketing firm that specializes in big, loud events for our clients. The splashier, the better. These are from some of our most successful campaigns." She walked slowly along the line of paintings. "This is for the Double M ranch up in Montana. They sell the world's best beef. See, says so right here." She smiled, pointing at a smaller frame beside the artwork. It contained an ad saying exactly what she just had.

"They're beautiful." She loved the Western theme of most of them. The one of the cowboy seated on a big black stallion. His

Stetson was low over his eyes, hiding his features. The figure reminded her of Trey. Her heart hurt.

Martha smiled. "That one was for the National Finals Rodeo." Her voice was wistful. Did she have a thing for cowboys, too?

"Well, enough of that." Martha turned away from the paintings. "I could spend all day here. Trudy has nothing but good things to say about you. She showed me some of the events you did for Marco. Very impressive."

"You know Marco?"

"I do. I've tried for years to get him to come work for us. He keeps refusing and avoiding me." Her eyes and voice grew distant.

"I don't understand." What did an event-planning job have to do with advertising? She opened her mouth to ask her just that when the woman continued.

"We create the ads, but each of these campaigns has a launch party. That's why we need an event planner. I'm very good at my job, which is coming up with the ideas for these." She waved at the paintings. "But don't even try to have me work with caterers and DJs and furniture rentals." The woman actually shuddered. "Just shoot me."

That was what Lisa liked best about her job. All the logistics and puzzle pieces to put together. She smiled. "I'd never be able to come up with an idea like that." She waved at the cowboy. "But I can easily make the world you picture come to life."

Martha grinned now. "How soon can you start?"

"What?"

"You heard me." The woman laughed. "I'm so far behind as it is. When our previous event planner decided not to come back from maternity leave, I nearly panicked. And after what Trudy told me, and after hearing that Marco hired you—I don't have to look any further. The job is yours if you want it."

Lisa couldn't believe it. The woman had barely interviewed her. "Are you sure?"

"I'm sure." The woman smiled and stood waiting.

"I'd love to. Thank you. I won't let you regret this."

"I know." The woman shook her hand again. "I have a meeting in five minutes, so I need to go. Can you come in tomorrow and start the paperwork?" She glanced at the beautiful watch on her wrist. "Ten tomorrow?"

Lisa nodded and watched as Martha hurried to the elevators. She waited until the doors closed before she rushed over to Trudy's desk. "Is this for real?"

"Yes." Trudy hung up the phone and gave her a hug. "I told her all about the Davis wedding." It had been a disaster that they'd managed to turn into a dream. "And the Macintyre party. She loved them both. I knew she'd like you."

They chatted as much as possible through a half-dozen calls, then Lisa decided she'd head home. She had a new job. An event planner job, not a waitress job. She'd hopefully have a desk and no need for those sturdy supportive shoes she'd spent so much money on.

Her new life was taking shape.

So why, when she opened her apartment door half an hour later, wasn't she more excited? Why had all her joy in life faded as if all the color had gone black and white?

Everything beyond the glass of the kitchen window looked the same. Trey glanced to the west and could still see the burn scar that marked much of the county. His grandfather had caused that fire, nearly costing so many people their livelihood.

Mom hadn't moved since she'd sat down to join him at the table. She wasn't reading the paper. She simply sat there, taking a drink every now and then, silent.

"I'm sorry, Mom."

"What for?" She still didn't move.

"For—I don't know."

"Then don't apologize." She finished her coffee but instead of getting up and putting the cup in the sink or the dishwasher, she simply pushed it away and folded her hands together on top of the table.

"You don't know everything, son." Her voice was so soft, but the kitchen was quiet enough that he heard her fine. She glanced over her shoulder at him then and the hurt inside her eyes was painful to look at. He made himself meet her gaze when he just wanted to break it and walk away. But he'd already done that. Fat lot of good that had done him.

"Then maybe if you told me, I'd understand." It wasn't a question, or a demand. Just the plain and simple truth.

Instead of a flare of anger, she sighed. "Someday you're going to have a family of your own and maybe you'll understand." Before he could respond or ask anything else, she stood up and turned around to face him. "Come on." She waved her hand, and he had to admit there was a flicker of something in her eyes. A flicker he hadn't seen in a very long time.

She left the kitchen and he followed. She walked down the hall, her steps sure and determined. She stopped at a set of double doors and put her hands on the brass handles. Time seemed to stop.

"You don't have to do this, Mom." Trey walked up beside her. "My beef isn't with you."

"Isn't it?" She was angry now. "You walked out on us all." She shoved the doors open. They would have slammed into the wall if not for the metal stoppers behind them. "You walked out on everyone because of that old fool." She gestured around the big room.

Pal's study. The room he'd spent so much of his time in. His kingdom's throne room. Trey did not want to be here. He'd been pleased to find the doors closed when he got home.

He looked around. Nothing had changed, and he grimaced. Were they leaving it as a shrine to the old man? He knew he didn't hide his reaction well. The big mahogany desk. The stiff leather chairs. The photos of Pal when he'd been young.

The damned painting up on the wall that depicted Pal on horseback. King of all he surveyed.

"I hate that picture," his mother said. "I think I hate it more now than I did when he was with us."

Never in his life had Trey heard his mother voice a negative opinion of Pal Senior. He stared at her. Shocked.

"You never knew that, did you?" she asked.

"Uh, no." Old hurts rose up to nearly choke him.

"No, you didn't." She turned and pointed an accusatory finger at him. "Because I always kept my mouth shut. He—" She swung her arm around and pointed at the picture on the wall. "He was my father-in-law, and no matter how much I hated how he did it, he built this home your father brought me to as a bride. You adored him, and on the whole, he adored you." Her voice trembled a bit. "I'd never ever speak negatively about someone who meant so much to you."

He stared at her feeling as if he'd stepped into an alternate universe. "I didn't ask you to do that."

"Of course not. You were a boy, a child when I first saw what kind of man he really was. I was a fool—I'll admit that. It was already too late. You adored him." Her voice cracked, and Trey heard the betrayal in his mother's voice, betrayal he was all too familiar with.

She'd put up with everything for him? Guilt made him cringe. "What happened?" Did he really want to know? He already hated his grandfather, and hearing he'd caused his mother the same pain wasn't going to help.

A thought flashed in his mind, an image of Lisa and Win. The way she'd hugged him when she'd found him in the caves. Envy wasn't any more pleasant than anger.

"My brother had inherited the land from my parents." His mother's voice had grown soft and brought him back to the present. She strolled into the room until she came to stop in front of the fireplace and tilted her head back and glared at the painting. A tear tumbled over her cheek.

Trey stepped forward, but when he went to put an arm around her, she pushed him away. "I know how you feel about Pal." She cried. "I understand his evil. He forced my brother into bankruptcy and when he couldn't pay the taxes on the land, Pal swooped in and bought it out from under him." She finally wiped at the tears on her cheeks. "That stretch by the beach you so loved? That was *my* father's land. Your other grandfather's land. Pal stole it." Bitterness spilled all over the beautiful room.

Trey had never heard any of this. Never knew any of these things. But while his heart hurt at the revelation—there was still too much missing. He almost didn't say anything. But time and his own pain had made him too overwhelmingly angry. "And you did nothing? Dad did nothing?" This new information only added to his ache to escape again.

This time the silence bristled with anger. Slowly, she spun around. "You think that little of your father and I?"

"I don't know anything." And he didn't wait to hear what she had to say next. Spinning on his heel, he headed to the door.

"Stop right there!"

Okay, he hadn't heard that tone in a long time. Slowly, he turned back around, fisting his hand to help focus his own anger. There were no words, at least not his. But she had the words and seemed determined to speak them. He waited, not so patiently.

"Why do you think we're still living in this house?" She stepped toward him. "Why do you think all of HH is managed by lawyers instead of your father?" She took a step and was so close she had to lean her head back to look into his face. "Because we did fight him.

We did make him accountable. The only reason there's anything left for you is because we made him sign everything into a trust fund."

She stepped away then and faced the painting. "Your trust, Trey," she whispered. "Not his. Not ours. The ranch is all that's ours." As if shaking herself out of a stupor, she shook her head.

"Money wasn't what I wanted." All the money in the world couldn't bring back the sense of home and family and idealism he'd lost when his grandfather betrayed him.

"I know that." She took a breath and shuddered. "But it all backfired."

"What do you mean?"

Bess walked to the door. "He wasn't the nicest person in the world, and I hated him sometimes. But he loved you, Trey, loved you more than anyone."

"He had a funny way of showing it." All the anger and bitterness resurfaced.

"That may be true, but when he hurt you…" She took a deep breath. "You hurt everyone else. You didn't just turn your back on him, you turned it on us, too." Her voice cracked. "Love is precious and not something to throw away. It doesn't come along that often. Pal may have been foolish enough to do that. Don't be like him."

She left then, not bothering to close the doors, leaving him alone in the last room he ever wanted to be in again.

Her words slammed into him. He was nothing like the old man. Nothing. But the longer he stood there, the more weight settled on his shoulders, in his chest where it hurt.

Trey watched his mother walk away, needing to process the new information—about his parents, his grandfather, himself—but mostly about someone else entirely.

Lisa.

CHAPTER TWENTY-ONE

THE OFFICE WAS quiet today. Martha was out scouting another venue for a campaign she was working on for next month and Trudy was off to a bird show. Lisa smiled. When they'd lost their last jobs and gone out to breakfast that morning all those months ago, she'd encouraged Trudy to pursue her love of showing her cockatoos. The woman had taken her advice to heart and wasn't making her job her entire life.

Lisa, on the other hand, was having a much more difficult time adjusting to this new life. Oh, it was a great job; the pay was more than she'd been making with Marco and she had so much freedom. It was what she'd dreamed of doing for years.

So why wasn't she satisfied?

Restless, she paced across the thick carpet to the wide windows. The office was on the twentieth story of one of Denver's highest towers. Martha was successful, and the office was prime real estate. The view of the Rockies was spectacular. Shadowed blue against the vivid azure of the sky, the white caps were almost hidden in the shade.

She couldn't look away. Her heart hitched. Trey was up there. Oh, not on those particular slopes. She couldn't see Telluride from here. At least, nowhere but in her mind's eye.

Glancing at her desk, she noticed the message that had triggered her thoughts. Her grandfather had asked her to call him. She wasn't angry at him, but she couldn't talk to him. Not now. Not until she got her tangled mind straight.

While Trey had been the one standing there and offering to buy the ranch, Grandpa had agreed to the deal. Wholeheartedly. Giving up on all the determination he'd held on to so tight. Selling away the secret he'd kept for years. Oh, she understood; she knew that he was marking time to the end of his life. Knew that after he was gone, there wasn't anyone who would protect the caverns.

Mom had already said she intended to sell the land when he was gone.

And while Trey had said the right things, had promised everything Win had wanted—would he really follow through? Would he keep his word?

It hurt almost as much that he was buying

her family's heritage as it did that she didn't trust him. It hurt. He'd never done anything to shatter her trust in him. But she just... couldn't.

And she didn't know why. She could not figure out what held her back from giving her heart to him, from letting him be a part of her life.

She wanted to. Oh, how badly she wanted it. But something stood in her way; something held her heart just out of reach.

"What's the matter?" Martha's voice startled her.

"I thought you were out."

"I was." The older woman stepped silently into the lush office. "How long have you been standing there?"

"Uh..." The sun was well down behind the mountains and the lights were coming on all over the city. Lisa turned around and leaned against the window's ledge. "I'm not sure what's the matter." She didn't want to upset the older woman who'd given her this dream job, but she had to be honest, with her and with herself. "I want you to know how much I appreciate this job. Appreciate you."

"Uh-oh. I hear a *but* coming." Martha came farther in and settled in the big desk chair that Lisa had vacated.

"No. Well, maybe." Lisa looked down. "I think I need to take some time off." Maybe she'd go someplace on a short vacation. Someplace warm. A beach. Not the snowy mountains.

"Oh." Martha slumped in the chair in relief. "I was afraid you were going to quit."

"Oh, no." She'd never do that. "But I'm not giving you a hundred percent right now."

"Because of your grandfather?" Lisa had roughly told Martha her concerns about Grandpa and the situation. She'd only hinted about Trey, though.

"Some. I just need to think."

Martha nodded, slowly, carefully smoothing out the papers on top of the desk. "I'll make you a deal."

The woman wasn't saying no. "Like?"

"Give me this next week. We've got two events, and I don't want to have to deal with them both."

"Oh, I won't leave you hanging." Lisa felt the smile of relief spread over her lips. "I'll finish up both of them, of course. Just knowing that the time is set will help."

"Good. Very good." Martha stood and walked around the desk. "Thank you. I am so glad you've come to work here, and I hope you stay with us." She put her hand on Lisa's shoulder, her multiple rings glinting in the fading light. "I'll focus on the Bryson's function if you finish up the ranch party. Then, how about you plan a two-week break."

"Sounds perfect." She'd have rather taken the Bryson account, but she'd already pushed her luck with her brand-new boss. She'd do as Martha asked. Lisa was only slightly surprised when Martha embraced her in a warm hug. She hugged the woman back hoping Martha could read her appreciation in the hug.

"All right, hon. Let's get to work so you can take off on that vacation as soon as possible." Martha grabbed the Bryson file from the desk, settling it in her arms like a schoolgirl carried her books. She left for her own office then and Lisa fought back the smile.

She'd been blessed to have Martha hire her. She wouldn't let her down.

Lisa took several deep breaths. The room was perfect. Since she'd been hired, she'd put every minute she had into this event. Her first solo project for Martha, it had to be perfect. She wanted to keep this job. So now she was here, an hour before the rest of the staff was scheduled to arrive. Making sure every single detail was in place.

The room looked beautiful. On the top floor of the Ritz-Carlton in downtown Denver, it boasted a wall of floor-to-ceiling windows. Beyond the thick glass, the city was just beginning to shift gears, the street and city lights slowly winking on.

The purple shadows teased the edge of the skyscrapers, and the Rocky Mountain peaks beyond. She'd timed the opening of the doors to this room to be in sync with the approaching sunset. It was as spectacular as she'd planned. She breathed a sigh of relief, then turned her back on the view. She didn't have time to relax.

According to Martha, this was her most important client so far this year. And while the woman owned and ran one of Denver's most successful advertising agencies, she had visions of growing even bigger. Lisa understood the drive to be at the top of the food chain. And she'd do everything she could to help Martha reach her dreams.

Enough, she told herself. There were details to check, things to do besides get lost in her own head.

On the opposite wall, the display was beautiful. And so familiar. She wanted to ignore it. Wanted to pretend she didn't see the foam board photo cutouts that looked almost real.

Rolling hills of snow. Thick, tall ponderosa pines. Stately blue spruce. She couldn't help smiling. Even a family of deer under one tree and a moose.

Her heart hitched. She'd spent hours with Robin, the graphic artist, poring over photos to use for this display. Only one final piece was covered, and Martha had worked on that one. The client was going to be here later for that unveiling.

Now, though, seeing it all put together— had she subconsciously chosen photos that resembled the cabin? Her heart hurt. She missed it. Missed her grandfather.

Missed Trey and the potential they'd lost.

Shaking her head, she spun away. The view. The photos. It was too much. She was losing her mind. She'd let her own wishes take over. What would Martha say? Was it what the older woman had expected of her? What if she'd screwed up?

"Oh, Lisa." The very woman Lisa had been thinking about breezed in through the double doors. She reached Lisa's side and gave her a brief, almost nonexistent hug. "That dress is perfect. I knew you'd look lovely in it."

Lisa had been surprised that the budget for this campaign had included clothing for them both.

Martha had said that was her normal mode of operation. "How do you think I get so many fabulous outfits?"

Now they stood there, both of them dressed to the nines, waiting for the room to fill with total strangers.

Martha gazed around the room, her smile growing. "You've done an outstanding job." She circuited the space, analyzing all the elements Lisa had just checked, her blue dress flowing around her ankles, giving just a tantalizing flash of sparkle across her toes.

"Do you think so?" Lisa tried to keep the uncertainty to a minimum in her voice. At Martha's frown, she knew she'd failed.

"Yes, absolutely." She reached up and gently patted Lisa's cheek. "Relax. You've met the client's wishes. That's what we're here for. Come. The caterers were downstairs when I came up. Let's make sure they can get in."

Happy for a task to focus on, Lisa checked the tables and held the door open when the catering crew reached the entry. Despite having put the menu together, and having done the food tastings weeks ago, her mouth watered at the scent of the luscious food.

"That smells heavenly." Martha spoke Lisa's thoughts aloud. With Lisa directing and Martha following behind to add the finishing touches, they had everything set up in less than an hour. Lisa breathed a sigh of relief. It looked nearly perfect.

Empty. But perfect.

Martha glanced at her watch. "They should be here any moment." As if on cue, the click of high heels on the marble floor outside echoed loud in the huge room. Men's dress heels soon followed. In just a few moments, the room was filled with dozens of people, all of them talking and laughing.

Martha waved to Lisa. "Mingle," she said. "Guide them to the displays. Talk up the ranch."

Lisa swallowed hard. It was easy to talk about a client in the abstract, but right now—this campaign, this client, reminded her too much of what she'd left behind. It was so similar...

Forcing a smile on her lips, she dove in, finding the people who looked the least likely to be interested in a high mountain ranch retreat. Martha left her side and did her own mingling in the crowd.

TREY STOOD ON the landing outside the ballroom. From here he occasionally caught a glimpse of Lisa. Her blue dress fit perfectly and flashed through the crowd like a sapphire in its polished setting.

"You gonna go in, boy?" Win's gruff voice cut through his thoughts.

He glanced over his shoulder at the old man. He'd never have imagined that the old guy could clean up so well. "You actually look human in a tux."

"You ain't half bad yourself." Win grinned and adjusted his bow tie. "But I ain't the one you're supposed to be impressin' here."

The only-too-familiar sound of rattling metal interrupted his response and they both turned. Hap and Sam were just stepping off the elevator.

"Sorry we're late," Sam said.

"Wasn't my fault." Hap glared at Sam as if silently telling him not to say anything. Sam just grinned back.

"Yer friend here needs to tell you something." Sam met Win's gaze. "Go ahead, Hap."

What were these two up to? Trey did not want them screwing up tonight. "Can this wait?"

"Yeah, it can wait." Hap headed for the open doorway.

"Oh, no, you don't. Tell 'em. Now."

Hap moved his walker back and forth nervously. "Uh, well, you know, uh, how you been workin' on this surprise here?"

Trey nodded.

"Get on with it, man. We don't have time for this," Win said.

"Fine. It was my fault." Hap glared at his friend.

"What was your fault?" Trey asked.

"Lance. I may have been the one to tip him off that there might be somethin' valuable on that land."

"What?" Trey turned around and glared at the old man. "How did you do that?"

"He and Lance were talking one day." Sam's impatience made him step in. "Hap was bragging about how much he knew about the land and town. When Lance mentioned trying to buy your ranch, smart mouth here said he remembered seeing a mine somewhere around there."

"You knew about the caverns?" Win's voice was loud and he shushed himself quickly.

"Not exactly," Hap admitted. "I followed your brother once." Hap looked down. "I even snuck back a couple times. I remember thinking I was gonna run away once, so I took a bunch of things up there. But then I got busy with life, getting married, and I couldn't find it later on. I thought maybe he'd find it if he was out looking around."

Win stared. "That was your box!"

"Box?" Hap frowned, then his brow cleared as he remembered. "I thought it fell down one of them holes." He shrugged. "Didn't think anyone'd ever find it."

No one spoke as all the information sunk in. Trey finally looked over at Sam. "How'd you find out?" He knew Hap hadn't volunteered anything.

"That's why we were late. Those two idiots who worked for Lance? Finally got a hit on some of the fingerprints at your place, Win. Arrested them two for breaking and entering. They sure were in a talkative mood." He winked at Trey. "Learned all kinds of things about what they've been up to for Lance."

"Like I said. It wasn't my fault." Hap gave his walker a shove and headed into the room.

"I'll go make sure he behaves," Sam offered and followed Hap. In the doorway he turned back and gave Trey the thumbs up. "Good luck." And then he was gone, too.

With a deep breath, Trey turned back to the doorway, hoping he hadn't missed his cue from Martha. Hap's revelation didn't change a thing. Nothing could at this point.

Standing there, he saw several more familiar faces. He'd given Martha total freedom in inviting people from Telluride. He was surprised so many of them had made the trip. Homesickness washed over him.

Would Lisa recognize them? Of course, she would. Would she figure everything out? He hoped not—not yet, not until he got everything accomplished.

WALKING THROUGH THE CROWD, Lisa did a double take. She could swear she'd spotted Trey. But that was impossible. He was still in Texas. Shaking her head, she focused on the couple beside her.

They were looking for a mountain retreat for their fiftieth wedding anniversary. "What's under that cloth?" Mr. Barnes asked, pointing at the hidden display.

"I don't exactly know." All evening she tried to rack her brain and pull up the items on the plan. Which one was missing?

"Guess we'll all see together, then." Mrs. Barnes smiled and lifted her drink in a salute.

After several other conversations centered on the mystery display, Lisa headed over to Martha. People were getting quite curious, and she didn't like not being able to answer. Maybe Martha would share a bit more information.

Just as she reached her, Martha smiled and waved at someone. Lisa turned to see who—and froze. Two men—two very familiar men—strolled into the room.

He *was* here. Trey was here, in Denver, wearing a tuxedo. And beside him, her grandfather strolled in, a wide grin on his face. Win's gaze searched the crowd, and when his eyes met hers, he winked, but otherwise he kept going.

What was he doing here? Her heart picked up the pace and she couldn't quite breathe.

Finally, Martha met them near the covered display. What was going on? Lisa pushed through the crowd, and as she did that, she saw more familiar faces. Where had these people been when she'd made her earlier rounds?

Turning her attention back to her boss and the men, Lisa inched closer though the crowd until she stood right in front of them. She didn't even try to smile.

But Trey smiled at her anyway. Lord, she'd missed him. Missed that smile, missed the way he looked at her. Missed the way he made her feel.

Trey tilted his head at her as if to indicate she join him. That wasn't going to happen. She stood right where she was, curiosity driving her crazy. Was this the same ranch? Grandpa's ranch? It had to be. What about the caves? What was going to happen to them?

Just like everyone else, she waited, which thankfully wasn't for long.

"Ladies and gentlemen," Martha said into the microphone on the narrow podium. The crowd took several minutes to quiet down. "Ladies and gentlemen," she repeated, shushing the last small group.

Finally, when she had everyone's attention, she introduced Trey. Lisa held her breath. What was he going to say? Anticipation drove her crazy.

With minimal fanfare, Trey explained he was the co-owner of the High Country Lodge and Resort. She liked the name and she wondered what Grandpa thought of it. His smile told her, though—he was happy.

Trey talked about the goal of the ranch, to provide a quiet, safe retreat for people to get away from the city. She recalled the pitch from the flyers, signs and brochures she'd been involved with creating.

It sounded like heaven. Finally, he reached over and grasped the corner of the drape over the last piece of the puzzle. The soft blue fabric swished over the sign and away.

Duncan's Dream was a cave that elicited a

gasp from the crowd. *Wait until you see the rest*, she thought. They weren't gonna believe it. She barely did anymore. She took a deep breath.

"Duncan found this beautiful cavern when he was a kid. Tragically, he was killed in Vietnam, so he never saw the realization of this dream."

Trey looked over at Win, who stepped up to the microphone. As her grandfather shared stories of Duncan, she smiled. His love for his brother was evident.

She liked this whole setup. Trey was grinning and Grandpa was happy—what more could she ask?

"And now I'd like to invite Lisa Duprey, the amazing event planner who created this beautiful party for you all, up here." Trey stepped back and applauded, a sound that quickly spilled over the entire center.

She *so* did not want to do this, but Martha gave her a pointed stare, and, for her boss, she joined the ensemble.

Trey looked handsome, but there was something in his eyes that wasn't usual. Was he nervous? Why would he be nervous? This was an amazing adventure.

"Hey," he said softly.

"Hey," she repeated. They stood there, gazing at each other for probably too long. But she didn't care. He was here. She was here. They could figure something out.

Finally, Trey reached into the pocket of his tuxedo and pulled out a folded set of papers. He double-checked them and then extended the bundle to her.

Surprised, she could only stare. "What's this?"

"Open it," he nudged.

She struggled for an instant with the pages, then, as they came into view, she blinked her eyes. Twice. This wasn't right.

"Why is my name on this deed?" she demanded of him, focusing on her grandfather the next instant. "You need to explain."

Trey smiled. "That's your portion of the ranch." He explained that while he would own the actual ranch and would offer it as a resort, he'd also be running cattle on the land and have horses. Win would retain the caverns and be partners with Trey in developing it for viewings.

It was perfect, but she still didn't understand why her name was on it.

"When I'm gone, it's yours. No one else's." Grandpa said softly.

They weren't going to let Duncan's dreams die. With a soft cry of joy, she threw her arms around her grandpa for a warm hug. But when she reached for Trey he hesitated. She hesitated.

"You came back." It wasn't a question.

"I said I would."

They looked at each other. "You did," she whispered. "I'm glad."

"Me, too."

"How's your dad?" Why was she stalling? It was just a hug, for heaven's sake.

"Better, thanks." They stared at each other for a long moment.

"Why are you here?" She finally blurted out.

"Someone much wiser than me pointed out recently that I've misinterpreted some things. She suggested I not throw love away since it's so hard to find."

"I… Love?" She was afraid to ask. Who had told him that? Why had he listened? Scary thought.

Slowly, reverently, Trey reached out and slid his hand to the side of her face. The calluses on his palm were still there and the gentle glide of his finger over her lips sent a shiver up her spine.

"Welcome home," she whispered just before he kissed her. Wrapping her arms around him, she kissed him back. *Welcome home.*

EPILOGUE

LISA SWALLOWED BACK the panic that threatened to choke her. Was this the right answer? Would this destroy everything she'd spent the last six months working for?

Trey had slept most of the way from the airport. She knew he was wearing himself out trying to function in two worlds. One week a month he flew home to help his mother care for Pal Junior.

The older man was making progress and the doctors were confident that soon he'd be back up on his feet. Titanium was stronger than the human skeleton, so it would hold his shattered pelvis and back together.

But what kept him going, she knew, was Trey. They were on the way to mending their difficult relationship. Titanium couldn't help with that.

Rubbing her knuckles over her eyes, she wiped away the stray tear. They were both such good men. They needed each other.

They deserved to have the father-son relationship Pal Senior had robbed them of.

But no matter how hard they worked, there was still something—someone—between them. That's why she'd come down here with him this time.

"Turn left at County Road Fifteen" the woman's voice in the GPS said. "Your destination is on the right."

"Wha…?" Trey lifted his head, sleep still clinging to his face. His confusion was obvious.

"Morning, sleepyhead." She smiled, enjoying the way the sunrise was painting the prairie bright red and gold. She followed the instructions, and turned onto a rutted dirt road. The big SUV took the road's unevenness easily.

"What are we doing out here?" Trey pushed up to a seated position, his brow wrinkled in a frown. He had to know where they were.

"Visiting." She didn't give him time to answer, but pulled through the curved iron gate that arched over the ancient prairie cemetery. She stopped just inside the gate and the silence of the still-sleeping morning was heavy. As the cooling engine ticked, the distant refrain of birdsong started up. She didn't recognize any of the birds, not knowing Texas wildlife as well as she did Colorado's.

"Lisa. Answer me," Trey said through gritted teeth.

"I told you." She pulled the keys from the ignition and as she shoved them in her pocket she opened the door. Jumping down from the high vehicle, she was surprised at how rock hard the ground was beneath her feet. Without looking at him, without saying anything more, she reached into the backseat.

The clink of glass was loud in the morning, but she didn't let it stop her. She curled her fingers around the neck of a bottle with one hand and then palmed the two stacked, smaller glasses. With her hip, she slammed the door and started walking.

Bess had given her directions to the grave and now she knew why Bess had told her she wouldn't need them. The small ancient cemetery held graves from pioneer days. Everything from worn wooden crosses to current-day stones etched with laser-cut designs filled the grown-over grasses. But none of them came close to the granite monolith smack in the center of the prairie.

"Is there a reason we're here?"

"Yep." She called over her shoulder but didn't stop moving. The thick grasses scraped against her jeans, loud and yet oddly calming. Predictable.

"Lisa?"

She kept walking, and he followed.

They'd nearly reached the stone when the sound of thunder startled her. She looked up. The sky was clear.

Trey frowned at the horizon. "What's going on?" he said so softly she almost didn't hear him.

Slowly, she walked over to the big, imposing gravestone. She had to tilt her head way back to see the whole thing. Good grief.

The sound of thunder came again. What was that? Then she spotted it—them. Half a dozen cowboys were headed their way and the thunder she heard was from their horses' hooves. The dust cloud that rose up behind them was impressive.

Lisa stood there and stared. What were they doing? Were those the guys from the ranch? She'd barely met any of them, but she recognized several of them.

They grew closer and she could see their faces clearly. But what surprised her most was finding Pal Junior sitting astride a horse. He also held the reins of another horse that was saddled but didn't have a rider.

Pal Junior was smiling and for the first

time she realized that he was finally well, finally recovered.

"What's going on?" Trey looked from her to the riders and back again.

Now or never. She hadn't planned on an audience for this, though. She walked over to the stone and set the bottle of whisky on a ledge. Then she pulled the shot glasses out of her pockets.

Without saying anything, she twisted the top off the bottle and poured two shots. "Time to take that drink."

Trey cursed and took two steps backward. He looked up at the men sitting astride all the horses. Looked up at his father.

"Chet," Pal Junior said, glancing at the foreman who'd come out of retirement to help at the ranch. "You brought it, right?"

The older man reached into a leather bag and came up with a bottle. "Yep. How's this?"

Pal Junior nodded. Then, as if on cue, the rest of the men moved. Each one of them pulled a shot glass from their pocket or their saddlebag. Chet dismounted and took his time filling each man's glass from the bottle.

Lisa wasn't sure exactly what was going on, but she knew each and every one of these men was here because Bess had told them what she had planned, and every one of them was here for Trey.

Her eyes burned with the gratitude she felt.

Pal Junior lifted his own shot glass in the air.

"You sure you should be drinking that?" Chet asked.

"Already checked with my doctor, so shut up, Chet. Lisa, can you hand Trey his glass? And don't forget yours. You're a part of us now, young lady."

Pal Junior smiled at her and she smiled, too. Then, carefully, she took the two shot glasses she'd filled and extended one to Trey.

Their gazes locked, and she wasn't sure what emotion she saw there, but whatever it was, she felt its intensity. The surface of the whiskey rippled as he reached out and took it from her.

TREY HAD AN IDEA what Lisa was up to. What his father and the hands had to do with it, he hadn't a clue. He waited patiently, feeling rather ridiculous standing in a graveyard with a shot of whiskey in his hand.

"Lisa didn't plan on us being here," his father said, looking only at Trey. "But I thought it was time. Son, I appreciate all you've done."

He cleared his throat. "Even though we've hurt you."

"Dad—"

"No, let me finish before I fall off this darn horse." Trey might have been upset at the reprimand in another time, and if his father hadn't laughed. He waited.

"My arm's getting tired," Chet good-naturedly complained. "Get on with it."

Once again, Pal Junior cleared his throat, and then he repeated the words they'd all said hundreds of times. "To a good and productive day, today and tomorrow."

He heard the voice of every single man there—as well as Lisa's higher-pitched, sweet voice—repeat the phrase. He did, too, only with a whisper and a whole lot less enthusiasm than the rest of them.

They all lifted their glasses to their lips and, just as he'd shown Lisa that night in the bar, tilted their heads back and took the full shots at once.

As always it burned, and he didn't take his eyes off her. She took it, too, though her eyes watered. He moved closer, making sure she was okay.

The sound of breaking glass shattered the quiet of the afternoon. Startled, Trey spun around, afraid his father had done as he'd predicted and fallen. But he was sitting tall in the saddle.

Then he noticed his father's shot glass. Broken into a jillion pieces at the base of the tombstone. In succession, each of the hands and then Chet tossed their glasses at the stone.

The afternoon sun glinted off the shards. The sharp edges of the glass, some in hunks, some small as dust, glistened up at him.

Trey looked over at Lisa and let the grin grow on his face. She grinned back and threw her glass down, just as the men had. Her laughter rode the afternoon wind and scattered over the prairie.

"You planned this?"

Lisa shook her head. "This is all your dad." She laughed again. "I love it."

"Me, too." Though he didn't look away from her. Not caring that the men and his father were all there, he pulled her into his arms. "Last one," he said and tossed his glass. The sound of it breaking seemed loud and echoed back at them.

"And that's done." Pal Junior's voice washed over them.

Without letting Lisa go, Trey gazed over at his dad. "Done?"

"Yeah." Pal Junior nodded. "No more nightly toasts. From now on the men of the ranch will go home to their families, to their homes when the day is done, not hang out until late for a toast. Time to build everyone's life."

They looked at each other for a long moment and Trey felt the weight of the past let its grip go. "You brought that horse out here for a reason."

Pal Junior grinned. "Wondered when you'd notice."

"Oh, I noticed."

"You've always loved him. He missed you. He's yours. The beginning of your herd up in Colorado."

"Oh, Trey," Lisa whispered, and her arms squeezed him tight.

"Thanks, Dad."

"You up to a ride?"

Trey looked down at Lisa; he opened his mouth to ask if she minded, but she didn't let him speak.

"Go on," she whispered. "I'll meet you at the house." She gave him a soft shove. "It's fine. We've got our whole lives to be together. Spend time with him."

Now seemed as good a moment as any for him to voice what he'd been thinking. "Was that a proposal?"

She looked taken aback for half an instant,

then her smile spread all over her face. "I do believe it was."

"Good." He reached out and pulled her back to him. "Saves me the trouble of asking if you'll marry me." He leaned in close. "But just in case, will you?"

Their gazes locked again and he wasn't going to look away until she said the one word he wanted to hear.

"Yes." She nodded.

The hands cheered and Trey thought he heard his father's familiar laughter. He didn't think any harder, though. He needed to kiss this woman, and needed her to kiss him back. Nothing else mattered.

"We're losin' daylight, boy," his father finally said and Trey pulled away.

"Meet you at the house, Lisa?" Trey confirmed before stepping away.

"Yeah. Now go. I always wanted to watch my cowboy saddle up. Old cowboy fantasy and all."

And that's exactly what he did. "Mornin', ma'am," he said, letting the deep Southern twang come through as he touched the brim of his Stetson. He winked at her. "We'll pick up where we left off then."

* * * * *

Get 4 FREE REWARDS!

We'll send you 2 FREE Books plus 2 FREE Mystery Gifts.

Love Inspired® books feature contemporary inspirational romances with Christian characters facing the challenges of life and love.

FREE
Value Over
$20

YES! Please send me 2 FREE Love Inspired® Romance novels and my 2 FREE mystery gifts (gifts are worth about $10 retail). After receiving them, if I don't wish to receive any more books, I can return the shipping statement marked "cancel." If I don't cancel, I will receive 6 brand-new novels every month and be billed just $5.24 for the regular-print edition or $5.74 each for the larger-print edition in the U.S., or $5.74 each for the regular-print edition or $6.24 each for the larger-print edition in Canada. That's a savings of at least 13% off the cover price. It's quite a bargain! Shipping and handling is just 50¢ per book in the U.S. and 75¢ per book in Canada.* I understand that accepting the 2 free books and gifts places me under no obligation to buy anything. I can always return a shipment and cancel at any time. The free books and gifts are mine to keep no matter what I decide.

Choose one: ☐ **Love Inspired® Romance**
Regular-Print
(105/305 IDN GMY4)

☐ **Love Inspired® Romance**
Larger-Print
(122/322 IDN GMY4)

Name (please print)

Address   Apt. #

City   State/Province   Zip/Postal Code

Mail to the **Reader Service:**
IN U.S.A.: P.O. Box 1341, Buffalo, NY 14240-8531
IN CANADA: P.O. Box 603, Fort Erie, Ontario L2A 5X3

Want to try 2 free books from another series? Call 1-800-873-8635 or visit www.ReaderService.com.

BETTY NEELS COLLECTION!

Buy 3 and get 1 FREE!

Experience one of the most celebrated and beloved authors in romance! Betty Neels will delight you with her signature brand of storytelling: happy romances, memorable couples and timeless tales of lasting love. These classics have been combined in 2-in-1 books for your reading pleasure!

Get 4 FREE REWARDS!

We'll send you 2 FREE Books plus 2 FREE Mystery Gifts.

FREE
Value Over
$20

Both the **Romance** and **Suspense** collections feature compelling novels written by many of today's best-selling authors.

Get 4 FREE REWARDS!

We'll send you 2 FREE Books plus 2 FREE Mystery Gifts.

Harlequin® Special Edition books feature heroines finding the balance between their work life and personal life on the way to finding true love.

FREE
Value Over
$20

Get 4 FREE REWARDS!

We'll send you 2 FREE Books plus 2 FREE Mystery Gifts.

Harlequin® Romance Larger-Print books feature uplifting escapes that will warm your heart with the ultimate feel-good tales.

FREE
Value Over
$20

READERSERVICE.COM

Manage your account online!

- Review your order history
- Manage your payments
- Update your address

We've designed the Reader Service website just for you.

Enjoy all the features!

- Discover new series available to you, and read excerpts from any series.
- Respond to mailings and special monthly offers.
- Browse the Bonus Bucks catalog and online-only exculsives.
- Share your feedback.

Visit us at:

ReaderService.com